The Disturbing Charm

The Disturbing Charm

Berta Ruck

MINT EDITIONS

The Disturbing Charm was first published in 1919.

This edition published by Mint Editions 2021.

ISBN 9781513282862 | E-ISBN 9781513287881

Published by Mint Editions®

 MINT
EDITIONS

minteditionbooks.com

Publishing Director: Jennifer Newens
Design & Production: Rachel Lopez Metzger
Project Manager: Micaela Clark
Typesetting: Westchester Publishing Services

Contents

Part II

PART I

I

The Coming of the Charm

"Yet I am bewitched with the rogue's company; if the rascal had not given me medicines to make me love him, I'll be hanged; it could not be else; I have drunk medicines."

—Shakespeare

The letter said:

". . . And this discovery, sent herewith, will mark an Epoch in the affairs of the world!

"Half the trouble in that world arises from the fact that human beings are continually falling in Love. . . with the wrong people. *Sir, have you ever wondered why this should be?"*

The old Professor of Botany stood looking at this mysterious typewritten letter, addressed to him, with the rest of his large mail, at the hotel in Western France where he was staying in the fourth autumn of the War with his young niece and secretary. He smiled as he came to the last words. "Had he ever wondered!" How many nights of his youth had been wasted in stormily "wondering—?" Strangers who write to celebrities do stumble on intimate matters sometimes.

He read on:

"Why should one girl set her affections upon the man who of all others will make her the worst possible husband? All her friends foresee, and warn her. She herself realizes it vaguely. But to her own destruction she loves him. What has caused this catastrophe? Some small and secret Force; one microbe can achieve a pestilence."

"Yes, indeed," murmured Professor Howel-Jones, nodding his massive old white head. He had been on the point of tossing the letter into the waste-paper basket, but something made him read on.

"Another young man, why must he desire the one pretty woman who can never give him happiness? She is 'pure as ice, chaste as snow'. . . dull as ditch-water; he, full of fire and dreams. He swears he'll teach her to respond to Passion; marries her. Another tragedy!"

How like himself again, the Professor mused, going back to the days when he had worn his Rugby International cap with more pride than he now wore his foreign degrees. That memory set him staring out of the big balconied window of his room, over the wide French lagoon, past the barrier of sandhills with their pointing phare, to where, miles away, the irregular white line of the Atlantic rollers crashed and spouted on the reefs. They had been crashing out those thunderous questions to the sands on his football days, they would be tossing their appeals to the sky long after his learning and his Nobel Prize were forgotten. Why, then, should an anonymous correspondent remind him of old unrest?

For all that, he went on reading:

"Each of us knows a list of these stories. How avert them? By seeking out and planting only in the right soil the root of good or evil, the Love-germ. All through the ages Man has recognized its existence; the ancients with their philtres and amulets. Shakespeare embodies it in an herb. We moderns accept it as an enigma; have you never heard it said of a woman, 'She is not actually pretty, but she has the Disturbing Charm, whatever it is'?"

"The Disturbing Charm!". . . Ah, he knew it! *She* had possessed it, the girl he had never married, the girl who had passed him over for his brother the sea-captain, and who had become the mother of Olwen, his niece. Olwen would be coming in a few minutes to straighten and sort all those drifts of paper on the roomy work-table which no hand but hers, in the whole of the hotel, was allowed to touch. He thought, half-amusedly: "Better not let that little Olwen get hold of this letter."

The letter ended:

"Sir, you shall not be worried with technicalities. Believe only this, that the life study of the writer of this letter has at last been crowned with success. In the small packet enclosed there is sealed

up the result of years of Research, with directions for its use. The
inventor lacks courage for experimenting. But you, learned Sir,
you, the gifted author of 'The Loves of the Ferns,' will not shrink
from responsibility in the cause of Science.

"Should you wish to procure more of the invention, there is
enclosed the address of a box at a newspaper office where you may
apply.

"With all good wishes from

Your obedient servant,
The Inventor

A deep genial laugh broke from the old man's wide chest.

He threw the letter and its enclosure on to the table, on the top of his notes for the chapter on "Edible Fungi."

"Mad—sentimental mad!" he commented. "Most lunatics think themselves inventors, that's why most inventors are considered lunatics." He drew up a chair and began making hay of the papers before him, in search of the other file of notes.

The large room which the Professor had had cleared of the bed and most of the other furniture was full of air and sunshine and of that polished cleanliness which few English rooms achieve. White walls and parquet floor shone like mirrors, mirrors like diamonds; the glass of the open windows was clear as the morning air that lay between the hotel and the pine-forest on the one side, the lagoon on the other. The resinous sigh of the pines mingled with the warm, lung-lifting breath of the sea. It was a glorious morning—too glorious for work indoors...

Professor Howel-Jones looked hard at his notes, but for once he scarcely saw them. He knew that the letter he had just read was the work of a sentimental lunatic, but for all that it had set a string vibrating. As the old man sat there, his brown eyes abstracted under the thatch of hair as white as seeding clematis, he looked like some clean-shaven modern Druid seeing visions. He did, at that moment, see a vision.

HE SAW AN ENDLESS PROCESSION of those people who have loved or married (or both) the wrong person.

He saw the lads who have chosen out of their class; barmaids, "bits of fluff."

He saw the girls who have married out of their generation.

He saw the flirts, who wear an attachment as they wear a hat, tied for life to the affection that is true as steel. (Dreadful for both of them!)

Also the young men who treat Love as a cross between a meal and a music-hall joke, plighted to the shy idealists.

He saw the Bohemian married to the curate.

Likewise the attractive young rake, fettered to the frump.

He saw the women born for motherhood, left lonely spinsters for want of charm to attract.

He saw the mothers who sighed for freedom, resenting the nursery.

He saw the Anything, wedded to the Anything *But*.

Yes; he saw for that moment nothing but the wholesale gigantic Blunder of the mis-mating of the world.

No DOUBT IT WAS ALL crystallized for him in one tender image; Olwen's dead mother, the girl he should have married. He sighed and smiled.

"Pity there's no putting things right, as that lunatic suggests," he thought. "There would be an invention worth boasting about! Wireless wouldn't be in it, or X-rays. Pity it isn't all true. . ."

A tap at the door interrupted his musings. The softest of girl's voices asked, "Are you ready for me, Uncle?"

"Yes!" he called out, jerking himself back into the world of realities. "Come in, Olwen."

Olwen Howel-Jones came in.

A small, but daintily made girl of nineteen. Just a handful of softness in a skimpy one-piece frock. A pale, three-cornered morsel of a face set off by sleek hair as black as her little French boots. Large eyes that seemed sometimes brown, sometimes grey; a mouth tremulous, but vivid as a red carnation—such was Olwen. She brought a ripple of Youth into that bare temple of Science that was her uncle's study. Something else she brought—a breath of tension, of impatience. A man would have passed it over; not so a woman. Already one woman in the hotel had said to herself, "I wonder who it is that child's so desperately in love with?"

Had she been in the room at the moment, that woman might have seen the answer to her question flame suddenly into the young girl's face as she stepped up to the table by the window. Under the balcony there was a sound of footsteps. Olwen pushed aside a great jar full of arbutus that stood at the further edge of the table.

"That's in your light, Uncle," she said.

The Professor's back was to her as the figures passed quickly out from below the balcony. He caught a glimpse of the two wounded British officers swinging off towards the *plage*. He caught the gleam of scarlet on khaki; heard a snatch of the rather husky boyish laughter of one of them; a scrap talk of the other. In a resonant voice with that particularly dominant form of accent, Scots with a dash of Canadian, there floated up through the clear morning air this somewhat arrested announcement:

"I'm the finest judge of women in Europe."

This the Professor caught, vaguely. What he did not catch was the sudden, still alertness into which there seemed to spring the whole body of the girl behind him. She was "aware" from head to foot; her white throat seemed to stretch, her whole being to strain; listening. The footsteps passed, the husky charming laugh of the one, the loud confident voice of the other. . . Life relaxed again in Olwen; mechanically her hands began sorting papers. No; the Professor had not noticed, her male relatives being avowedly the worst observers of a girl's psychology. . . even had he seen, he probably would not have guessed which of the two young men who had gone by was responsible for that sudden transitory illumination of his niece's face; whether it was the black-eyed Staff Captain who had lost an arm, or the blonde R.F.C. pilot who had been shot down last April. . . Well, they'd both gone now; nothing more of them to be seen until the *déjeuner*. . .

Olwen dragged her eyes back to the disorder of the writing-table; she tossed up her head with a rather forced sprightliness, and laughed.

"*What* a mess! Worse than ever, and I'd put everything so beautifully tidy last night! You *are* dreadful!"

"Never mind, Olwen *fach*," he said, with a hand on her shoulder. "There won't be much work done this morning. I'm going into the woods. Just hand me my specimen-case. . . ah, here. And file the June numbers of that Danish magazine—where on earth did I put 'em?—ah, there. Then there are a couple of letters to copy into the book, and that's all. You can come on and find me; I shall be where we went yesterday with Mrs. Cartwright and that young What's-his-name, the flying officer."

He set aside the two letters to be copied, planting upon them, as a paper weight, one of the enormous pine-cones that he had picked up in the forest. Then he slung on his specimen-case, took up his indented grey hat, smiled and nodded to the girlish figure at the table, and went out.

Olwen, left alone, stretched her arms over her head. "*Oh!*" she sighed, desperately. She moved the jar of arbutus into place again; picked out a spray, dark-leafed, berried with scarlet and orange, tried it against the dull serge of her frock. Then she tilted her chair back so that she could just see herself in one of the gilt-framed mirrors. It showed her a forlorn little face.

"He'd never *look* at me, I know," she told herself.

She thrust the spray of arbutus back into water and turned to her work listlessly enough.

HALF AN HOUR LATER THE listlessness had finished.

A miracle had begun to work!

For the Professor's niece and secretary was pouring breathlessly over a letter that she had found on the table under a file of notes for J. Howel-Jones's great work on Agarics.

With shining credulous eyes she turned from that typewritten letter to the little packet that had been enclosed in it. Then she turned to the letter again. She read:

> "*Half the trouble in the world arises from the fact that human beings are continually falling in love. . .* with the wrong people."

She read the astonishing suggestion:

> "*Each of us knows a list of these stories. How avert them? By seeking out and planting only in the right soil the root of good or evil, the Love-germ.*"

She read further, this profoundly hopeful comment:

> "*Have you never heard it said of a woman*, 'She is not pretty, but she has the disturbing charm, whatever it is'?"

Finally she read this, the sentence that set her trembling:

> "*In the small packet enclosed there is sealed up the result of years of Research, with directions for its use.*"

It lay in her hand, the packet which she had taken up as gingerly as if it had been turpinite, or something else capable of blowing her out through the window and past the long wooden pier, across the sparkling *Baissin*, over the sandhills with their lighthouse and into the Bay of Biscay where those rollers foamed and roared. . .

The old Scientist had said "Madness!" This girl longed to accept every word of it; partly, perhaps, because every loving woman secretly believes there must be some Power of this kind, could she but find it—the power to compel the love she covets. Here it was.

Hastily she broke the wrapping; it disclosed an inner packet and a paper. In small characters there was written on the paper:

Directions for Use

"This charm must be worn, *hidden*, about the person of him or her who wishes to test its efficacy.

"It may be hidden about the dress or person of someone who does not know of its properties; its power will work, nevertheless.

"A small portion of the charm will suffice.

"Constant use does not wear away its power."

Olwen, bending closely over the inner packet, sniffed at the pleasant musky scent that rose from it.

"*Oh!* . . ." she breathed. . . Were those steps outside the passage? . . . She sprang up. . . Swiftly, almost guiltily, she dragged down the low collar of her frock; she thrust the packet and paper into her bosom. They crackled against the soft mauve ribbons of her underbodice.

"Supposing I'd *got* it!" she thought, and her whole heart lifted. She pressed her hands to her breast.

Supposing that under her own small and fevered hands (dimpled, faintly stained from the carbon of her typewriter) she held it, that recipe for setting right the Blunder of the world! Ah, if she'd got hold of it really, the Love-germ, the microbe of mischief and delight!

The Disturbing Charm itself!

Then what would come of it?

II

The Accepting of the Charm

"What I can do, can do no hurt to try."

—Shakespeare

That day, since the Professor chose (as he often did) to give lunch a miss while he wandered and pottered about in the Forest, he sent his niece into *déjeuner* alone. Her he never allowed to miss a meal; he held that young people must eat plenty and often.

Bareheaded, with a scarlet knitted coat over her frock, the girl threaded her way through the little round iron-legged tables and past the tubs of flowering cactus outside the piazza of the hotel. She pushed open a window and entered the big light *salle*. All one wall of it seemed to be windows from ceiling to floor, giving on to the *plage* and to that stretch of lagoon, and sandhills, pointed by that lighthouse. The other high walls were panelled with mirrors that reflected a dozen times the hanging chandeliers, the rococo gilded curves of carving, the moving heads of the visitors already at the tables.

The reflections of little Olwen's own head and shoulders, black-and-red like a lady-bird, appeared repeated in the picture; she did not see it.

It was another image that she sought. . .

Her bright glance, searching the thronged and buzzing place, fell on two empty chairs at the long table that ran down the middle of the room.

Ah! "They" weren't in for lunch, then? Nothing to be seen of "Them" until the *dîner*, perhaps. With a sigh of resignation Olwen Howel-Jones turned to the table for two near the end window where she was accustomed to sit with her Uncle.

But before she sat down, the tall Englishwoman in brown, who was sitting at the little table next to hers, caught the girl's eyes, smiled, nodded, and with a swift leaning forward of a supple body that made her look like the figurehead of a vessel, accosted her in a deep, rather attractive voice.

"I say! Are you alone today? So am I. Have your lunch at my table, won't you?"

"Oh! thank you, Mrs. Cartwright; I'd like to," said the girl, pleased. She took the chair opposite.

Mrs. Cartwright, who had been at the hotel for some days before the Howel-Joneses had arrived, was the widow of an Indian Army officer, the mother of two boys now at school in England, and a journalist under several names.

This was why, when she said she was as hungry as a hunter because she had been working like a nigger all the morning, Olwen asked her, with a shy smile, "Were you being 'Miss Claudia Crane' or the 'Wanderer through Western France'?"

"For a change, neither," returned Mrs. Cartwright cheerfully over the omelette which the frail little Italian waiter had brought to her. "I actually went back to being 'Domestica' and I turned out two thousand words of wisdom on ration-recipes—just for the pleasure of charging them eight times what my price used to be when I navvied for that paper regularly. What have you been doing—taking down sheaves of notes from that wonderful-looking old Welsh Nationalist, your uncle?"

The Professor's niece, as she answered that she had done nothing but tidy up and answer letters, was still absorbed by the thought of that epoch-making letter that she had read before she had even seen that it had not been left there for her to copy with the others. Her whole being was so taken up by the memory of what the letter had claimed for the powers of that hidden packet (now drawing warmth from the softness of her breast where it lay) that she only had half an ear for the talk of the woman opposite to her.

The Disturbing Charm. . . Could it be anything but a fairy-tale? How many of that heterogeneous collection of people gathered there in that very dining-room—the English visitors, the little knot of uniforms on leave, the French family parties—how many of them would laugh incredulously if they were told what she, the celebrity's niece, was treasuring at that moment inside the bosom of her frock?

There she sat, demurely eating a plateful of those Edible Fungi of whose forest lives her Uncle made such a study. Yes, she sat hiding something that might change not only the current of her life, but of their lives as well. Perhaps it was true. What a thought!

"SOME NEW PEOPLE HERE TODAY," chatted Mrs. Cartwright, who never seemed to look at anyone or anything in a room (Olwen had noticed that) but whom few details escaped; just as her eyes did not seem to be glancing about, so her lips hardly moved; but they had the habit of letting fall comment after comment, softly, casually, on every one of those details that the eyes above had noticed. "What a typical Hotel Spinster that is in the corner there! You can just see her over that young French soldier's head when he ducks to tuck in his napkin; yes, that survival in the expensive tweeds and the hair-net. Stays so old-fashioned that when she bends she comes away from the top of them as if it were over the rim of a vase into which she's been poured. How fatal it is to allow oneself to crystallize into the mode of the year when one was twenty-one! (But you, lucky child, don't even know what that mode is going to be.) English? Yes, of course. No wonder Prévost calls England 'that positive reservoir of old maids'!"

"Poor thing!" murmured Olwen, glancing at the new-comer, and of whom she now caught a clearer glimpse. She saw a woman of perhaps thirty-four or five, with uninteresting brown hair, elaborately dressed, an equally uninteresting brown face with a large nose and timid eyes that wandered from face to face.

Olwen thought, "No; I can't imagine anybody liking her—in *that* way!" Then she thought with a little start, "But if it were true—if all women were allowed even a tiny grain of that Charm, there would be no such thing as an 'Hotel Spinster.' No old maids in the world! How lovely!"

"Enter several characters from a French novel by Abel Hermant," pursued Mrs. Cartwright, as the door of the *salle* nearest to their table swung open and admitted two ladies in deepest mourning, an old gentleman with a red speck in his button-hole, and a boy of four. "The son of those old people has just 'fallen on the field of honour'; the lovely young Madonna is his widow; that's his little boy. What a splendid child!"

The little French boy that followed his grown-ups so sedately down the room was as dark as a damson and clad in a white tunic that showed his dimpled arms and his strong brown legs. He left a wake of smiles. The Hotel Spinster put out a finger and touched him as he went by.

"There. I knew she'd do that," commented Mrs. Cartwright; that deep soft voice of hers running out in the sort of monologue that scarcely moved her lips. "That woman's fonder of children than anyone here, and a better hand with them, I bet. Did you see the little boy smile back at her? Only at *her*. Yet Fate has decreed that she's never to have a chick or child (though what point 'a chick' would have I never could fathom). Private means. Stodgy connections in Debrett. Left with a house of her own, probably, crammed with mahogany and Coalport—and no man's ever looked at her in her life."

"Dreadful!" murmured little Olwen; and her hand went up involuntarily to her breast.

(If that letter was true, what a gift she had it in her power to bestow upon that woman; upon any woman!)

"The latest in British officers, I see," ran on Mrs. Cartwright, pursuing the nonchalant soft stream of comment as she pursued her lunch. "Staying here on his pay. Giving as much for one *déjeuner* here as would keep him for half a week at some little pension in the town, where he ought to be. *Very* new; *very* temporary commission. He had a talk with me in the lounge just now. A nice frank little Cockney. Told me he was a shop-assistant before he joined. '*And the next, Madame?*' Poor lad! The next is that he's learned what it is to be considered IT, and what the insides of the best hotels are like, and the chief seats at revues. He's learned Bubbly-tastes on Beer-pay. Overdrawn everywhere. What *will* he go back to in civil life, if he goes back? Another tragedy of the war. Dozens of them! . . . Pleasant little pink face, too. . . His only hope would be to get some profiteer's heiress to marry him—"

"Yes, he might do that," agreed little Olwen, again conscious of that packet at her breast. She looked down the tables at the rosy, undistinguished young face of the Second Lieutenant of whom Mrs. Cartwright had been murmuring. One of the waiters was deferentially endeavouring to understand this British officer's French. The boy looked self-conscious; at sea. Even a man might be glad enough of some magic that could bring him Love and Fortune, thought Olwen. Some men were without charm, just as some other men—ah, yes!—were all Charm.

Here Mrs. Cartwright, still seeming to look another way, followed the young girl's glance as it turned again to the objective that it first had sought—to the two empty places at the long table.

"Captain Ross and Mr. Awdas have gone into Bordeaux for the day," commented Mrs. Cartwright. "I hope they'll bring me back the fountain-pen ink and the 'Vie Parisienne,' and the brown darning silk that I commissioned them to get—" and here, quickly, she turned away as if to gaze out of the window at the little motor-boat that was making its way up the lagoon, where the tide was high, to the wooden pier. Actually, her movement was to avoid seeming to stare at the face of the girl before her, where Consciousness had again flamed out into a live and lovely red.

"So *that's* it. . ." she thought.

"I *wish* I didn't blush!" Olwen Howel-Jones was scolding herself angrily. "I *am* a little idiot to blush at the sound of the man's name! Nobody in the whole world thinks of doing such a thing nowadays; it's like wearing your hat on the back of your head! Yet here I am, going on like this as if it were *Eighteen* Seventeen! I *do* wish to goodness I had another sort of skin. Mrs. Cartwright might easily have *thought*—!"

But Mrs. Cartwright was talking pleasantly on about the journey to Bordeaux; about the forest of Les Pins, the air of it. . .

"Such a becoming place, too," she laughed. "Makes you feel well; look well. May I make a personal remark, Miss Howel-Jones? You yourself are getting twice as pretty as when you came here."

"Oh, no," protested the enraptured girl. "No one could—no one has ever called me pretty!"

"No? But they will. Perhaps you are only just growing up to it," said Mrs. Cartwright with a very kind glance into the face opposite to her. "So many people make a virtue of blurting out unpleasant truths; why shouldn't one tell the truths that aren't unpleasant? Today (I saw it when you came in) you are quite lovely. You look as if a charm had touched you."

Little Olwen's whole heart went suddenly out in emotion and gratitude towards the woman who had said this thing.

Only the very young can realize how much they mean—the very first compliments to the very young girl! Especially to the very young girl in Love; she who feels the special need of beauty, the special need of encouragement to think herself beautiful.

And now here was a clever woman (who knew what men admired, and who had seen so many lovely people) pronouncing her, Olwen, to be "quite lovely."

Oh, Event!

As she went up after luncheon to her room—the replica of her Uncle's study, with its parquet floor and high balconied window—she felt there was nothing she could not have done for this Mrs. Cartwright.

To do something for other people; that was the wish that filled the child's heart in its overflowing mood.

Throwing a look to her hair and eyes in the glass, she thought of the woman whom Mrs. Cartwright had classified so promptly as the Hotel Spinster. She thought of that woman's meaningless but "good" clothes, of the hungry eyes which she fastened upon that little French boy seated at table with his mother. How the Spinster had watched that mother bending over her child, turning his chair, showing him how to hold his little silver spoon shaped like a wine-taster, folding his napkin for him; ah, how she'd watched!

"Poor, poor thing!" thought the soft-hearted Olwen. "Anyone could see how she would love a little child of her own—"

And then she thought of the other rather "out of it" guest at that hotel; the very young New Army subaltern whom Mrs. Cartwright had said was living a life to which he hadn't been brought up and which he must leave again unless he could find a rich wife. Not an attractive type, thought Olwen (forgetting that for her at the moment there existed only one masculine type that showed any attraction whatsoever). It wasn't likely, she considered, that he would find anyone to care about *him*.

"Poor boy!" She felt quite motherly. For she was the type of girl whom personal emotion drives outwards to include the world in her thoughts, rather than the commoner type of lover who is driven inwards, upon concentrated narrowed sympathies. Ever since she had come to that hotel and had fallen in love, Juliet-fashion, with the first glance at a good-looking male face seen across a dinner-table, the little creature had longed for everyone, not only herself, to be lucky in Love.

She found it horrible that in this supreme matter everything must be left to Fate, to Chance, to the merest Toss-up.

No woman could lift a finger to help either her own love-affair or anybody else's. The pity of it!

But wait—Again the delighted thought thrilled her—If that discovery were true? . . . The Disturbing Charm! If that could really help. *If*. . . after all?

What was it that Mrs. Cartwright had said to her?

"You look as if a charm had touched you."

Could that have meant more than her friend had known?

Olwen threw another wondering, searching look into her glass. . . Was it her imagination, or did she look prettier already than she had ever before seen herself? *Oh*. . .

She stood there, reflected; an image of Uncertainty hovering between belief and doubt. "Uncle wouldn't believe a word of it, I'm sure," she told herself. "I'm sure he thought he'd thrown the letter away. He may be quite right, of course. It sounds nonsense. Yet—"

(*"As if a charm had touched you,"* Mrs. Cartwright said, knowing nothing.)

"The writer of the letter said it was the result of years of research," pondered Olwen. "If he could give years, surely I can give just—just a *try?*"

She paused, hands clasped upon her breast.

"Shall I? Shall I? . . . Supposing I tried the effect of the Charm upon somebody else, first? Somebody here? There are at least two people besides myself in this hotel whom it could help. . ."

Then she thought defiantly, "The inventor said he shirked responsibility. Well, *I* wouldn't! If it doesn't do any good—well! There's no *harm* done! I—"

Another second's pause. Then the decision.

"I will. Yes! I *will* try it!"

Half believing, half longing to believe, and wholly excited by the thing, the girl began busying herself as if in answer to some mysterious Command.

She opened a drawer of her toilette-table, taking out a square work-basket in which reels, scissors, thimble, and darning skeins were packed into the smallest possible compass; Olwen being as neat in her habits as her uncle was chaotic. From another corner of the drawer she took a carefully rolled-up length of the mauve satin ribbon she used for slotting through her underclothes. From this she cut enough to sew up into a tiny sachet.

Then she sat by the window and stitched, the young Welsh girl into whose busy, dimpled hands there had fallen this maybe tremendous Power. While the autumn sun glowed redly on the bodies of those pines without, while the border of far-off Biscay rollers tossed their cloud-like columns of white against the sky-line, she sat at her needle like a Fate with a face of a grave-eyed child, the mouth of a flower.

In a few minutes she had the square of satin ready for filling. She drew the packet from her bosom; opened it with a hundred precautions; poured into the sachet a little—a very little!—of the musky scented powder.

The packet itself she bestowed at the bottom of her work-basket, locking that carefully away. Yes; some of that was for *her* to wear again, but not now. Later on.

BERTA RUCK

The curious fact persisted that she would wish to see first the effect of that Charm upon another wearer.

She had stitched up the sachet before she had answered her own question, "Whom shall I give it to first?"

III

The Launching of the Charm

"A field untilled, a web unwove,
A flower withheld from sun or bee,
An alien in the courts of Love—"

—Kipling

Accident decided it for her.

As she was running down the broad red and white steps at the front of the hotel, Olwen met, coming up, the woman whom Mrs. Cartwright had noticed at lunch for her hopeless well-off spinsterishness. The Spinster carried a guide book, a flowering-plant in a pot with paper round it, and a bound map.

She wore over those expensive tweeds of hers those furs which none but the young and radiant should venture to wear; grey squirrel. Her face was blank.

It lighted into a tentative smile as the young girl turned and ran back a few steps to the top, waiting for her.

"Good afternoon; we mustn't cross on the stairs," Olwen called. "It's unlucky!"

Was it her fancy, or did the Spinster look pathetically pleased because some one had said "good afternoon" and had made a playful remark?

Up the steps she hastened, rather stiffly, her figure being of the kind that seems all clothes.

When she got to the top she said, with a shy, effusive little laugh, "Oh, are you superstitious?" and before Olwen could answer, she hurried on, "Oh, can one order tea here, at any time one likes? Could I order it in my own room, do you think?"

"I think so," said Olwen, surprised.

In spite of the gap in their ages, this woman of thirty-five seemed to speak as if she were a new girl, just arrived at school. In spite of her "set" figure, her mode of dressing, her big nose, there was—yes! something of suppressed schoolgirlishness about her yet. Some are born with the saddle to wear, some with the spur, says the proverb. This Spinster had the look, not only of having been born with the saddle, but of having been for years under the spur of others. Her timid eyes were those of a dog who has been turned adrift. They fastened upon Olwen.

"This is a lovely place, isn't it?" she hurried on as if afraid the girl would leave her. "Have you been here long?"

"About a week."

"Oh, have you? I have only just come. I came just before lunch. I saw you at lunch, with a tall lady in brown. Are you staying with her?"

"No," Olwen said, "I'm here with my uncle; I am his secretary."

"Oh, are you? How nice. I am not with anybody," volunteered the Spinster. Clutching her guide-book and plant and fixing the girl with that timid yet persistent eye, she seemed ready to stand there and talk for half an hour. "You are the first person I have spoken to here. I'm quite alone."

These were the three words which—with all the unspoken, unconscious pathos behind them—went to Olwen's heart. She tightened her fingers upon what she held in her hand, and she thought to herself, "*Here's* someone who needs the Charm!" Then she thought, caught back a little, "I can't give it just to the first person I meet. Oughtn't I to see a little more of her, first?"

The Spinster's next remarks seemed to fall in with this plan.

"I oughtn't to keep you here talking, without any hat on. . . Oh, d'you always go without a hat in the woods? . . . I must just put this plant down; do come into my room a minute, won't you? It's only on the first floor, just at the top of the stairs; yes, do—"

It was the best room in the hotel to which Olwen followed this new acquaintance of hers; and it seemed crowded with belongings, all very obviously costly, and all—curiously enough!—quite incredibly *new*.

"Oh—couldn't you—couldn't you have tea with me?" was the Spinster's next suggestion. "My name is Walsh; Agatha Walsh. Do have tea with me. Please. I'll order some now—"

She rang the waiter's bell; and in halting French she ordered the sallow little Italian to bring up to her room tea for two.

"*Simple?*" asked the waiter.

"Oh—what does he mean?"

"He means do you want just tea," explained Olwen, "or anything with it?"

"Oh! Everything there is. You like cake, don't you? Girls do," said the Spinster with that timid, friend-hunting glance. "Jam, and pastries, and things. Tell him to bring everything, please."

"*Complet*," ordered little Olwen, feeling a woman of the world in comparison with this stranger who was abashed before waiters.

"Oh, how well you talk French," murmured the other. "Do sit down here. I wonder if I shall ever be able to talk it quickly. I've never been in France before, do you know? I—Isn't it funny? I have hardly ever been *anywhere*!"

"*Haven't* you?" said Olwen—who herself had known her native Wales, Liverpool, the South Kensington Museum, and some other museums in Paris.

The Spinster broke into further confidences. "Oh, no. You see, I lived a very secluded life. I had to. I lived with an elderly cousin of mine in Buckinghamshire, oh, quite in the country. Here she is."

From her silver-strewn table the Spinster took an ornate oval frame. It enclosed the portrait of an old lady in a Victorian cap of lace and ribbons, with beetle-brows and a mouth of steel.

"Yes, this is Miss Walsh; the same name as mine, you see. She never left her house for the last fifteen years, you know. A beautiful house; such grounds! We never went out of them, except the half-mile drive to church every Sunday. And of course we scarcely ever saw anybody, except just the Rector and the old Doctor," the Spinster confided to Olwen. "All that money—But, poor thing, she was never really well. Of late years she had to have everything done for her; everything!"

"I suppose *you* had to do it!" volunteered Olwen, with a glance at the portrait and a pang of pity for the woman who showed it to her. The girl was too young to read the whole story as Mrs. Cartwright would have done; soaring years of a woman's youth harnessed to the bath-chair of a bitter-tongued tyrant in shawl and cap! But she guessed that the "poor thing" might more appropriately be applied to Miss Walsh the younger.

"Oh, well," said the Spinster, gently, "she only had me in the world. Except her nephew. She quarrelled with him. He was very outspoken, and—well, they quarrelled. He should have come in to her money, you know. She made another will only just before she died, poor thing. That's how—" She gave a gesture that seemed to take in the new portmanteau on the floor, the winking silver-backed brushes on the table, her own tweeds and furs, the wide view from the window, and the waiter bringing in the tea-tray. "It all came to *me*!" concluded Miss Walsh, diffident, amazed. "I can scarcely believe it *yet*! I couldn't believe I could leave the place and go away for as long as I liked!"

Olwen asked, "What brought you? Why did you come here?"

"Oh! because there was nowhere for me to go. I went to London because I'd only been there once in my life. Then I went over to Paris because I'd never been there. Then I stuck a hat-pin into the guide-book to see where I'd go next. It came out here. It seemed like Fate, didn't it? So I came."

Olwen looked at her as she poured out the tea. Her wrists clanked with gold curb bracelets (of a pattern as obsolete as was the enormous brooch of plaited gold and turquoises at her throat; the heavily set rings on her fingers, no doubt jewellery of the late Miss Walsh). They were chains that had fettered a patient slave—but she was a slave no longer.

"I'm so glad!" said little Olwen, impulsively.

"Oh! Thank you." Her hostess smiled as gratefully as if the girl herself had helped to alter that will. "I knew you were sympathetic. I could *say* things to you. One can *talk* to some people, can't one?" she added, as the waiter went out. "I thought at lunch what a sweet little face you had, if you don't mind my saying so. There—there's a charm about it! What is your name? . . . Olwen Howel-Jones. . . Is your tea right? I didn't even know they had proper tea in France now; my cousin never would go Abroad because she said they gave you no tea. . . Olwen! How pretty. How old are you? You don't mind my asking, do you? Nineteen? I was just nineteen when I went to live at the Grange—Miss Walsh's house. Nineteen. . . I always liked young people; but of course we never saw any. My cousin disliked girls as a rule. Even the servants were quite elderly. I—sometimes" she went on in a rush as of the pent-up confidences of years, "I longed to see something young, do you know? I suppose *you've* always. . . Brothers and sisters? Lots of cousins? How nice! And lots of friends, of course. . ."

She stopped, she fixed her eyes musingly upon the dainty creature helping herself to cherry *compote* and ended with a shy, quick involuntary question.

"Are you engaged to be married?"

"Me?" exclaimed Olwen with a swift turn of her little black head against the hotel easy chair. She laughed, with the traditional girlish rejoinder, "Oh, dear, no! I don't suppose I—"

It broke off short on her lips.

Footsteps, two sets of footsteps, were tramping up the polished shallow stairs outside the closed door. A man's voice rang out as it had rung out that morning under her Uncle's balcony. That accent which was as penetrating as Scots mist, as clear as Canadian frost, reached her ears in the giving out of this dictum:

"What I demand in Women is, firstly—"

Here a door above slammed, cutting off the rest.

Ah, thought Olwen, "They" were back again already, were "They"?

This breathless thought made her lose the thread for a moment of what this Miss Walsh, the wealthy waif, was pouring out to the first friendly soul she had encountered in the place.

Then the girl in love dragged herself back to that polished comfortable room, that tea-table, that woman who had stuck a hat-pin into a guide-book to decide where to go.

"Oh, you know, I often used to wonder if I should be an old woman before I'd ever made friends with anybody. I used to sit winding wool for my cousin and looking out of the morning-room window at the rhododendrons. Such rhododendrons! Every spring they came out. . . a wall of pink! Then they dropped their blossoms on the lawn. . . a carpet of pink! Every spring they came again. Not the same flowers; fresh flowers every spring. Fresh flowers. . . But the springs went by, and of course I knew that I should never come young again—Oh, what is that?"

For Miss Walsh, taking up the tea-pot, had caught sight of something that Olwen had laid down on the tray while she spread the cherry jam on her biscuits. Hastily Olwen picked it up again. It was the sachet into which she had sewn the Disturbing Charm.

In a flash she thought to herself: "Yes! she *is* the one! This poor dear, who's never had anything! Before she's quite too old! Something ought to be done!"

". . . Fifteen—sixteen of those springs," Miss Walsh was murmuring again, "and such appleblossom. But looking at things alone makes spring so much sadder than winter. . . Of course, you'll never have to understand that—my dear."

Olwen was thinking definitely and finally, "I must try the Charm upon her. I *will*. It's probably rubbish. . . But if it isn't—! Now how do I set about getting her to wear it? I can't say, '*Tuck this inside your blouse and you needn't be lonely any more, you'll begin to have people falling in Love with you!*' How shall I—?"

The method seemed to dart ready-made into her head as she held out on her pink palm the tiny square of mauve satin, scarcely larger than a postage-stamp.

She turned upon the Spinster the appealing smile that had made "little Miss Howel-Jones" such a successful worker on the last Welsh Flag Day, in Liverpool.

"Will you buy one? I'm selling these," announced the inventive Olwen. "They"—(then to herself, "*Quick, what shall I say?* ") "It—it's for the Croix Rouge."

"Oh, is it? Oh, yes. What's it supposed to be? A scent sachet? How pretty," exclaimed Miss Walsh, taking the thing in her hand. "Yes; of course I'll buy one. Where is my little bag?" (Bag, of crocodile and purple satin, produced.) "I'll give you something at once."

The "something" proved to be a hundred-franc note.

"Oh, no! Not all that!" gasped the impromptu Red Cross Flag seller. "It's only a franc! I *can't* take any more!"

"Oh, but of course you can. It's for the soldiers," put in Miss Walsh, a look of surprise crossing her mild, Roman-nosed face. "Of course you must take it. I like giving things. . . There! Where's the little sachet? How sweet! Did you make it yourself? I must put it in among my writing-paper." (Case produced, all Bond Street pig-skin and gold-monogrammed A. W.)

Olwen hesitated. Of course the Charm would be of no earthly good *there*, even if it were of any good at all, she thought, half fluttered, half ashamed of herself. One curious thing she had noticed about this Charm already.

Alone with it, the whole incredible theory seemed real. Brought into contact with other people, it appeared nonsense. Still, since she was going to give it a trial, she might as well do it properly. For a moment she listened again to the lonely, talkative woman.

"Oh, you know, I've always longed to give things! Only I've no one to give to. Shopping is lovely, but not when it's only for oneself—"

"No," absently from Olwen (who sometimes felt she had all Carnarvonshire commissioning *her* to shop for them as soon as she got to town). "That sachet—" she ventured presently, eyeing the case. "It's supposed to be a mascot, you know. To bring you luck."

"Oh?"

"Perhaps you don't believe in it? But if you wouldn't mind. . . To please *me*," said Olwen. "I mean to please the Red Cross! If you'd *wear* it!"

"Oh, I must wear it, must I?" (Case opened; sachet pinned by a large pearl bar to the front of the thick white satin shirt.)

"Er—Not quite like that," from Olwen. "It—I believe it has to be worn hidden. Out of sight somewhere."

"Oh, yes. Very well." (Sachet unpinned, and refastened to the brocade lining of the tweed coat.) "There!"

"But you take off your coat in the evening, don't you?" demurred Olwen, quite anxiously.

Not alone this woman's history might be changed by the wearing of a Charm, but her own. It was her love-story, Olwen's! for which that Charm was to be put on trial, too. She drew breath quickly.

"Miss Walsh! I'm so sorry to bother you! But it's something that has to be *always* worn about you. Please would you mind pinning it right inside your blouse? Or—or to the top of your stays! French people often do wear a sachet there, don't they? Then I shall—I mean you'll always be sure about it. . ."

"Oh, very well!" agreed Miss Walsh, smiling. She turned her back modestly upon Olwen, and by the movement of her elbows seemed to be busy with countless fastenings. Then she reached for a gold lace-pin from her pin-cushion. There were more jerks and fastenings-up, and presently she turned smiling to the girl.

"I have safety-pinned it right in *there*," she announced, patting a slab of satin over Heaven (and Heaven alone) knew how many layers of Jaeger, whale-bone, coutille, and solid white embroidery, and long-cloth. "There! Will that be all right?"

Olwen gave a little sigh; a breeze to carry the ship of this Adventure. It was launched!

"Thank you," she said. Then she glanced at the hundred franc note in her hand. "But I do rather feel as if I'd got this under false pretences!"

"Oh, no!" smiled the Spinster. "If the little mascot does really bring me so much Luck, it will be worth a few more francs, won't it?"

"Yes, indeed," agreed the demure Olwen, feeling as if she exchanged a mental glance with the unknown Inventor of that Charm. "It will be worth it."

IV

The Charm begins to Work

"Bescheidenheit ist eine Zier',
Doch weiter kommt man ohne ihr."

—Boche Proverbs

N o woman can get me to call her pretty," enunciated Captain Ross, "until I've seen her walk."

The fiat, delivered in that ice-ax voice of his, cut through the polyglot murmur of the visitors gathered in the shining bare salon, all mirrors and decorations of artificial iris. The voice continued to hold forth.

"Feet first; then figure. That's how it comes with me. Then hair. Fairrrr hairrr. Must be fair-to-golden. A woman who isn't bland"—this is how he pronounced it, but his hearers assumed it to mean blonde—"a woman who isn't bland is only half a woman to me."

This saying was given out on the evening of the day when the Charm had fallen into the hands of Olwen Howel-Jones.

She was sitting there at the time, on a red plush sofa next to her Uncle, at the edge of the group formed by Mrs. Cartwright (who wore a tawny-golden tea-gown and was knitting a khaki sock), Mr. Awdas, the young flying officer who looked so appropriately like an eagle with his bold features and the head that was so narrow in comparison with his wide, wing-like shoulders, and Captain Ross, the one-armed Staff Captain, who was discoursing to them on the subject of Women, of whom (as he had been known to remark) he was the finest judge in Europe.

Olwen's little jet-black head was buried in the current number of "Femina," which she had picked up from the oval, crimson-covered table in front of her, but she was devouring every word of the homily on Women.

That Captain Ross should notice a girl's feet was glad news; her own feet being not merely tiny, but of a gratifying shapeliness. But her heart seemed to sink suddenly down into the slippers that shod them, when she heard the further "demmannd" that Beauty must be fair-haired. Ah, he would never look at *her*, then!

She never, apparently, looked at him. For, regarding this one man for whom she would have given her eyes, the artless Welsh maiden had learnt Mrs. Cartwright's art of seeing without seeming to do so.

What she seemed to see were those glazed full-page French fashion-plates.

What she did see were every look and turn of the man at two arms-lengths from her, lounging in the red plush chair with its ornate écru mats. What she saw can be seen by each girl in love; "the Heart-wish Incarnate," a glamorous, radiant creature indeed!

And—What was really *there*?

Let us borrow the eyes of the others, who were not in Love with this Captain Ross, to describe him.

Young Awdas, the flyer, would have told you, *"A top-hole fellow. Bucks rather; but you get used to it. Capital chap."*

Professor Howel-Jones might have said, mildly, *"He has somewhat definite opinions, even for a man of his youth; but we allow that to those youngsters who have endured more in three years than we in three-score."*

Mrs. Cartwright, in writing to her sisters at home descriptions of every one staying at Les Pins, had set down:

"Captain Ross. Special Reserve man. Keen soldier. Came over from Canada to join in '14. Arm lost on the Somme. Shell-shock; and gas—that's why he's here for his chest, which is bad again.

"About 30; looks more. Thick-set, dark. Scarlet tabs suit him. Imagine Charles Hawtrey when young and two stone lighter; imagine a handsome black Tom-cat with a woman's mouth, from which issues a strong accent with the eternal 'Is that so—o—oh?' punctuating its speech; well, there you are. Sometimes he seems entirely Canadian; at other moments the complete Scot with every R burring like a cockchafer on a window-pane.

"Right sleeve tucked into pocket. Amazingly quick and clever at doing everything with left hand; getting notes out of case, managing siphon, lighting cigar.

"Eyes, hard brown, watchful as a robin's (I don't think they see anything, but he hates me).

"Would not be good-looking but for the lower half of his face; that mouth really beautiful, tenderly curved and sensitive, and constantly showing an even row of the milkiest teeth in the world.

"Intensely sure of self (to put it kindly).

*"Has the look that one recognizes as the trace of women's
eyes and lips upon his face, but nothing that counts up to now,
I think."*

The man thus unknowingly summed up brought out his cigarette-case with that clever left hand of his and proffered it first to the woman who had summed him up and then to Jack Awdas.

This was the tall blonde flyer, who was sitting beside her; a striking young figure. A woman would have noticed first his eyes and the changeful expressions that darted swift as racing planes across their blueness. One was an eager, anticipatory look. *"What have you for me?"* it demanded of Life. *"Will you be wonderful? Shall I be satisfied?"* One was a look of joyous mastery. *"Love me,"* it seemed to say to Fate herself. *"Give me and tell me all that I ask, for I am impatient Youth, and must be served."* One was a look less often seen; it was the "yonderly" look, the glance of those favoured (or cursed) with a glimpse now and then beyond the kindly curtains of the Flesh and of Everyday. . . It seemed to question a surprised *"What? I can't quite see. . . What? . . . I heard something. . ."*

Needless to say that the youth himself was entirely ignorant that any of these signals could be read. Generally, he was healthily unconscious that there was anything to be signalled.

To the French people in that hotel he was known as Monsieur de l'Audace.

His observer, his squadron, and several enemy airmen could have told you that he deserved the nickname, but no other decoration had been granted to him. In that last ghastly dive from the clouds he had so nearly lost, too, everything that was his; however, health and strength and full power of limb were returning now, and youth, and sleep o' nights, and careless gaiety. Quite often now his laugh rang out; it was still a trifle husky, as was his boyish, nonchalant voice. (One of his many wounds had been in his throat.)

"Go on, Ross," he jeered amicably. "Let's have some more of your priceless pointers on the Sex. What was the one you gave me today going along the sea-wall? Oh, yes; 'Never make love to a woman with a pink chin; she's older than she looks.'"

"Why, that's quite true," put in the deep voice of Mrs. Cartwright, mildly. She crossed one long, gold-draped leg over the other, and threw an amused glance through the cigarette-haze at the finest judge of women in Europe. "D'you mind if I put that into a book, Captain Ross?"

"You'd better not put anything I say into any book you write," the Staff Captain advised her, with a short laugh (while Olwen, head still deep in the journal, drank in every syllable of the assured voice). "Your public wouldn't stand for it, Domestica."

"This would not be a 'Domestica' book," returned the writer, with a little tilt of her brown head over her knitting. "This is a little book I'm going to bring out seven years hence, for my own two boys. A sort of manual to help them when they go courting. 'The Guide to the Girl,' I shall call it."

"The title has one very all right sound," laughed Captain Ross. "But if you'll pardon my saying so, Mrs. Cartwright, I guess I could compile that book considerably better than what you could."

"Not you!" declared Mrs. Cartwright. "Most of those manuals are written from the point of view of the man. That's where they fall short. *I* should make the Girl herself do the advising. I should let her give the 'pointers,' as Mr. Awdas calls them. I should divide them into little chapters: '*Of Proposing*,' '*Of Presents*,' '*Of In-Laws*,' '*Of Caresses*'—"

"'*Of Caresses*,'" took up Captain Ross, with another laugh, "is going to get you banned by the libraries."

"Not it. I," said Mrs. Cartwright, knitting, "shall not treat the subject in—in that way."

"Then that manual of yours isn't going to help your boys a lot," affirmed Captain Ross in his most final tone. "For, see here—"

"Olwen *fach*," said the Professor, suddenly taking his pipe out of his mouth and looking over the smudged black sheet of "La Patria," "isn't it time for you to go to bed?"

"Uncle!" came indignantly from behind the fashion-plates: "It's only half-past nine!"

A smile went round the little group of the English about that table; the eyes of each turned upon Nineteen who was being treated as Ten years old. She would have kept up the screen of her "Femina," but Mrs. Cartwright, finishing off a row of her knitting, put it aside, and drew nearer to the girl.

"May I look at them with you?" she said, pleasantly, and the two shared the fashion-drawings, while the men watched; Captain Ross, with a curl of the lip and a remark about Women and their fairrrrm conviction that, because clothes are drawn one way in a picture that's the way they'll look when they've gotten them on.

Mrs. Cartwright lifted her head quickly, but it was not to retort to this. She had suddenly seen something (as usual, without looking at it) that surprised her. Then she dropped her head again.

"My dear!" she murmured to Olwen in an amazed little laugh. "Did you ever know such a thing? There! Coming in through the dining-room door, now! You can see her in the mirror, behind those French children playing draughts. It's the Hotel Spinster we were looking at, at lunch today," chattered Mrs. Cartwright in the soft stream that scarcely moved her lips. "The woman I said had never had a man to look at her. Can I believe my eyes? She's got a man with her now!"

"Miss Walsh?" exclaimed Olwen, gazing with all her eyes into the mirror that showed her this group.

Miss Walsh, in a fur coat, had evidently just come in from the Forest; she carried a bough of arbutus, and her cheeks were pink from walking in the clear night air. Close beside her came the man—yes! the male, masculine man who was her companion; the sturdy blue-clad French sergeant who had been at the table d'hôte. Across the intervening groups of people he was seen to be all smiles and gestures, the traditional gallantry of his nation spoke in the very bend of his back as he opened the door, bowed again, clicked his spurred heels. Miss Walsh was holding out her hand; her lips parted, obviously in one of her characteristic "Oh's"—the pink upon her cheeks deepened as she took leave of this cavalier. One could almost hear her struggling French. She looked back again; another bow, another click of the heels from her escort. Then the sergeant marched back down the room, beaming satisfaction painted upon every line of his face, bold, swarthy, and somewhat bull-necked. He was what his own family described as "beau garçon"; a fine figure of a man. He disappeared, through the ante-room, towards that wing of the hotel inhabited by the management; Monsieur Leroux (bald, amiable, the shape of a captive balloon), his three pigtailed daughters of exquisite manners, and his alert wife (who ran everything—including him—in the hotel).

"Heavens!" exclaimed Mrs. Cartwright absently, as she took up her knitting again, "that must have been Madame Leroux's nephew. Her sister's son, the *artilleriste*. I heard all about him the other day. Gustave Tronchet his name is. Madame told me that he was coming here *en perme* as her guest, seeing she had no son, and that he loved to eat well and to be *bien* generally. I suppose she is introducing him—!"

"Some romance!" laughed Captain Ross, jerking his head towards the door through which the fur-clad form of the lonely traveller had disappeared. This was the first remark of his to which Olwen had paid scant attention. As suddenly as if some one had called her, she sprang up. She had dropped a kiss on her Uncle's thistle-down locks, had given her hand to Mrs. Cartwright, had launched a shy glance and a "good night" in the direction of the others, and had darted away, a slim sprite in grey with touches of black, almost before the two young men could rise to their feet.

Mrs. Cartwright was still thinking of the stiletto-eyed French manageress who had introduced her nephew to the occupant of the best room in the hotel.

"What family spirit!" she admired. "What sense of possibilities! What respect for Power—I mean money. What an admirable nation they are. . . Will ours ever learn foresight and thrift from theirs?"

"Ours—that is, mine—has family loyalty very strongly too," the Professor joined in. "The Welsh, my dear lady, are as clannish in that way as the French; they'll do anything for 'my nephew.'"

"They've an eye skinned for the dollars as well," volunteered Captain Ross, his robin-like eye twinkling as he took out a cigar. "What's that saying—ah, yes, God made a Welshman, and God made a Jew, but thank God he never made a Welsh Jew!"

The Professor stiffened a little; and Mrs. Cartwright, seeing this, drew the conversation back to the worldly aspects of germinating Romance. . .

The drift of all these remarks would have been entirely lost upon Olwen even had she stayed to hear them.

For she knew better. She knew that it was not Madame Leroux, the manageress, who was responsible for the coming together of a travelling spinster and of a French soldier on leave. She, Olwen, knew what was responsible for those attentions, that talk, that interested, deferential smile on the part of the man who had attached himself to her new-made friend. Olwen knew what had attracted him where no man had ever been attracted before. Yes! She knew! This was the work of the Charm that she herself had seen hidden away so near to an unsought heart. . .

This nephew of a French hotel manageress. . . of course he wasn't exactly the sort of admirer who belonged in Granges with grounds full of rhododendrons, but he was a *man*, triumphed Olwen. There'd be others, people that Miss Agatha Walsh could think seriously about; but he was the *beginning*! He'd shown the success of her experiment. The

Charm *could* work. That letter was *not* all nonsense! It was all true! And since the Charm had worked for Miss Walsh, it would work for—well, others! Joy, oh joy!

Bursting with joy, in fact, the girl darted out of the *salon*, scampering upstairs in all haste to overtake Miss Walsh, and to hear more of this.

She hoped to catch her up at her bedroom door, but already Miss Walsh had gone in.

Olwen knocked; was asked, "Who's there?"

"Only me—Olwen!"

"Come in," was the muffled answer. It came from behind a handful of Miss Walsh's hair, quite abundant and almost pretty, now that she had removed the flattening net and taken it all down. The first glance showed Olwen that it was not just "down" for the night. There was a side glass in Miss Walsh's hand; a thick loop of her locks was coiled up at the back, ready for the side "bits" to be drawn across in a simpler fashion than the upholstery of puffs and curls. Yes! She was seeing how she looked with her hair done a different way! Ah, sign of the times, that could spell only one thing: M—A—N!

"I—I only came in to say good night to you," Olwen began (really longing to ply with questions; how—how soon did It work—what happened—).

Miss Walsh turned a face as transfigured as Olwen's own above her quilted dressing jacket.

She looked ten years younger. She held her head at almost the angle of those who have *not* been born with the saddle. All fluttered and flushed she was, but delighted; a once bleak landscape that a sun-ray lightens. For it is your lifelong teetotaller who, rescued from Death, perks up at the first sip of restorative. It was the elder Miss Walsh's cloistered companion who was responding to that tonic: masculine attention. She turned a new smile upon Olwen.

"Oh, it's you," she exclaimed, with new notes in her voice. Then she broke into the breathless talk which was to her as new a function as shopping for herself.

"I've been out!" with a wave towards the arbutus-bough on her table. "Oh, it is such a lovely night! Oh! You've no idea how glorious the stars looked, peeping down between the branches of the pines! I've *never* seen them so wonderful, never. I went for a stroll in the Forest after dinner, do you know—Oh! You saw me come in? Oh, I never saw you. Yes; I—I went with somebody—" she babbled on. "That Monsieur

Tronchet, the French soldier. He is a sergeant. . . but everybody in the Army is anything just now, aren't they? He showed me the Avenue leading out into the woods. . . Was it very extraordinary of me to go out for a walk with him? Oh, I don't think it matters, do you? Everything's so different. . . in France. He spoke to me at dinner; I believe I'd taken his place by mistake—then we talked—"

"*Ah*," came softly from Olwen, standing there listening, listening to her witness for the power of the Charm. It had forced this man to speak; it had drawn him! . . . "Oh, and he's such a delightful person," Miss Walsh poured out between gasps. "He has been telling me such a lot of the most interesting things about himself and the War! He spoke slowly, when I asked him. I could really understand most of it. He expresses himself so wonderfully! The French all do, I suppose. But he finds the English so sympathetic. Oh, and what do you think? You won't laugh, I know; you're so sweet. I am going to be his *marraine*. God-mother, that is. They all have them in the French Army, he tells me; somebody who just writes very often and takes an interest. He told me he hadn't any. So I promised. We are to write to each other when he gets back to the front. Oh, and tomorrow—what do you think? He is going to take me across the lagoon in the motor-boat!" breathed Miss Walsh, and her eyes were now those of a child who has been promised a fairy treat. "I don't think any one has ever taken me in a boat before. This is a wonderful place, isn't it? I am so glad I came!—Oh, are you going to bed now? I shall see you tomorrow. I feel as if I knew *such* a lot of nice people already! Good night!" and her door closed upon a very happy face.

Equally excited, and even happier, little Olwen sped up another flight of stairs to her room. Stars danced in her eyes. It was true! It was all true! she rejoiced. *Now—!*

Yes; now, Captain Ross, *en garde!* Stipulate as you choose for the colour of Beauty's hair; swear that no woman is Woman to you except a blonde. One little sooty-haired brunette is now no longer to be cast down by your specifications. Say what you like; she has confidence in what she is going to do.

SHE BURST INTO HER ROOM, snapped on the lights, ran to the drawer, snatched out work-basket, thimble, needle, silk; now the mauve ribbon! Now the packet containing that so potent Charm!

Then down she sat again to work as she had worked that afternoon, but in all certainty instead of doubt. Snip—snip—snip. Three lengths of ribbon, and to each a sachet.

"I'll have to buy yards and yards and yards of this ribbon presently," thought Olwen feverishly as she stitched. "And I'll have to send to that address for all the Charm that they can send me; all that there is in the world!"

She rolled a sheet of note-paper into a little funnel; and through this she filled—ah, so cautiously!—the sachets with the musky, seed-like powder.

She sighed: "*What* a pity that I've only got enough here for four of us!"

V

Further Plans for the Charm

"Je dirai qu'une femme ne doit jamais écrire. . .

"Je ne vois qu'une exception; c'est une femme qui fait des livres pour nourrier ou élever sa famille.

"Alors elle doit toujours se retrancher dans l'intérêt d'argent en parlant de ses ouvrages, et dire, par exemple, à un chef d'escadron: 'Votre état vous donne quatre mille francs par an, et moi, avec mes deux traductions de l'anglais, j'ai pu, l'année dernière, consacrer trois mille cinq cents francs de plus à l'éducation de mes deux fils.'"

—Stendhal

Now so far one charm-sachet was accounted for. It was safety-pinned into the high busk of Miss Walsh's almost obsolete corset. The second Olwen now hung about her own neck. Even in sleep she would never be parted from it. Let her absorb its potency every hour of the day or night! Therefore she sewed to the square of mauve satin a piece of pink baby-ribbon, tied it in a bow and slipped it over her head. *Her* charm!

There were (until she obtained more of that magic stuff) two sachets left.

Over these she pondered, running her needle into the flannel leaf of her needle-book.

"There's one thing to be seen yet," she meditated. "I've seen it work once. It's been a success all right with a woman. The question is—Will it work with a man? I must try."

So the destination of the third sachet was decided. That young and pink-faced subaltern should have it; he who had such blushing struggles with his French and who seemed to have no more friends than had Miss Walsh; he who had told Mrs. Cartwright so frankly that he was an ex-shop assistant, with the joys of travelling first-class (and of living to match) gone to his boyish head. Yes; the disturbing

Charm should be applied to help him. She would think out the "how" tomorrow.

But the fourth sachet? To whom should she give that?

Perhaps it was the passing thought of her writer-friend that brought in its train a bright idea.

Mrs. Cartwright!

"Why shouldn't I give her the Charm? Why shouldn't she enjoy life a little bit more before she's quite, quite an old woman?" thought the girl. "Of course she's not young; older than Miss Walsh even. And not pretty—well, how could any one be pretty at forty—even though her clothes do seem to fit her, and she does run up and down those sandhills as fast as I can. She's awfully jolly and nice, though; so kind, too! I daresay she'd like to be married again. I daresay she's tired of always writing and writing. Tired of living all by herself when those boys of hers are at school. I daresay she'd like to have somebody nice and sort of settled-down to help her with them. Now if only she could attract somebody! Somebody like that—"

Here a second brilliant idea flashed into that well-willing, impulsive little black head of Olwen's. She uttered it aloud, the name of this "somebody" who might be suitably attracted by Mrs. Cartwright—even at forty.

"*Uncle!*"

All alone in her room, Olwen clapped her hands over this idea. Swiftly it began to enlarge itself.

"Yes; why not Uncle? The very person! He's old, but then that's all the better; for her. He's just the right age, in fact!"

Professor Howel-Jones was a sturdy seventy; and to Nineteen the gap between forty and seventy, seen vaguely down the perspective of the years, is scarcely noticeable, particularly when it is the man who is seventy—men generally being of themselves younger than women. (Or so we are told.)

"Yes; it must be Uncle. He's such a dear. A widower, too; and I'm sure he ought to have somebody nice to be a comfort to him, always there. Not only me. Besides, I might be—"

She hardly dared yet to finish to herself the thought, "Besides, I might be getting married and leaving him any time now!"

So she pursued her ingenuous scheme. "He ought to have a nice wife. He really ought. And Mrs. Cartwright would be splendid—for him. He does like her. He was talking to her for hours in the Forest the other day about that essay of his on Welsh Flower-names. He calls her 'My dear lady' always. And she likes him; why, only at lunch today she said something about 'that wonderful-looking old Uncle of yours.' She admires him. Now, if she only had enough Charm to *attract* him," thought Olwen, "so that he would ask her to marry him, I'm sure she'd be only too glad to! I don't suppose any one else has ever asked her to marry again... but I would so like her for a kind of Auntie," decided the young girl, hastily taking out her needle again and threading it with pink silk.

Another length of narrow ribbon was stitched to one end of the fourth sachet.

It was destined for the neck of Mrs. Cartwright.

At Olwen's age a thing is considered better left undone, than not done at once.

At once she decided to take this gift to her friend.

So, still dressed as she had left the *salon*, Olwen slipped quickly out of her room and down a sharply-angled corridor, passing as she went the old Frenchman with the red speck in his button-hole and the elder lady in mourning.

Olwen glanced up at the numbers on the doors.

... "22," that was Mr. Awdas's room; she had overheard him telling Madame that he would remember *vingt-deux* because it was his own age. "23," next to it on the right; that was Mrs. Cartwright's. Olwen hoped that she had not yet gone to bed.

She tapped.

"*Entrez!*" called Mrs. Cartwright's deep voice, rather absorbed.

Olwen entered, to find the writer apparently ready for bed, but at work.

Her green shaded lamp was alight on the table, where she sat with a pad before her.

Her brown hair hung down in two plaits over a Persian robe of raw white silk, almost seamless, gold-girdled, and with stars and islands worked in gold thread; a relic of her time in the East. Another relic, perhaps, was the mingling of faint discreet scents that hung about the room: sandal-wood, orris, kuss-kuss, and rose.

She looked up; then sprang to her feet as she saw Olwen Howel-Jones, still dressed as she had gone to bed some time before.

"My dear—Anything wrong?"

"No! No, thanks," said Olwen. Then involuntarily and surprised,

"Oh, Mrs. Cartwright! how wonderful you look in that dressing-gown! Your arm, when the sleeve fell back, was like a little statue my Uncle's got in Liverpool, copied from the British Museum. A Tanagra, he calls it. You look exactly like that statue, you do really."

"Do I?" returned Mrs. Cartwright, with a passing glance down her own long outlines from the shoulder to the narrow Turkish-slippered foot on the mat. It was no news to her that she possessed, even yet, some lines that sculptors centuries dead would have loved. Like many another plain-faced woman (as she was self-admitted) she had her special vanity. Her own pride of limb was as arrogant as it was secret.

"My boys are going to inherit my absurdly long legs, I think," was all she said, lightly, smiling down into the vivid little face of the girl who had come in, and wondering what had brought her there so late.

Olwen held it out, the Charm dangling at the end of its long ribbons. As she was hastening along the corridor she had wondered what excuse she could bring with it. Now she felt that it was unnecessary display, that invention of the Red Cross Charity Sale which she had palmed off upon poor Miss Walsh. The truth—or a small portion of it—seemed to blurt itself out to Mrs. Cartwright.

"I've got something here that I've made for you," explained Olwen, flushing a little. "It's—it's a luck-charm. Like a touchwood or a swastika, only—only different. There's something in the sachet that will bring you very good luck if you always keep it on where it can't be seen. Don't ask me what it is," she begged, lifting her earnest little face that the elder woman found so touchingly pretty. "And please don't open it. Only always wear it, will you, please?"

"Thank you so much; of course I will. I can do with any good luck that's going just now," smiled Mrs. Cartwright. She slipped the ribbon over her head and tucked the sachet inside the soft folds of her Persian robe. "There! It's like a scapular that the little French children have; I remember seeing a flock of them once, trooping in to bathe off the coast of Normandy, wearing nothing else; their little bodies each marked by the black scapular, were like pink tulips freaked with one dark stripe. . . May I take it off when I wash? Good. Now I'll expect it'll bring me luck for finishing the last chapters of my serial."

"Are you going to sit there and write all night?" asked Olwen, with an eye on the half-covered pad.

"Oh dear, no! Just another hour or so, perhaps. I was only recopying a paragraph, and then I found I was in the vein and could go on. But you—you mustn't lose your beauty-sleep," she added, gently smiling at the pretty creature in the doorway. "Good night!"

"Good night!" said Olwen, with a final glance at the edge of that pink ribbon showing above her friend's unconscious neck. She sped away—to dream, as she hoped, of all that Charm might be expected to bring her, but in reality to the dreamless perfect sleep that is Youth's heritage.

The half-gentle, half-amused little smile hovered about Mrs. Cartwright's lips for a moment, then gave way gradually to the look of blank absorption as she bent her brown head over her pad, writing rapidly, filling a page, tearing it off, to add to the pile at her feet, filling another.

IT HAD BEEN A LONG apprenticeship which she had served to this job of hers, since she had first been left as a young widow, to fend for herself and two babies on the pension which her country judged sufficient for the families of the (Old) Army. Ream after ream she had written on the once so fully discussed subjects: What to do with the Cold Mutton; and, How to Keep a Husband's Affection Warm.

To say that this occupation thrilled her would be overstating the case, but Mrs. Cartwright had preferred it to the thought of letting some other man pay for her board and lodging, some man who was not her Keith. This alternative had been hers more than once (in spite of little Olwen's conjecture that she had never been asked to marry again). She had refused; working on, in her poky "rooms." . . . At all events, those cold-mutton articles had put plenty of nourishing beef-gravy into little Keith; and when Reggie had nearly gone out with bronchitis she had settled the doctor's bills with her brightly-written instructions as to always keep a smiling face and a dainty blouse for when Hubby got back from a hard day's work in the office. A fortnight's fresh air at Margate had been supplied to the small convalescent by his Mother's "Chats to Engaged Girls," which discussed "how many and many a foolish damsel brings shipwreck upon her life's happiness by her failure to realize that her fiancé cannot be expected to give up for her sake every hobby, every recreation, every chum that he possesses," etc. etc.

When this sort of journalism became superannuated "Domestica" adapted herself swiftly. Business-like columns on Emigration and Fruit Farming for Women paid for the boys' first reefer-coats. Their school-kits came out of the long serials to which she had at last attained, and which became a never-failing joke with those of her acquaintances who had cultured literary tastes.

"My *dear* Claudia, I see you've been and gone and done it again, in the 'Morning Mail,'" they had smiled. "Another of your sugary fullertons—I mean 'A thrilling new story, by Miss Claudia Crane! You can begin today!' You don't expect Us to, I hope?"

"Oh no," Mrs. Cartwright had said, also smiling.

After all, these literary tastes of her acquaintances were no more "superior" than the thickness of her new woollies that she was then going on to buy for her sons' wear.

Moreover, the woollies were of more use.

(Furthermore, they were harder to come by.)

AT THE JUNCTURE WHEN MRS. CARTWRIGHT enters this story she was able to make any holiday pay for itself twice over; witness her "Wanderings in Western France." It was about this time, too, that she had begun to afford not only the warmest underwear for Keith and Reggie, but the silkiest for herself.

Even yet, she discovered, silk "things" were a joy to her again. So were her perfectly simple *suède* shoes. All these years she had lived and toiled for Reggie and Keith; she was only just beginning to find herself in this toiler. She was beginning to discover other relics, beside the Eastern embroideries and the scent, of the woman whom she had thought to be left dead beside her merry soldier husband.

Surprising. . . Life was still surprising; interesting. Let people take it out of her "fullertons" if it amused them. . .

She completed the "sugary" paragraph that brought her instalment to the required "curtain," wrote "*To be continued*" beneath it, and smoothed the blotting-paper down over the pad with a sigh of relief.

"There!"

She rose, stretching the tall symmetry of herself under the Persian robe, then glanced with raised eye-brows at her watch.

So late? She had not realized the flight of the midnight hours. Everybody else in the hotel would be asleep.

Mrs. Cartwright snapped off the lights. Guided by a thin streak of moonlight on the floor, she stepped to the window, flung first the shutters then the windows open, and stepped out, all shimmering and ghostly, on to her balcony. She stood—accustomed to air about her—looking out on the moon-bathed scene below. The *Baissin* was a sheet of silver; the belt of sandhills silver-grey. No words can give the whiteness of the Biscay rollers, silent with distance, tossing their columns of foam to the vast and lambent sky. Stars were as pin-points. Reassuringly near, the lighthouse raised its taper finger, on which the light sparkled like a jewel, now white, now red.

Mrs. Cartwright, enjoying all this too much to feel cold, stood watching.

Why did people sleep away the best part of the twenty-four hours? Why scuttle away and hide from Beauty within the ugliness of their own houses? It was only once in months that a woman stood as she was standing at that virgin hour, able to lose herself in the solitude, the freshness and silence and light. She stood, dematerialized, part no longer of a woman's warm and pulsing body, but of the sea and sky themselves. . . White, red. . . White, red. . . the phare light flashed almost in time to the soft breathing, that could be heard, in that perfect stillness of her body. *She* was outside it. . . *Ah!* What was that?

With a start so violent that it seemed to wrench her, Mrs. Cartwright came to herself again, and to—what Horror was this?

Through that perfect stillness a cry had rung out, sudden as a shot. Close beside her; it came from the right. It was a man's voice crying hoarsely, "*Got* him!" Then another cry, of agony; a scream. . .

What was it?

VI

The Clutching of the Charm

*"Fights all his battles o'er again;
And thrice he charged the foe, and thrice he slew the slain."*

—Dryden

"Un aviateur, un de ces demi-dieux dont l'existence sur terre doit être courte. (La lumière dont ils procèdent les rappelle bientôt. On croit qu'ils tombent, mais ils remontent.)"

—Marcel Astruc

It came from the right, therefore it must be in the bedroom next to hers on the wall encircled by the balcony.

Quick as thought, Mrs. Cartwright ran a few steps along the balcony. Yes; the next window stood wide open. She dashed into the room, flooded with moonlight; white light that showed up, clearer than a star-shell, the figure of Mr. Awdas, the young wounded flying-officer, sitting bolt upright in his bed, with his eyes still closed, his mouth too working, and his face as the face of Death itself.

She ran to him, took him by the shoulder.

"Wake up! Wake up!" she called, clearly and firmly, in the voice which had often delivered her small son Keith from the bane of his childhood, nightmare. "Wake up, it's just a dream!"

A great shudder rocked the young man, he opened his eyes. Their wild stare met the woman's face, the woman's white-clad figure bending over him. "Oh Lord! Sister," he muttered. "It all came again. Oh, Lord! I thought I was crashing. I—"

Shuddering again, shaking like a leaf, he threw out his hands and grasped Mrs. Cartwright's arms, his fingers burying themselves in her flesh. "Don't leave me," he sobbed, hoarsely. "For God's sake don't leave me, Sister!"

Before Mrs. Cartwright could speak the door of his bedroom was flung open. There burst in a group of people in night attire, a group heterogeneous and agitated as on a raid night or at a fire, roused by the alarm of that sudden scream in the darkness, demanding "Qu'est-ce qu'il y a donc?" . . . "What's up? . . ."

Mrs. Cartwright, pinned in the grip of the young man's shaking hands, had only time to realize two of these people, the portly French manager, draped in an eider-down and looking (as she afterwards said) a perfect advertisement for Michelin tyres, and Captain Ross, in violently-striped pyjamas, when she saw the door gently but firmly closing upon all of the invaders but Captain Ross.

In a curious medley of idiom Captain Ross was reassuring the others.

"It's all right. *C'est seulement* Monsieur de l'Audace. He's been drrrriming again; *songe*, crasher; *comprenez*? Pardon me, but please *allez vous en*. I guess we can fix him, me and this lady. *Bon nuit!*"

A final glimpse of open-mouthed faces, seen over dressing-gowned shoulders, and then the door clicked upon the murmuring, dispersing throng. Captain Ross, barefoot, turned back to the bed where his friend, utterly unnerved, was shaking as if with fever. His fingers still gripped the arms that had first been held out to him; his wet forehead was now pressed to a woman's shoulder, as if to shut out from his sight a vision of horror.

"Oh Lord!" he groaned.

"All over, Jack. Put a pipe on," said Captain Ross quietly.

And Mrs. Cartwright glancing at him over that rumpled head buried on her shoulder, beheld a Captain Ross quite new to her; not merely the finest judge of women in Europe, but the fine comrade of men. It was with an admirable mixture of gentleness and matter-of-factness that he spoke, moving as he did so quietly and quickly about the room; closing the shutters, to banish the ghastly radiance of the moon; turning up the yellow, mercifully ordinary lights; finding flask, a tobacco, pipe, and matches; handier and swifter with his one arm than many a man with two.

"Put a pipe on, man. Here. No? All right; presently. Rotten luck; I thought we were clear of these attacks. It's this darned moon. . . He was shot down in the moonlight, I heard. . . We used to get 'em every week one time, Mrs. Cartwright; the whole ward pulled up standing, and the girls on night duty thinking it was blue murder, I guess, the first time. I knew when I heard him; we were in hospital together."

"He thought he was still in hospital when he saw me," put in Mrs. Cartwright softly.

"Is that so? You only reached him first by seconds, I guess; I was up before he'd finished hollering," said Captain Ross, with a glance at the spent boy who was leaning up against the woman, his face still hidden, his breath coming in gasps. "It was a baddish go, this trip. A drink, man?"

Young Awdas shook his head without raising it. "I'm. . . all right. Dashed sorry. . . all right in a second. . ."

"Give it him presently," murmured Captain Ross; then glancing at the woman beside the bed, "There won't be much sleeping for him or me; but it's no reason why you should lose your night's rest, Mrs. Cartwright. I'm staying. No need for you to wait up any longer."

But at this, those clutching hands of the boy gripped her tight again, closing upon the silken folds above her breast. She answered the quick involuntary appeal, feeling herself caught back to the times when little Keith, waking in fright, had clutched her, and cried: *Don't go Mums! I want you to stay with me!*"

"I'm not going," she said, just as she had said then. She let herself slip down in a sitting posture to the edge of the bed.

Captain Ross paused, with another swift glance at the group.

"You'll stay with him?"

"Of course."

"I guess he's better in your hands; I'll leave him there," said Captain Ross with a nod. He glanced about, picked up the thick dressing-gown that lay over the bed-rail, and tucked it like a railway rug about her. Then he turned to the door. "I'm just across the corridor. If you want anything, just call, ever so softly. I shall hear."

He went out, leaving Mrs. Cartwright to the oddest vigil she had ever spent. For the first time she found herself watching through the small hours in the company of a wounded lad who had come through that Hell which is not always left behind on the battlefield. They bring some of it away with them, too many of these boys! its fiery traces still impressed upon mind and brain and nerve, however plucky. Its memory persists, robbing them of laughter, despoiling them of that dreamless perfect sleep which is Youth's heritage, making of night a thing to be dreaded.

So this young airman, who had been shot down in an air duel one moonlight night last spring, must live it through again and again before he might live it away. . .

Presently he raised his head. He began to mutter.

She listened, pitifully, knowing that the lad scarcely knew even yet whom he was holding—save that it was human, and friendly, and warm. He scarcely cared to whom he was babbling in hoarse little snatches, incoherently—save that it was a woman, and kind.

"Five—five of them! Five Australians!" he began, suddenly. "You know what splendid fine chaps. . . I had to watch. . . I was lying. . . out there. . . pinned under the wing. They. . . they tried to get at me with stretchers—six times they tried. . . came across No Man's Land. . ."

"Yes; but you were dreaming," she said, in the most soothing tone of her deep voice. "You just had a bad dream—"

"No, No! It was what happened," he said hoarsely. "They were trying to bring me in after I'd crashed. Those blighters. . . turned a machine-gun on to them. They did in five. I—I saw it!"

She could only look at him, only give him the comfort of her touch, could only put out to him, silently, all the pity that was in her.

He took one hand away for a moment, passed it back over his hair in the known gesture of the flyer who adjusts his crest like cap, then returned his clasp to her arm.

He began again:

"I. . . I never take an Australian's salute in the street without remembering. . . that! . . . I had to lie there. . . couldn't lift. . . finger. Five of them, were stretched out. . . killed. . . Just for me! My God! Think of it—" He seemed about to break down once more.

"Hush!" Mrs. Cartwright said, steadily. She bent her eyes upon his. "Hush! One can't think like that. It's impossible."

"Those splendid chaps—"

"S'sh! Remember only that they were killed doing one of the finest things a soldier is called to do," interrupted the soldier's widow, quickly. "Remember that their people would be proud to know how it happened. They volunteered to save you; took their chance. Think how your own people would have been proud, Mr. Awdas—"

"Yes," he muttered, letting her hold his eyes, clinging to her for the strength that had slipped.

She repeated, firmly: "When you see Australians in the street, think only of *that*!"

"Yes," said the youngster, simply. "Yes. . . All right, I will."

When he next spoke there was a thought less strain in his husky voice.

"I'm everlastingly sorry, routing people up like this. They got quite fed-up in the hospital. . . I couldn't help it. . . Falling, falling—oh, it's beastly. . . So weird, too. . . You wouldn't think. . . Well, I couldn't *take* more than about two and a half minutes to crash, could I?"

"I suppose not," she said, forcing herself to be as matter-of-fact as Captain Ross had been.

"Two and a half minutes; well, it seemed a *week*, at least. Absolutely. It always seems a week till I come down. . . Down, down, down—I seemed to have time to think. . . no end of things. I yelled out to my observer. . . That's why I always shout in those dreams of mine. . . I was falling, falling; and calling out to my observer, trying to make him hear. He was killed."

"Was he?" she responded gently—not too gently, lest he should melt.

"Yes! He was dead before we came down. Jolly good chap, my observer. (Ross knew him.) Ferris, his name was. The first time we went up together over the Boche lines, I remember his saying to me: 'Now, when you hear a dog bark, don't take any notice; it's only Archie!'"

Here the ghost of a smile seemed hovering about the young flyer's face. Mrs. Cartwright did not speak; but surely the warm sympathy that flowed from her caught him in some restoring current. His voice grew less strained with every sentence.

"It's—it's a funny thing how fond one gets of one's observer; the man one's always with. Each of you depending so much on the other, I suppose; being for it together, always together. You've no idea what pals one gets. I—I sometimes think there can be nothing like it. We *were* pals; I was sick; they'd done him in—"

Mrs. Cartwright nodded; listening to the husky English boy's voice, that seemed to fill this room of a sleeping, silent French hotel, and hearing also in her heart that immortal plaint of the young fellow-soldier mourning down the ages—"*I am distressed for thee, my brother Jonathan. . .*"

"D'you know, I sometimes think there can be nothing else in the world as good as just friendship. To be absolute friends with some other fellow," young Awdas said presently; shyly, but earnestly looking into the woman-face so near him. Without speaking a word, Mrs. Cartwright was encouraging him to talk on and on. Yes; let him talk—of Friendship or the Differential Calculus, if he liked; anything, rather than let him be haunted again by this useless, this unreasoning Remorse that he had been the death of five other brave men—or by this dream of falling,

falling. He talked on, sitting up; taking his hands at last from her (badly-marked) arms and clasping them about his knees.

"Absolute friends," he mused. "Understanding everything the other chap means, or doesn't mean. Not minding if he's ratty sometimes; being ratty yourself if you want to, and going off on your own, knowing it'll be all right whenever you come back. Good times or rotten times, always with him. Not seeing each other for ages, perhaps. Then finding him just the same. Caring for all the things you're keenest about; barring the same things. I don't think it could be ever exactly like that with a girl."

"Never," murmured Mrs. Cartwright; "the girl will be more to you or less to you, but not the same."

"A girl would never be more to me," said young Awdas, and now his voice sounded almost normal. He broke off suddenly, and turned to her protestingly. "Mrs. Cartwright, I don't know what you must think of me. Keeping you up like this—Good Lord! it's three o'clock. Sitting there, catching cold—?"

"I'm never cold."

"And I'm all right now. Please—please do go to bed."

Mrs. Cartwright smiled obstinately. "My good young man, I am on night-duty. You called me 'Sister' yourself when I came in. I am going to be 'Sister' for once."

"You're too good," he said, with a sigh of obvious relief that she was not going. "I couldn't sleep. . . but why should you miss yours?"

"I couldn't sleep now, either; I couldn't have slept. I'd only just finished working when you called out. I shall stay"—she tucked the dressing-gown a little more closely about her—"and—No, I won't have a cigarette. I'll light one for you, however. And here's your drink, and I shall just stay and talk to you until you go to sleep."

"Too good," he said again, taking the cigarette from her hand and giving her a shyly grateful glance. "I've been bucking no end—I don't know why—I don't generally talk a lot."

She knew it; knew also that the distraught boy would not have talked to a man as he had let himself babble, almost hysterically, to her. (It is only women, the so-called talkative sex, who could give statistics of how much men talk, and of what they will talk, upon occasion!) Up to that night, he had not exchanged a dozen sentences with her since they had been staying at the hotel. That same evening, when Mrs. Cartwright and his friend Ross had chipped each other in the *salon* over her "Manual of Courtship," had been the first occasion

BERTA RUCK

that Awdas had found himself sitting next to this tall countrywoman of his.

But now he turned his eyes upon her as if she were all that is meant by the word Home.

These wakeful, solitary, strange hours had made them friends such as two years of ordinary companionship could not have seen them. Both knew that never again could they be mere hotel acquaintances.

She looked at the face that was falling at last into lines of composure; no longer a white mask of strain and anguish. Colour was coming back, and a smile took the place of that intently thinking ghost behind the blue eyes. He lifted that small head, set so eagle-wise upon the wide shoulders, breathed more deeply; and she knew that it was she who had restored him, this fallen cloud-sweeper. Fancifully she thought of his daring job as something still verging on the super-human; after all, these flying lads, with their freedom of one element more, are the half-gods of our time. She thought of that myth of the other half-god Antaëus, who, to gain fresh life, must draw it from the touch of earth; and she remembered that Woman (that last creature to be civilized) is still generations nearer than man to the healing soil. Yes; she had healed him.

Without showing him that she did so, she studied his face, with its soft fruit-like oval that does not survive the first quarter of a century. Twenty-two! He seemed, as most young soldiers do nowadays, more than his age. Yet in some ways he looked younger.

After a puff or two of cigarette-smoke had risen into the air, she asked gently, "Why did you say, just now, that a girl could never mean more to you than friendship?"

He said simply, "I don't know. Perhaps it is because I don't really know any girls much. They've never come my way."

"Not?" she exclaimed, scarcely believing this.

He said quite seriously: "You know it makes a lot of difference when one hasn't any sisters. I haven't any; there were just three of us; me, and my brother in the Navy, and the Nipper—the youngest. (Cadet Corps.) My people live in the country, you know—Kent. It's not a bad old place; orchards and a moat for punting about on when we were kids, and the paddock. We had quite a decent time. But there were no girls in the house."

Mrs. Cartwright suggested "Other people's sisters?"

"Not often. My mother used to try and get girls to stay with her sometimes, but—" He moved his wide shoulders. "It was rather a wash-out. When there aren't other girls to come for, you know. There's a sort of feeling of their having been dragged in. Everybody's shy and stiff. At least, they were; the girls who came. I suppose that's why I haven't thought much of girls. They always seemed a nuisance, and self-conscious, you know. Wooden. Glad when it was time for them to go, and I can tell you *I* was. They were thundering difficult to talk to."

Mrs. Cartwright, always ready to hear of the bringing-up of boys, gave thanks inwardly that her Keith and Reggie possessed countless girl-cousins who were to them as sisters; creatures dispossessed of glamour, but a channel into those fields where glamour ripens. Then she said, softly, to this other boy: "But when you went away from Home, when you came up to Town, and—oh, all that sort of thing, like other young men of your age, surely you met plenty of girls who were—well! Easy enough to talk to?"

He nodded slightly. "Oh, yes; one met those. But—" There crept over his face the look that some think is more often to be seen in these days of Emancipation than in more guarded times; the scrutiny of the young man who is at least as fastidious in his love affairs as the young woman. "They weren't very amusing either—or, probably, I wasn't—to them. Of course, one knows lots of top-hole fellows who were always about with girls. Permanent address: 'Stagedoor, Frivolity,' sort of thing. But when I got leave, I'd just as soon go round with my people, or poor old Ferris, or some other fellow—"

He had finished his cigarette, and leant his fair rumpled head back on the pillow.

Mrs. Cartwright, watching it, knew suddenly and certainly that—but for his own mother and his nurses at that hospital—she was the first woman who had seen it thus.

Then she could hardly check the smile that rose to her lips; for there was stealing over his face a look that made it not merely boyish, but little-boyish. A film was blurring those keen blue eyes; he opened them more widely, precisely as she had seen the eyes of little Keith open widely, obstinately, against her breast when he was dropping with the sleep that he defied. Young Awdas, she saw, was fighting down a well-disguised yawn. For a moment there was silence in the bright, isolated room. Then he said, "Mrs. Cartwright, do go to bed."

"I am not sleepy."

"No, nor am I," with a drowsy smile. "If you go, I'll get out a book and read until it's time to get up."

"Don't do that," she said. "I suppose you wouldn't try and go to sleep for a bit?"

"I couldn't." The blue eyes opened again fixedly upon her face. "I—"

It seemed in the midst of the sentence that his lashes fell against his cheeks, closely and suddenly as the lashes of her babies used to fall. In the idiom of those old days he was "off," he was "down."

Afraid of moving, to snap off the lights, lest she might disturb the sleeper, she sat on, watching that peaceful face, that broad chest heaving rhythmically. She sat, watching him; or letting her glance take in the room with his neat, soldier-like appointments; his folding-case for brushes and shaving-kit, his one photograph (obviously of his mother) in a celluloid glazed frame, his leather writing-case, with his name and the name of his Corps printed in ink on the cover. Her eyes upturned to him, as she sat—thinking. . . thinking. . .

It was nearly five o'clock when the door opened cautiously, and Captain Ross, that adequate campaigner, entered, with a Service dressing-gown over his zebra-stripes, and carrying two steaming cups of excellently-made tea. His glance fell upon Jack Awdas, slumbering like a child. Mrs. Cartwright, rather cramped, rather chilled, and rather drawn in the face between her straight-falling plaits of hair, was still sitting there like a statue, in a white robe with gold patterns, from the folds of which there peeped an end of narrow pink ribbon—the ribbon which held, hidden at her breast, and all unsuspected, a Charm.

VII

The Spreading of the Charm

"When England needs
The sons she breeds,
And there's fighting to be done,
No matter where,
You will find him there,
The Man behind the Gun. . .
It's Bill, Bill, Billy, Billy, Billy, Billy, Billy Brown,
Of Putney, Piccadilly, Camden Town;
Why! It's Mister—
Bill, Billy Brown—
Of London!"

—Fragson's Song

The following morning brought a small disappointment to that little plotter for the commonweal, Olwen Howel-Jones.

No Mrs. Cartwright at *déjeuner*!

Olwen (knowing nothing of that vigil of the night before, or of the slumber into which the woman, drained of vitality, had dropped as soon as she returned to her room) imagined her working through luncheon-time.

Too bad! For now it must be postponed, the sight of how that Charm, given to the writer, would affect Professor Howel-Jones. It could not begin at once then, that Darby-and-Joan pairing-off that so suitable match which little Olwen had planned. What a pity! Still it was not put off for long, she cheerfully hoped.

The other wearer of the Charm was also absent from the midday gathering in the *salle*, but that was all to the good, Olwen had passed Miss Walsh, with her hair done in that new way! speeding off as excitedly as an Early Victorian to her first dance; speeding down to the pier, where the motor-boat awaited her, with Sergeant Tronchet. Madame Leroux had put up a basket of provisions for them, and they were going to make a picnic of their excursion across the lagoon.

Captain Ross came in to lunch with his friend Mr. Awdas, but so late that the two young men crossed the path of Olwen and her Uncle (who had finished their meal early) in the hall. The girl had paused here for a moment to slip into the Red Cross collection-box that hundred-franc note which had been bestowed upon her yesterday by Miss Walsh.

Captain Ross noticed her action.

"You're making a mistake, Miss Howel-Jones," he said banteringly, and smiled as he might have smiled at one of the little pigtailed daughters of the manageress. "That's not the box you put ten centimes into and get two sticks of candy."

Olwen, half in delight that he had spoken to her, half in resentment that it was in the tone he might have used to a child, raised her pointed chin on its white childish neck, looked down under her lids, and demanded, with what she considered great stateliness, "Who wants *candy*?"

"All little girls, I guess," returned Captain Ross, his robin's eyes twinkling, his perfect teeth flashing in another teasing smile. Olwen, glancing under those dropped lids at this somewhat showy vision of black-and-white-and-brown-and-scarlet-and-khaki, felt that she would die for him.

There was a magic about him, she thought; even if he were dictatorial or teasing, or seemed to think rather a lot of himself—a magic! At the same instant she remembered that, yes! There was a secret magic about her too, now. A magic that had proved itself unmistakably once; a Charm that she herself was wearing. Confidence seemed to rush, in a warming flood, about her heart.

Quite defiantly she tilted her black head, and looking straight over Captain Ross's shoulder, she laughed, for pure joy of her secret.

"*You* don't know everything about girls!" she told the finest judge of women in Europe.

And before the young Staff-Officer could retort, before he could even open his eyes over the temerity of this chit, this schoolgirl, who had said this thing to him (*Him!*), those little French boots of hers had skipped away, carrying her upstairs towards the study where she must type out the notes which she had taken down for her Uncle in shorthand that morning. Those boots fitted the chit's ankles like a coat of black paint, he noticed as he looked after her, too amused to be annoyed, of course. The piece of Impertinence—! Awfully neat. . . They disappeared, the little twinkling heels. He went on to join Jack Awdas at table.

Olwen, at an angle in the corridor a floor higher, ran into the young *femme-de-chambre* for that floor, carrying over her arm a khaki tunic.

They stopped to smile and to exchange "*bonjours*," these two girls much of an age and much of a race, for Marie came from Brittany, and already the Professor and his niece had amused themselves by finding out how many Welsh words the Breton maid could understand; the simple words which were the same in her own tongue.

"I come from cleaning the buttons of the English monsieur, his better tunic," explained Marie, in French, smiling as she held out the khaki coat.

"It is not of Monsieur de l'Audace?" asked Olwen.

"No, Mademoiselle. Of the other English officer, young, young, who does not talk French too well; Lieutenant Brrrrrrown," returned Marie. "Can Mademoiselle tell me what decoration is that he has?" Olwen gave a look at it.

"It is the ribbon of the Military Cross—it's like your Croix de Guerre," she said. "I didn't notice that he'd got that."

"He" was the pink-faced New Army officer of whom Mrs. Cartwright had spoken to her.

She remembered, in a flash, that it was he for whom she had intended that fourth share of the Charm, still in the pocket of the serge dress that she wore. She had not yet made up any plan as to how she was to press the Charm upon him. The plan came to her then and there, as she stood in that corridor.

"Hold Marie," she said, suddenly. "I have a *porte-bonheur* for this officer." She took out the sachet. "Say nothing to Monsieur," she impressed it upon the little maid, all smiles and delight to be included in a secret. "I am going to hide it in his coat."

And, taking hold of the coat, she slipped the sachet full of the enchanted powder into the slit-like pocket at the waist where men keep tickets.

"There! . . . Probably Monsieur will not find it; but all the better. It won't matter, even if he does not know it is there."

The Breton maid nodded. "A *sachet à preservation* then? I know them. We have them also, Mademoiselle. It is to avert all danger from the soldier who is to wear it, is it not?"

"No. Not precisely that," said the young Welsh girl. "It is to bring to him—well, Happiness of the best."

"Love, then. Ah, *là là*! I doubted myself of that!" declared the young *bonne*, bursting into ripples of laughter. "I go now to take the coat to Monsieur, who does not suspect. But no, Mademoiselle, I will say nothing to him of this; nothing, nothing, nothing at all!"

Olwen thought, as she went on: "Now Marie probably imagines that I am in love with this dreadfully uninteresting little Mr. Brown, and want to attract him to being in love with me! When I've never spoken to him in my life, or even seen what he's like when he's close to one!"

But that afternoon she both saw and spoke to this Mr. Brown.

They were returning, she and her Uncle, from one of those wanderings which the Professor loved to take out westwards from the hotel. For a couple of miles they had tramped along the hard sands at the foot of the great dunes wherein pine-trees were buried up to their lower boughs; then, leaving the sands, they had scrambled up the sandhills into the pine-forest that bordered them.

Its fragrant aisles stretched for miles bisected by paths, spread with a rich terra-cotta carpet of pine-needles. Already the Professor had slipped his pipe back into his pocket, for the notice "*Défense à fumer*" appeared again and again tacked up on the trunks of the great pines that made of those miles a perfect factory of turpentine.

With their faces towards home, they caught sight through the pines of a figure that repeated for an instant the effect of the pine-trunks themselves, brown-clad, long-lined, and slender. It stooped at the foot of a tree.

"My dear lady," said the Professor, taking off his hat to the figure, which was that of Mrs. Cartwright, "you look like Daphne, being changed into a pine rather than a laurel."

Mrs. Cartwright laughed as she rose to her feet. She had been putting into position a fallen tin cup, shaped like a flower-pot, and left to catch the resin as it oozed stickily from the trunk. Most of the firs in this part of the forest had a tin blade, that had scored them down, left plunged into the bark.

"Delightful, to be able to turn into any sort of plant, rather than be bored by the wrong man," remarked Mrs. Cartwright lightly, dusting her hands.

"What a pull for those nymphs! Must have made it worth while to live in a world where there was no tea. I am ready for mine, though—"

The three went on homewards together, the Professor walking between Olwen and the writer, who found herself once more admiring his Druidic head and still-active frame. In precisely the same spirit she would have admired some stately, ivy-grown keep that had once echoed to the shouts of archers; she was scarcely the type of woman who becomes an "old man's darling—"

But little Olwen was busily thinking: "Now! I do believe the Charm has begun to work. Didn't Uncle say she was like Daphne?—and doesn't she really look younger today? It's *begun*! And see how she's smiling at him and talking to him about Anatole France. . . But I wish they'd leave off about books and begin about themselves. I wish I could run on and leave them to come home together (but they both walk as fast as I do any day, bother them!). If only we could meet somebody that I could fall behind with, and let Mrs. Cartwright have Uncle all to herself—"

This wish was fulfilled at a turn in the path where there was a clearing in the symmetrically spaced pines. Three paths converged towards a sort of oasis of heather and undergrowth, surrounding a hut of untrimmed pine-branches. Huge blackberry runners, purple and green, flung themselves before the door of it. And there stood, fixedly regarding the place, a boyish figure in khaki with an ultra-floppy cap at a rakish angle on his head.

"Are you thinking of taking that house, Mr. Brown?" Mrs. Cartwright asked him laughingly, as they came up.

Mr. Brown gave quite a jump before he turned and saluted the party.

Up to now they had known this young man as one very fond of his food, always sitting on the back of his neck in the most comfortable chair he could find, eternally smoking cigarettes, and evidently bent on getting his money's worth out of the hotel. But it was a different young man who now turned his pink face and pop-eyes on them. They'd evidently interrupted him in thinking over something; thinking hard.

He echoed Mrs. Cartwright's last words. "Thinking of taking that hut?" he repeated, in a voice that seemed to bring a breath of crowded A B C shops, of Tube-lifts and cheerful workaday London generally into that stately French glade. "Well, d'you know, that's a wheeze. It's a dashed good idea. I was just that moment thinking that something would have to be done!"

"What about?" asked Mrs. Cartwright, as the party halted.

"Why, about everything, the whole blooming thing," returned Mr. Brown, pushing his floppy cap to the back of his head. "This is just about beating me, I give you *my* word. Look at me, what am *I* doing here?"

Mrs. Cartwright said: "Evidently you're having a look at your new house?"

He said: "I don't mean here this minute, in this Epping Forest sort of show. I mean *here*!"—he spread out his hands as if to take in the whole of Western France. "Of course, they told me I'd got to go to pine-woods when they gave me three months, and a cavalry fellow, at Sister Agnes's, told me here was better than Surrey, and gave me the address, and it seemed quite natural to take it and think—Blow the expense. But I wish—I tell you what I wish."

He dropped his voice confidentially.

"I wish this blessed War was over, and me riding in a third-class carriage again!"

Before any one could speak, he went on with his candid and good-humoured grouse.

"I've got to go first, with these colonels and company promotors, and people. The trouble is, I like it. Too dashed well I've got to like it. I never used to think of all these things coming to me when I was serving behind the counter; nor the customers neither, I'll bet. And now nothing but the tip-toppest hotel's good enough for me, and me posted in Cox's 'star' department. R. D., refer to drawer! Got it in my pocket now; show it to you. I could have sworn I'd got the money, you know. Still, here's the cheque—"

He said it with a disarming and engaging honesty, as if the whole story might be read anyhow in his pink, snub-nosed, and ordinary face. Mrs. Cartwright and the Professor found it impossible to help liking him as he stood there, the little Briton who gave no further thought to the tense horrors of Suvla Bay, where he had won his Cross, but who confessed his liking for the best hotels. But as for Olwen, she was watching him anxiously; for his hand had gone to the pocket where she herself had hidden that "*porte bonheur*." He fumbled. At that moment his finger and thumb must have encountered it. . .

"No—what's this?—that's not the cheque—must be in my case," he went on, taking the hand out of the pocket. (Olwen breathed again.) "Well, now something's got to be done. They'll wait at the hotel, I daresay, if I don't leave this place altogether. And I like this place." He looked round the empty hut again, as if he half expected to see a Willesden estate agent's name round the corner. "Not half a bad idea of yours, Mrs. C. I might send for some camp-kit; sleep here—do the picnic touch—"

For a few moments they stood, discussing forest regulations and to whom the would-be camper-out must apply. Then, four abreast, they turned to go on, the sea-breeze meeting them.

"Mind the barbed wire," exclaimed Mr. Brown, flipping with his cane at one of those giant brambles. "It's caught your skirt," to Olwen. "Allow me."

He bent down and unfastened the hook-like thorns from her frock. This kept the two behind the Professor and Mrs. Cartwright, whereat the innocent Olwen rejoiced. She could not guess that not only did the Professor seem at least as old to Mrs. Cartwright as he did to his own niece, but that the Professor himself, though he found her a sympathetic listener, could never at any age have wished to make love to this lady. For he was a "type"-lover. To him any woman who was not tiny and black-haired (as Olwen's own mother had been) was only, to quote Captain Ross, "half a woman. . ."

But they were talking together, easily, interestedly, as they walked ahead through the wood. And even though the subject might only be of Celtic Folk-lore, Olwen felt already that she saw her wish coming to pass before her eyes.

She turned to her other experiment with the Charm.

Mr. Brown had slipped his fingers again into the pocket into which he had first hunted for his dishonoured cheque. And this time he brought out the hidden sachet.

He stared at the small mauve object.

"Now what the dickens is this?" he demanded, genially bewildered. "Don't remember where this came from—"

Olwen, inwardly terrified lest the young man might in his ignorance toss the precious thing into the arbutus bushes, said with outward carelessness, "It looks like a mascot; better not lose it."

"Looks more like the little square bags they used to fasten on to the ladies' covered coathangers in the Haberdashery. With scent inside 'em. I've no use for perfumery—"

Olwen was now sure he meant to throw this gift of the gods away. With a hasty gesture she snatched it out of the young man's hand.

"It is a mascot; I've seen others like them!" she told him, as they came in sight of the hotel. On the piazza Captain Ross was smoking, with his friend, the aviator; Mrs. Cartwright and the Professor had joined them.

Olwen realized that Captain Ross was also staring down on to the pine-bordered road, at herself and young Mr. Brown, who had stopped short, and was still looking at what she held, the treasure that he had discovered in his pocket.

"But how did it get in there?" he demanded.

"Somebody might have slipped it in without your knowing. But anyhow," said Olwen, taking a resolution, "*I'm* going to slip it back for you now, to bring you luck!" And she did slip it back into the khaki pocket. "There! You know where it's come from this time. You'll keep it there, won't you?"

"Anything to oblige," laughed Mr. Brown, and the two young people walked on to join the party on the piazza, who were waiting for them.

Olwen thought, "It's rather annoying that he's going to leave the hotel, and live in a hut like the Wild Man of the Woods *just* when I want to watch how the Charm will work with him! But if it *does* work, that's the main thing, after all."

She added aloud, looking into the pink and puggy face that had outstared Danger and was now staring at Bankruptcy, "Take care of it, won't you? You won't throw it away or let it get lost or anything?"

"Not for all the Eau in Cologne!" Mr. Brown assured her with a mock-flourish as they ran up the piazza steps together.

Those robin-like eyes of Captain Ross were fixed very watchfuly upon this young Mr. Brown as he appeared, laughing and chatting as if he were quite old friends with the Professor's niece. Then the young Staff officer looked from him to her.

For a girl who wasn't bland, she was (he thought again) quite neat. . .

The chit didn't look at him. . .

And what (Captain Ross wondered) was that keep-sake that she was handing to that fellow?

VIII

The First Engagement by the Charm

"Artill. 38 ans, célib., sér., demande marraine affect, désinteressée."

—La Vie Parisienne

Astonishment, incredulity, excitement and delight, reigned in the hotel at Les Pins.

One thought only pervaded the place, from the topmost attics inhabited by Marie the Bretonne and the other *femmes-de-chambre*, down through the other floors to the wide *salons* and to the shut-off wing that was the domain of the management. One topic alone set all tongues there chattering, in English, French, or Canadian-Scots. One piece of news was now being discussed before any *communiqué* from any of the fronts.

It was the news about Miss Agatha Walsh and the nephew of "the management," Sergeant Tronchet.

They were engaged to be married.

This was sudden, as everybody commented one after another. This was quick work. For, how long had Miss Walsh been staying at the hotel? Two—three days? And had she ever met this man before? Never?

One moonlight walk in the pine-forest, one expedition by motor-boat across the lagoon, half a dozen conversations at table d'hôte, an encounter at the post office where Miss Walsh had gone to buy picture postcards of the Côte d'Azur, another stroll in the forest, a game of draughts together—this had been all the preparation necessary for a declaration from the bull-necked, swarthy French sergeant to the English lady-all-alone. The deed was done. He had asked her to become his wife. She had accepted him. No; there was no mistake. The pair were going about looking as if they were newly-elected king and queen of the Gironde, and those visitors to whom the engagement had not been announced in French by Sergeant Tronchet, had been told in English by the radiant, tremulous, blissful Miss Walsh herself.

Madame Leroux, all smiles, had confirmed the news herself in each instance. Monsieur Leroux had taken the little tramway into Arcachon to blaze it abroad at his café. The three little pigtailed daughters fluttered about the villas of Les Pins in their red-and-white check frocks, twittering like starlings on the subject of the *fiançailles*, and spreading the news that Mademoiselle Ouallshe was sending to Paris for presents for each of them, and had said that they were to call her Tante Agathe! The wedding was for soon—for almost immediately!

Excitement rose higher and higher; it might be observed that the delight seemed, if anything, on the French side; the astonishment on that of the English visitors.

Little Mr. Brown turned from his plans for furnishing the woodcutter's hut for himself to open his candid and bulging blue eyes upon this new event in the hotel. He was, as a matter of fact, the first of those who heard the news to refer to a certain element in it.

"I say; look here," was his comment. "That chap's all right, I daresay; but are his people and all that quite class enough for the lady's family? I don't know about foreigners, of course. And of course I don't pretend to be Anybody, myself. But what'll her people at home think? Won't they— Well, *socially*, I should have thought it would have been considered a bit *Rum*!"

Mrs. Cartwright told him, quickly and quietly, that this marriage was not complicated, on "the lady's" side, by any people at home, and turned to Olwen to confirm it. Olwen, who was wide-eyed with a mixture of feelings, which she was surprised to find were not all happy ones, agreed that Miss Walsh hadn't any relations.

And presently Mrs. Cartwright was writing to her sisters: "*A marriage has been arranged between the French Sergeant and the Hotel Spinster I described to you in my last. I think an excellent plan. She wants marriage, he wants money. Translated into English, it is brutal and horrible. But these clear-eyed French make something so different out of all that.*

"*She is madly in love with him, for the same reason that Eve fell in love with Adam in that Garden; he's the first man she's ever seen. The gap between their worlds is no wider than the gap between her and the world generally. Up to now (35, my dear!) she's belonged to the Great Unkissed.*

"*He is proud of his achievement, and, consequently, proud of her. I expect he will make her an admirable husband. They'll live in this country, his people will be her people. He will be affectionate, and genuinely fond of her, as only a Frenchman can be fond of the wife who has brought him money, and at whom he would not have looked, but for her income!*"

Olwen, behind that startled gaze of hers, was realizing that she, and she alone, was responsible for this projected marriage and for the way in which it would turn out, whether for good or ill.

She had been the first person in the hotel to whom Miss Walsh had confided the great news. With the tremulous face of a girl, with a girl's faltering delight, the Spinster had called into her room an hour before.

"Oh, Olwen, come here a minute. (I'm going to call you Olwen.) Oh, I must tell you first. You were the first person who spoke to me here," she cried. "Oh, can you believe that it was only last Thursday? You said that it would bring me luck—that Charm you gave me. Oh, my little Olwen, it's brought me all the luck and happiness in the world! That's nonsense—I suppose! Still, I *am* the happiest person in the world. Kiss me. Pierre is so wonderful! You see what's happened? Oh, yes, you must guess—"

Olwen, hardly believing her ears, still guessed. She left Miss Walsh, her small ears buzzing with the woman's pathetic gush of confidences, her mind a welter of emotions. Perhaps the chief feeling was fright. . .

It was so powerful, then, that Charm? She had not expected this. Not only the swiftness of the wooing, but a definite engagement! . . .

And a marriage to be expected shortly. . . And to—well, *not* the sort of person whom Olwen, the disposer of the Charm, had meant to see attracted to the wearer of her amulet. At least, she had not expected to see him *accepted*—! She had hoped—for what? Well, not the first man who asked Miss Walsh; not the man who—who looked rather like their village policeman at home! and not for it to happen in three days! It was rather frightening. Could one count so little upon the way in which that Charm was going to act? Perhaps after all it was not going to prove the unmitigated blessing of the human race which Olwen had at first seen it. . . Oh. . . Misgivings thronged upon her. For a moment she felt inclined to wish that she could take the Charm by force, if necessary, from Miss Walsh—undo what she had done. That she could steal the Charm away from Mr. Brown's tunic-pocket. That she could snip the ribbon that tied the Charm round Mrs. Cartwright's long slender neck. . .

As for the Charm that rose and fell with the gentle curve of Olwen's own breast, where it lay, well, that would be all right. For her, Charm or no Charm, there was no question of attracting the wrong man. For her there was only one man in the world; his right sleeve was tucked into his jacket-pocket, and as he smiled teasingly down at her his teeth were a flash of snow across the brown of his self-confident face. For her the Charm that attracted him could only be a beneficent thing.

But what about those others? she mused, doubtfully, over her typewriter.

In Mrs. Cartwright's case, the Charm was not working as swiftly as in the case of Miss Walsh. She seemed, so far, on the same terms with the Professor that she had always been; as ready to listen to his interpretations of Welsh names—"Olwen," for instance, meaning "White Track," and belonging to a maid of Celtic mythology in whose path daisies were wont to spring up—as interested in his special subjects. As friendly at table d'hôte or in the evenings; yes, as friendly. . . but no more so! At their age, Olwen thought, people strolled into Love, perhaps, instead of falling into it, as they did at nineteen.

In her own case, she thought—and she hugged the thought!—the Charm did seem to be working. Not at that perilous speed with which it had served Miss Agatha Walsh; not yet with results which meant these definite and pole-axing announcements! Still. . . wasn't it working a little?

Without looking at him, the girl had several times been aware that Captain Ross's dark quick glance had sought her out as soon as she appeared, and that it had followed her as she went out. Several times since the encounter in the hall, when she had told him that he "didn't know everything about girls," he had stopped to talk to her; always to "rag" her with some question or comment. But he had stopped.

Often she thought: "That means nothing! He never could think of me seriously. Why should he?"

Then again she felt that a time must come when he would stop longer, say more.

She waited for that time, outwardly indifferent, just as a branch studded with the brown scentless swellings of mid-winter waits for the spring that shall see them break into sweetest buds. She waited, fixing her bright gaze upon some point beyond her idol's broad shoulder as she answered his greeting with some snippy girlish flippancy, while her heart whispered—ah! what volumes of tenderness. She just waited; biding her time as a girl needs must, whether or not she knows of some secret Charm that backs her power.

She waited. . . but now waiting and secret watching, uttered retort and unuttered yearning, were all alike tinged with a new apprehension.

That Charm! What unexpected way of its own was it going to take *next*?

IX

Unforeseen Effect of the Charm

"Does the wood-pecker flit round the young ferash? Does the grass clothe a new-built wall?
Is she under thirty, the woman who holds a boy in her thrall?"

—Kipling

It would have been a shock to little Olwen had she realized what other result of the Charm was manifesting itself already at that moment.

Probably the first, imperceptible manifestations would have been lost upon this quite young girl.

Had she noticed the gravitating towards Mrs. Cartwright's chair of an evening of Captain Ross's friend, the young flyer, had she observed the gradual way in which it was becoming a matter of course that when the writer was not working he was in attendance upon her, had she known of a bouquet of late roses, bought in the Ville d'Hiver and sent by the chambermaid to Room 23, had she heard what boyish confidences about flying, and Work, and Other Fellows, and even Home were being poured into an ear well used to hearing of such things by a tongue not well used to talking to women—well! Even had she known all this, Olwen would have looked upon it much as she looked upon her own impulses when she stooped quickly to pick up a pair of dropped spectacles for the old French lady, the little dark boy's grandmother, or held open the door of the *salle* for her to pass out. It was merely "manners."

Further, if she had known of that night which Mrs. Cartwright had watched through with him, putting all her own Force between him and the forces of Horror, little Olwen would have thought she saw the whole reason for the young man's attentions to a woman nearly twenty years his senior. It was gratitude. How natural!

Manners, and gratitude. . .

This is what Olwen would have thought, and what Mrs. Cartwright herself would have said. It is true that the elder woman should have known better. Later, she might have confessed that she did know. At the time. . . Well—

There is one subject in the world upon which more barefaced lying goes on than upon any other half a dozen subjects put together: sport included. The discussion of it turns nine men out of ten into what Captain Ross might describe as "a darned fabricator."

Golf and salmon fishing cannot compete with the lying records of Love! Food it cannot be that the golfer and the fisherman cling *in their own hearts* to the fabrications that they fling abroad.

Whereas, regarding the matter of Love, men (and even women) can actually believe exactly what they wish to believe.

This was not Mrs. Cartwright's habit. She was a woman sincere with herself as a rule. Into the lives of the sincerest of us there trespasses the exception that shows up the fallibility of human rules.

So when she told herself that this growing attraction towards her of the boyish Flying-officer was a normal and delightful friendship, she believed it herself; she insisted on believing that the look in his young eyes as they followed her movements was not the look she had been used to see in the eyes of Captain Keith Cartwright and of a dozen other men; yes, she made herself believe that her own more joyous mood was not the life-giving zest that every woman feels when she is admired, desired—and at no other time.

She deliberately believed it was the glorious autumn weather that made her feel this stimulant in the air, in the sea-bordered forest, in the society of young people; that amusing Captain Ross, little Mr. Brown, the pretty Howel-Jones child, and Mr. Awdas, for instance.

With pleasure she accepted Mr. Awdas's invitation, one afternoon, to walk through the forest with him and down to the oyster-beds, the pride of that part of the country. She thought that Captain Ross was coming too, but it appeared that Captain Ross and the little Brown boy had gone for a walk in the opposite direction, to prospect around that woodcutter's hut.

She and the young flyer set out together, walking lightly and quickly in step; their shadows, flung on the road in front of them, showed a curious likeness that one would not, looking at the pair, have noticed, he so blond, and blue-eyed, and boyish—she whimsical, brown-haired, plain of feature. But the shapes of both, blue silhouettes on the white road, were young and supple, both characteristically small-headed, wide in the shoulder, slim in the flank, and long from hip to knee. Seeing them from their shadows only, one might have guessed a brother and his sister swinging easily along together.

The shadows broke, striping the red bodies of the pines as they entered the forest from the road.

"It's jollier walking further up," said Mrs. Cartwright, taking a path to the left. "We get glimpses of the sea all the way along; this way."

He followed her in silence. He had been in a silent mood all day, she had noticed. She asked him, looking back with a little glance of concern, if he had not been sleeping again.

"Oh yes, I've slept all right—slept like a top," he reassured her from behind. The path was so narrow that they could only walk one abreast through the arbutus bushes. He told her: "I haven't had any bother at all since—that night—"

"Good!" said Mrs. Cartwright heartily, but he had not finished speaking; he was concluding in a low voice, "that night when you were such an angel to me."

"Oh, please don't!" she laughed, looking ahead. "You make me feel like something off a Christmas card of my childhood; it's not a bit like me, believe me." She was not looking at him; she did not know, just now, that his eyes were fastened on the lithe brown length of her as she made her way through the bushes that seemed to catch at her, offering their bouquets of white flowers, their jewels of orange and scarlet, as she passed.

Presently they grew less thickly, the arbutus bushes; they seemed to fall back into the forest.

The two people walking, reached a little rise in the ground, and now a rush of salter air was mingling with the warm pine-scent that hung everywhere about them, and now there was a familiar sapphire gleam through the pine-boughs that showed black and fringed against sea and sky.

"One can't walk for long in this wood without coming upon that glimpse of the sea outside," remarked Mrs. Cartwright, gazing at it, and taking in a deep, enjoying breath. "Sea through pine-needles is so like the blink of very blue eyes fringed by thick black lashes! It reminds me so of a man I was once very much in love with—"

Quick as a shot came the interruption to what she was saying; a hoarse curt "Don't!" over her shoulder; a hand that clutched at her upper arm, and then dropped as soon as it had touched her.

She wheeled, startled. She faced the angry, hurt, and jealous eyes of a man.

Jack Awdas, looking steadily down into her astonished face, repeated in that husky, angry tone; "Don't. Don't do it! Don't talk to me about any man you've loved. I can't bear it. D'you see? You—I—You mustn't."

She said nothing, in the extreme of surprise. He said nothing more either. It is possible that he was as startled as she was by the declaration that had broken from his lips, and whose sound was still ringing in their ears. The boy had not meant to say it. He had not known what he had meant to say; his mind had been, as it were, filled by some luminous and bewildering and concealing mist.

Now a breath had blown aside a corner of that mist: he caught a glimpse of the heights and depths that it had been hiding—for how many hours, how many days? He did not know. Only it seemed to him that since that night of his bad dream, since his eyes had closed upon the sight of that woman watching, lovely with Pity, he had woken up to a new world.

It was full of strangeness and unrest, that world; it was full of sudden thrills. It held impatience to hear her voice, to touch her hand. It held longing and mystery. It held worship of a laugh or gesture from her. It held amazement at oneself; incredulity that one could feel these things. Now, he found, it held also Pain. . .

This woman had been made part of his life by that vigil shared. He could not bear the thought of her in other men's lives; couldn't bear to think of it, much less to hear of it in words. . . It couldn't be. She was his!

They walked on in silence, these two English people from the hotel; each treading a maze of hidden thought as they went. No word of it escaped them for the present. Jack Awdas was the first to speak.

He said, his husky voice once more composed: "You haven't had a look at this place yet, have you?"

"No," replied Mrs. Cartwright, also in the accents of every day. "You know the way, don't you?"

"Yes; Ross and I explored the oyster-beds the first day we came over. Rather interesting. I thought perhaps the place might come in useful to you as—as 'copy.'"

"Oh yes," murmured Mrs. Cartwright, out of the labyrinth of her thoughts. . .

It would have augured ill for the next chapters of her serial had she depended for "copy" upon what she was to see of that French oyster-park that afternoon. Neither she nor the boy, who was her guide, had anything but a cursory eye, an abstracted mind, to give to that lightsome, airy picture of wide sea and sand, mapped out with stakes and sills and basins, and peopled with busy barefoot women in their picturesque garb of black sunbonnet, print jumper and long scarlet trousers.

Up and down the narrow paths stepped those long slender feet of Mrs. Cartwright, shod in the brown canvas *sandalettes* of the neighbourhood, with lacings that clipped her to mid-calf like the *cothurne* ribbons of a dancer. Before her tramped the high leather boots of the Flying-man; crunch—crunch—crunch, over the gravel and chipped shell. But still the paths that each was treading remained those of the secret labyrinth. . .

SHE, BEHIND ALL THE LIGHT composure of her manner, was more than disturbed. She was touched down to that mingling of inner tears and inner laughter, which was her very self. He cared for her, then, this charming lad, whose heart so far had known only his own people, only that other lad who had been his observer and his chum. He loved her. There could be no mistaking the tone in which he'd blurted out: *"Don't talk to me about other men you've loved; I can't bear it!"* Yes; he was hers—just as Keith Cartwright had been hers, and young Rolfe, who was killed on the Frontier, and Rex Mannering in Nineteen-oh-one, *and* the man whose sea-blue regard had laughed through such black fringing lashes, and the others. She ought to have known. Here was this boy. . . At twenty-two! . . . She had seen such affairs. . . She had watched, not too sympathetically, the mature woman who receives the attentions of her son's contemporaries. Once she had heard a friend of hers, in all the glory of her twenty-four summer, declare, "It's such an *elderly* habit, letting youths *younger than oneself* fetch and carry for one. And oh, Claudia! I don't think you or I will ever have to know the humiliation of loving a *boy!*" Mrs. Cartwright had lost sight of this friend, who was a year older than herself.

Perhaps the unforseen had happened to her too. Certainly Mrs. Cartwright had never dreamed that this thing would ever happen to herself; to become at her age the object of a lad's first love. It made her feel, at the same time, suddenly old—and suddenly young.

Outwardly unchanged, she let her gaze sweep the flat stretches of sand before her, and then rest upon a *parqueuse* who waded by, a vivid figure in scarlet and black, carrying a square rope-bottomed oyster-basket.

"Wonderfully picturesque those wide black sunbonnets the women wear," Mrs. Cartwright commented. "Curious to think they're a survival of our occupation of this part of France, all those centuries ago."

"Are they? by Jove," was all that young Awdas replied. "That's interesting."

But for him, too, what he said was as a man talks in his sleep; what he saw about him was less clear than the landscape of a dream. In his heart the boy was awed and exultant. He had told her. It had leapt from his lips, rather. He was conscious of new power within him; something of the feeling that had been his on the morning when he had first gone up on a "solo." Now she knew what he had to say to her—for he *would* say the rest of it presently. Not yet; not yet. . .

They pottered about the oyster-park, talking of oyster-culture. They had tea in the town, discussing the various tea-shops of their preference in London and Paris. Then he asked her if she were too tired to walk home and would like to take the little tramway; he knew he ought to ask her that, but he hoped inwardly that she would agree to walk. He breathed again when she protested that she was never tired. They took to the forest-path again, now gilded by the sun's rays, pointing through the pine-trunks; beyond the fringing branches the glimpse of sea and sky had changed from corn-cockle-blue to saffron-yellow. They walked, talking of those other fair woods of France that the War had turned into treeless, blasted wastes, spun over by webs of barbed wire. And then they came to that rise in the ground of the forest where the arbutus bushes seemed to fall back, and whence they had caught the first glimpse of the sea. It was here that he had spoken, on their way out. It was here that, on their way home, silence fell suddenly upon them. As if by tacit consent, they stopped walking. He turned to her.

"No," said Mrs. Cartwright hastily, as if he had said something. "No, no."

"Yes," said Jack Awdas, quietly and steadily, and just as if no time had elapsed between his first hurt "*Don't*" and this. "I am going to talk to you about it. I must."

"No, no. Please don't," gently and unhappily, from her. "It's better not. There's nothing to be said."

"Oh, isn't there, by Jove!" exclaimed the boy. "There is everything. I must tell you. I—Well, you know now, of course. I do care for you, most tremendously."

Tall woman as she was, he was looking down into her face as he went on quickly, composedly. The intensity of what he felt took from him all shyness.

He said: "I never thought it was in me to care so awfully about anybody. It's all come"—he sketched a gesture with his long arm—"like that! In me! I can't tell you what it's like. When I've heard other fellows talking, I've thought—But I see now it's absolutely true. Only more so. None of them cared as I do. They couldn't. They hadn't met—you."

"Please don't." She pressed her lips together. "I ought not to have let you say as much." She tried to meet his eyes frankly, but that young ardour in them disconcerted her. She looked aside, leant a hand on the hard red bark of the pine nearest to her. "Of course," she concluded (very feebly, as she felt!), "I am so glad you like me, Mr. Awdas. . . I hope we shall always be. . . great friends. . ."

"Friends?" echoed the boy. He put back his small head and laughed. "Like you? But I want you to marry me."

She looked at him, at a loss for just the right words.

He persisted, still smiling. "But, of course, you've got to marry me."

Now she gave a little hopeless laugh, glancing about as if to take on to her side the tall old trees, the distant sea, the sunset-clouds. She said, with an attempt to put the conversation on a more natural basis, "You know, you mustn't talk nonsense to me—"

"Why nonsense?" quickly. "This is dead earnest."

She said quietly: "Mr. Awdas, how old are you? Twenty-two, aren't you?"

"Yes; but look here! That's got absolutely nothing to do with this—"

"Everything," said the woman. "You're twenty-two; I am—"

"I don't want to know," he broke in. "You're—you. You've got nothing to do with ages, or age. You're so wonderful. There's nobody in the world like you. I love you," he ended, in a mutter. "I want you to marry me."

There was a lump in Mrs. Cartwright's throat as she said ruefully, "I might be your mother."

He cried out impatiently: "Oh, dash it all! So '*might*' Madame Leroux, or anybody else, be my mother! The point is, they don't happen to be. You don't either. You aren't. And you're going to be my wife. Don't you see how I care for you?"

She was struck by the stark simplicity of him. He cared so much, then, that he should not think of its not meaning everything to the person beloved, as well as himself. He was looking down at her not only adoringly, but masterfully. To him this new love was so wonderful that it must needs be omnipotent. Sorry, and touched more deeply that she had dreamed, she sighed as she stood there in the wood and set herself to argue.

She went over them all, the old, the obvious, the stock facts that have proved themselves for centuries, the truths whose lasting light is put out only by the transient fairy glamour of Infatuation.

"You see, this is a passing thing. This happens to almost every young man once in his life. He looks back and laughs at it."

". . . fatal to marry out of one's generation!"

"In a little time you'll know how right I am—"

". . . ten years hence you'd look at me, and see I was an old woman. You'd still be a young man. It would be horrible!"

The boy looked at her and smiled as she spoke, and she knew that the words meant nothing to him, the lips that uttered them were everything.

She said, resignedly, "Let's walk on," and they walked on down the narrow path between the thickening clumps of arbutus; this time he led, his head turned over his shoulder to watch her as she followed.

He began again (without alarm, it seemed): "You won't marry me, then?"

She was a little reassured by the cheerfulness in that husky boyish voice. She had flung cold water, then, to some purpose? He was ready to listen to reason.

"My dear boy, my dear child!" she exclaimed, laughing more naturally. "You weren't *born* when I'd been living for years and years. I was growing up and married when you were running about that paddock at home in a jersey suit. I'd been round the world when you were going to public school. Marry you? I shouldn't dream for one instant of such a thing. Not for one single instant."

"Just because of *ages*?" he tossed back over that wide shoulder as they went. "Is that all?"

"Isn't that more than enough?"

"What, just because you've lived in this world more years than I have? Eaten more breakfasts and dinners? Had time to wear out more pairs of shoes?" the boy took up quite gaily. He pushed aside a bush that straggled right across her path, offering his bouquet of white lily-of-the-valley-like flowers, growing on the same bough as the berries of scarlet and orange. Arbutus! She knew she would never see the plant again without being reminded of this hour. To her and to these others here with her it would always mean "that time at Les Pins. . ."

He broke off a spray, held it towards her. "Look, you're like that," he told her, more softly, and for the first time rather bashfully. "I was thinking so yesterday, in the woods. You may have been grown-up, and—and have known things and all that; that's ripeness and fruit, I suppose. . . Yes; but, at the same time, you kept on being. . . white flowers, and buds. . ."

She shook her head, silently refusing the flattery that she knew was meant sincerely.

But she took the spray from his hand, tucked it into her brown coat (tucking in as well an end of Olwen's pink ribbon that had escaped again).

The look of joyous mastery flashed into his eyes. He went on, fondly teasing, "Come to that, I've seen and done more things than you have in all that long, long life you talk so much about. I've been *up* further, anyway, haven't I?" He tilted his crested head towards the pine-tops. "And *you've* never crashed down a mile and a half from the clouds; now, have you?"

"Ah—" she said, and checked a little shiver. The sun had set now; it was growing dark under the trees.

"Let's walk faster," said Mrs. Cartwright, hurriedly. "Let's get in. And—we won't talk about all that any more."

He said nothing. His whole heart was filled with the utterly boyish, utterly obstinate Will-to-Get.

X

Divagations of the Charm

"There's a girl wanted there, there's a girl wanted there,
And he don't care if she's dark or fair,
There's a nice little home that she's wanted to share."

—Song of the Past

The scene with which the last chapter closed would have been further undeniable proof to Olwen of the too-potent success of her talisman, had she known of it. But how about the working of the Charm, as it had been mapped out by herself?

As it was, guessing nothing as yet of how it had drawn to her friend, Mrs. Cartwright, the adoration of quite the wrong man, the girl was already in a mood of dissatisfaction. Chiefly, perhaps, because half the day was over, without a word or look for her from Captain Ross. It is true that the young Staff officer had announced the evening before that he guessed he was going to take the following day out in the open. But if her Charm had been strong as she had hoped it, Captain Ross would scarcely have wished to leave the hotel for an entire day while she (Olwen) was in it? Yet, how magic had been its effect in the case of Miss Walsh and her sergeant! They (the fiancés) were now inseparable, rather to the scandal of the French contingent, new to the code of the English betrothed. Olwen scarcely had a word with her friend, except for good night! Well, the unchaperoned Miss Walsh was entirely happy. That was one ray of brightness in the gloom of little Olwen's mood, for even she was now coming round to Mrs. Cartwright's expressed view that it was better to be happy with a quite unsuitable partner than to be bored with one who is apparently "cut out" for one. So much for what the Charm had done for Agatha Walsh.

But what about Olwen herself? What about Mrs. Cartwright? What about little Mr. Brown? . . . To the girl, in her present impatient frame of mind, there seemed to be absolutely "nothing doing," as Captain Ross would have said.

That very afternoon, when she and her Uncle were closeted together in that bare, shining study-room of his, she had tried to draw a discussion of Mrs. Cartwright into the rewriting of the Professor's article on old Welsh flower-names, but the old man was not to be diverted from his own subject.

"Never mind Mrs. Cartwright's new dress now, Olwen *fach*," he'd said, indulgently, but firmly. "Clothes, clothes, and stuffs—! Get on with this, now—" And he had laid down close to her typewriter a further page of notes, in his all but indecipherably small handwriting:

> "Fox-glove—*Bysedd cwn* (Hound's fingers).
> Mullein—*Canwyll yr adar* (Bird's candle).
> Cotton-grass—*Sidan y waun* (Moor silk).
> Snowdrops—*Clych Maban* (Baby's bells). . ."

Olwen had tapped out a dozen of these names on a fresh sheet of paper, thinking, rebelliously: "Well, I don't see that these are any more important than 'clothes and stuffs' that one's got to *wear*! Certainly not half as important as an awfully nice woman whom Uncle might be marrying all this time. I do call it a waste—" Then, as she pushed the roller of her machine along the carrier again, a more optimistic thought had struck her. "Perhaps he's making up his mind to propose to her *now*."

"Perhaps he won't—Good gracious, what handwriting! What's this?

"'Briony—*Paderau gatti* (Cat's Rosary).'

"Perhaps he won't just say a word to me about Mrs. Cartwright, or how that goldeny jumper suits her, on purpose. *He's afraid I might guess!*"

Then the optimism had faded again into gloom. . . Mechanically she finished her work, stamped the letters, tidied up the table after her Uncle had gone. She ought to write home, she knew. She owed letters to Auntie Margaret, who kept the big rambling house in Carnarvonshire for the family, and to her sisters Peggy and Myfanwy, and to some of the cousins. (The Howel-Jones family was as big and rambling as that old house of theirs.) But Olwen was in no mood for writing any letters of her own. She took out some picture postcards of the place, one showing the edge of the pine-forest silhouetted against the sea, one of the *Baissin* all a-flutter with the sails of yachts (a flight of giant butterflies) on regatta day, and one of a wave, marbled with foam, about to break on Biscay shore. On these Olwen scribbled messages to her home-people; then she took them up with her Uncle's letters, and ran out of the hotel to post them at the little bureau opposite to where the tramway started for Arcachon. Then, since there was nothing else to do until dinner-time, she turned to ramble in that forest that seemed to fling out its green, deep arms towards human beings clustered in their houses and villas, their hotels, and their chattering groups between its edge and the margin of the sea. That forest seemed to draw them as if it too held at its hidden heart some disturbing Charm, thought Olwen fancifully, as she roamed out westwards, apparently alone, but always in her thoughts accompanied by a sturdy compact form in khaki with scarlet tabs, his right sleeve tucked into his pocket, his gaze confident as the tone of his voice. Only, in her inmost thoughts, that voice was not wont to tease and laugh, and "rag" her, as in everyday life. She put, into the unexpectedly beautiful womanish mouth under that toothbrush moustache, the tone and the words that she would have wished to hear from it. . . and one can hazard a guess at the feelings of Captain Ross and of most other young men could they but listen to the dream-language given to the dream-images of themselves by the girls who are interested in them.

Little Olwen's guileless imaginings, for instance, murmured, "Olwen! My sweetheart! My own, sweet, sweet little girl! No, no; I have never cared for any one else in my life. All my life I have been waiting for You; the one girl who was made for me. Tell me you've never cared for any one either; ah yes, darling! Tell me. Do tell me. I shan't be able to sleep all tonight unless you do—" Thus the Captain Ross of Olwen's maiden reverie.

"Then," she mused, with her head down and her eyes on the unseen carpet of pine needles, "I'd tease him for half an hour before I did tell him there'd never been anybody, *seriously*, but him. And then at last—yes, then I'd let him kiss me. Two or three times running, even," decided this abandoned Olwen, as she roamed the forest that might have been Arden, or Eden, or the woods of her native Wales, for all she noticed of it in her daydream.

Into that dream there broke a loud and cheerful shout of "Hullo, hullo, hullo, hullo!"

Olwen jumped on the path, glanced quickly to the right, and then found that she had reached, without knowing that she had come so far, that clearing among the pine-trunks where the paths converged upon the woodcutter's hut.

Upon that place the hand of Change had fallen. Those giant bramble-runners had been thrust aside from the entrance to it; a pile of green canvas camp-kit leant against the log-wall; a khaki coat and a service cap were hung upon the outstretched arm of the nearest tree; and, just within the open doorway, a small figure in shirt-sleeves was standing working. With the end of a bough, used as a maul, he was driving four stumpy stakes at right angles into the pine-needle strewn floor of the hut.

"Harry Tate, in 'Moving House,' that's what this is supposed to represent!" explained Mr. Brown cheerfully, as Olwen came up. "What d'you think of my little grey home in the West? Palatial and desirable family residence, is it not? (Not.) Standing in its own park-like grounds." He dropped the maul. "Allow me—"

He lifted the little green canvas chair out from among the pile of the other things, pulled the four legs of it into position, and set it on an even piece of ground close to the doorway.

"Take a pew, Miss Howel-Jones," said Mr. Brown, and Olwen sat down, laughing. In a whisk the shadowy and adorable companion of her dream had been for the moment banished. She turned to this substantial but unthrilling young man of everyday life.

"Are you really going to live out here?" she asked.

"Got to," said Mr. Brown, with a business-like nod of his bullet-head. He returned to his post just inside the doorway, and went on driving in his stake. She watched him; asked him what those were for?

"Table," he explained between thumps. "They're lending me a table-top from the hotel. (Very decent the old girl was as soon as she realized I wasn't going to do a flit without paying my bill.) These stakes are going to be the four legs, d'you see? Then I stick the festive board on top of 'em. Old Ross is bringing it along presently; he's been lending a hand."

"Oh, has he?" said Olwen, looking round with great interest at the rest of the furniture. "Are those all the things you've had in Camp, I suppose?"

"Things somebody's had in Camp," grinned the little subaltern. "I think—Yes, that is my bucket, with 'Brown' painted on it; but none of the other things seem to be mine. I've snaffled a lot of other fellows' kit. But then, they've snaffled mine—or where is it? The bed's marked 'Capt. Smith,' and the bath 'Robinson'—I'd better paint Crusoe in front o' that, eh? Monarch of all I survey touch."

She watched him as he drove in the last stake; then he turned, put down the clump of wood with which he had been hammering, and began to drag out the light, canvas-covered furniture.

"Shall I help you with that?" suggested the girl, idly, half rising.

He waved her back with his pink hands. "No! No! You sit here and watch me and talk to me. Having a pretty young lady to look on and make things pleasant when you're doing a job of work; what could be nicer?" prattled little Mr. Brown, picking up the camp-bed that, under his short arm, gave him rather the appearance of an ant carrying a twig. "There! I'll have done the lot before Ross comes back with that table-top; I bet he's getting in another drink while he's about it. Talking of drinks, won't you allow me to offer you a little light refreshment? Such as my humble mansion can afford; here you are—"

As he spoke he took his knife out of his pocket and gave a cut at one of those ten-foot bramble-runners that had sprawled before the doorway of the hut. He held it out; it was covered with clusters of those soft, juicy blackberries that grow largest in the shade.

"Try our fresh gathered fruit, at market prices," chattered the London-bred lad; he took the cut end of the prickly runner and stuck it between two logs of the wall, just to Olwen's hand. "There you are, you see. Help yourself, won't you?"

Olwen picked and ate a couple of the sweet cones, black and glossy as her own little hatless head. Then she held out half a dozen on her pink palm to her host. "Won't you have one?"

"Chuck it in," he said, from where he was squatting turning over the things in his hold-all, which was spread out on the ground almost at her feet. "Three shies a penny, Miss! Try your luck—"

He put back his head, opened his large pink mouth. He looked almost like a big bull-pup, to whom the girl was teaching, with lumps of sugar, the trick of "Trust" and "Paid for." Smilingly Olwen took aim with one blackberry after another, missing twice to each one that she dropped into the mouth not so far from her knee; a babyish game enough! But their combined ages scarcely reached forty-two. Their laughter rang pleasantly through the trees, greeting the ears of Captain Ross as he strode up with the light wooden table-top tucked under his left arm.

And it was quite an idyllic little picnic group that met his eyes in that woodland glade of green and russet-brown: the little lady-bird of a girl, black-headed and red-coated, enthroned there on that camp-chair set under the trees, and taking aim from a handful of fruit at the open-mouthed, wholesome-faced boy kneeling before those absurdly small boots of hers.

Perhaps the little slinger of blackberries aimed more successfully, at that moment, than she knew; hitting, as Woman often does, another mark than the one at which she looks.

Perhaps the Authority on Woman was not too pleased to see another man allowed a glance at his (the Authority's) special study, even at a stray page of it?

But it was with quite a genial "good afternoon" that Captain Ross set down the table-top beside the other furniture.

"Well, that's that, Brown," he said.

"Ah, thank you," from the other young officer. "Much obliged, I'm sure. Now, we'll fix this on to here——"

Olwen darted forward to help with the table-top, but the two young men had managed without her.

"That's the ticket. Now, Ross! What about this for a scene in a Canadian lumber camp? Yes; there's water over there, and I've got my old spirit-kettle. Might turn an honest penny, too, by giving teas in the forest. Parties catered for, eh? The Old Bull and Bush touch. Who speaks for the job of the pretty waitress?" with a cheerful grin at Olwen. "What, are you going on, Ross? I thought you'd come to lend a hand at my flit. Don't go. Stop and watch me work, anyway."

"I guess not," said the Staff Officer, with a flash of his splendid teeth, and with the gesture that always tore at Olwen's sympathy, the forward shrug of the shoulder that should have moved his right arm. "I'd just hate to think I was in anybody's *way*——" He saluted, without looking at Miss Howel-Jones any more than she was looking at him.

Another moment and his scarlet tabs had ceased to brighten that glade of a French wood, that heart of a Welsh maid.

Poor little Olwen sat there by Mr. Brown's hut, feeling as if she could with her own hands have pulled it down about his ears, just for sheer exasperation. It's true that he, Mr. Brown, was wearing the Charm that her own hand had tucked into his pocket—but that had no power over her here. Here she was, left! Left for the rest of the afternoon, possibly, in the company of a young man whom she didn't care if she never saw again. *He* could talk to her, it seemed; *he* could pick blackberries for her; *he* could suggest that she would make a pretty waitress.

But the one and only young man for whose attentions and compliments she would have wished—what did *he* do? Just chucked down, with a careless word, the table-top that he had been to fetch, and made off without a look or a thought for her, she told herself.

Yet she was wearing, as she always wore, hidden away next her heart, the disturbing Charm!

What was the meaning of that?

But for the engagement which it had already brought about, Olwen would have been forced to the conclusion that it was all a fraud, that Charm.

Couldn't be that for some people it possessed power, for others none at all?

Had it only no effect when it was worn by her, Olwen?

The "no" to this question came almost as she was asking it; but not in the way that the girl had wished.

Little Mr. Brown, having been busy as he chattered, unheeded by her! for the last ten minutes, had now moved into position the whole of his effects—except the canvas chair on which Olwen was sitting. His blue bulging eyes had glanced in her direction several times, as he pulled and shifted and set straight. Now he looked again, and at length.

"I say, you know, you do look top-hole, sitting there like that," he told her, suddenly. "Wish I'd got my little kodak that I had to leave at Southampton after all; I'd take a snap of you, just as you are. Sitting there, as if it were your own little place, and all—"

He paused, still looking at her with his head on one side. He had taken his coat down from the bough, and stood, one arm in a sleeve of it, while he considered Olwen as if from a new point of view.

He said: "It's just what it wants—what any house or cottage or anything wants. The little missus. . . You'll be having a house of your own, o' course, one day."

Olwen shook her head. "Never," she said, with all the gloom of a temporary conviction.

"Oh! Come! Don't say that," Mr. Brown besought her, cheerily. "Course you will. All girls say they'll never marry, and all girls *do*, after all. All the pretty—All the ones like you, I'm sure."

"I shan't," persisted Olwen, a trifle cheered however. "*I'm* not pretty."

"Oh! Who's fishing for compliments?" laughed Mr. Brown. He jerked the other arm into his coat and began to fasten it. "If you don't mind me saying so, you're the prettiest girl in the place by miles. You are. I'm not the only person in the hotel who thinks so, either."

"Aren't you?" said Olwen, with a lift of her head, and of her heart. "Who—?"

"Why that old boy who keeps the hotel; old Leroux. He said you were '*très jolie*' the other day, when you were passing the steps. I said 'wee, wee, *très*.' You've got such ripping eyes."

"I don't think they're anything," said Olwen, disconsolate again.

"They are," insisted little Mr. Brown, his pink, ordinary face becoming dignified by his sincerity. "And it's not only—not only that you've got a lovely little face. There's—well, I don't know what there is about it."

"A charm, perhaps," suggested Olwen, with would-be irony; but he took up quite gravely: "That's it! Just what I meant. A charm. One sort of feels glad there is the kind of think walking about. It's like the song

> '*When we was in the trenches*
> *Fighting beside the Frenchies,*
> *We'd 'a' given all we 'ad for a girl like 'er,*
> *Wouldn't we, Bill?*
> *Aye!*'

Or something of that sort. Really now. Seriously. It is awfully topping to know there *is* a girl like you!"

Olwen shook her head again, laughed, deprecated. . . Impossible to assert that she was offended at his homage, even from the wrong young man. She listened as the guileless Brown went on to tell her it was a very lucky man for whom she'd be making a little home, some day; and, by Jove, anybody might envy him—

"Very nice of you to say so," murmured Olwen, pink-eared, and ardently wishing that Captain Ross had stayed on to hear this declaration.

The next remark of Mr. Brown's seemed to have nothing to do with it.

"Well, the War can't go on for ever."

"No, I suppose not," said Olwen, uncertainly.

"And I suppose—Well, it oughtn't to be quite as hard for a chap to get some sort of a posish of his own afterwards," said little Mr. Brown, thoughtfully, and as if he were already looking ahead, to a time when he should no longer wear that uniform, that belt that he was fastening as he came and stood nearer to the girl, looking down.

"I mean to say, I'm not going back to any stuffy shop and serving a lot of old trout—I beg their pardons—ladies with two and a half yards of écru insertion, pay at the desk, please. Not much. 'Tisn't the life for me; I know it now. They ought to find something different for me, after this. They've got to. Don't you think so?"

"Oh yes," agreed Olwen, a little vaguely.

"Well! There you are! All sorts of things might happen, with luck, even if it's no good planning 'em out now," took up the cheery boyish voice; and then there was silence for a moment under the pines.

Then lowering the voice, he said: "I say, I'll tell you something. That little mascot I found"—he touched his coat—"that you tucked in there for me, I'll always keep that. Nobody else shall touch it, you bet."

Olwen rose from the chair, putting her hand on the back of it. She was suddenly a little fluttered, as if by some ripple in the atmosphere, set stirring by some small and secret Force. The ripple was setting towards her this time; not from her, as she was wont to feel when she was putting out that childish soul of herself towards another man. But it touched her, the tiny Disturbance.

"Don't you want this chair?" she asked quickly.

Little Mr. Brown put his own hand on the back of it, closing his fingers for one moment over Olwen's—his fingers that had handled laces in a ladies' shop, had handled a rifle later, and, later still, a blood-stained revolver. . . Decency and honesty were written on every line of the little fellow's face at that moment; and even if he were of a pattern that everyday England turns out by the thousand—well, so much the better for England.

Quite simply, and as one stating a fact, he said to the girl beside him: "I don't suppose you've ever let any fellow kiss you?"

He himself had no doubt kissed girls in dozens, but he knew now that even to mention the word to this girl was a different thing. It did not need Olwen Howel-Jones's aghast little "*What—?*" to forbid him to go further than the word.

He took his hand away with a little rueful laugh.

"'*Archibald*, certainly not!' Eh? *I* wouldn't have tried."

"No. Of course not," said Olwen, repressively, but feeling a trifle shaken. Who would have thought of his saying such a thing to her? Who would have dreamt that the Charm would threaten to work to cross-purposes like this? Her small face took an invulnerable look. She swept some bits of blackberry leaves off her skirt, and prepared to turn homewards.

He walked with her to where the trees met the telegraph-posts of the shaded road.

There, as he said good-bye to her, this little young officer added, with a wistfulness: "But I would give anything to!"

XI

THE FEASTING OF THE CHARM

"There's that that would be thought upon,
I trow, beside the bride.
The business of the kitchen's great,
For it is fit that men should eat,
Nor was it there denied."

—Sir John Suckling

Crowded hours were to follow that quiet afternoon in the forest.

A morning or so afterwards Olwen darted out into the hall, where she had caught a glimpse of the bride-to-be going past in a great hurry.

"Miss Walsh—!"

"Oh, Olwen," said Miss Walsh, stopping breathlessly. "Oh, I do want to talk to you, but I haven't a moment. It's the lunch today, you know, the *déjeuner intime* for all his relations and friends. They've had the cards—"

Olwen nodded; she had sent her "*faire part*" card home to Wales as a curiosity.

"It's to be down in Madame Leroux's own sitting-room; she says better so than having the party in the *salle* after the hotel visitors have had lunch," explained Miss Walsh, always breathless. "Oh, I feel I must go down and see if I can help her, but it is so difficult to understand when she will talk French so dreadfully fast—"

"Let me come too," entreated Olwen, eyes suddenly alight. "Let me help, do! I can generally make out even her fast French."

"Very well—if *you* ask her!"

Madame Leroux was talking faster French that morning than they had ever heard from her before. They found her in the basement, a whole region of the hotel that was unknown ground to Olwen, peopled by a tribe of workers whose sallow faces she had never seen before, and who were flying hither and thither on errands undreamt of on the upper floors. Even so the stoke-hole of a liner is unthought about on its polished decks.

The manageress was in the *appartement* that adjoined the kitchen, a domain smaller but pleasanter of aspect than any of the big rooms above, and more comfortable, except for one narrow space that was neither kitchen nor *appartement*. This space between the walls seemed to be a sound magnifier of the rumbling service-lift, the whistles of speaking-tubes, and the hissing and running of every water-pipe in the place. The door into the huge French kitchen stood open, giving a glimpse of marmites, burnished copper pans, crocks, and five-decker cookers; of vegetables piled haystack high, of ramparts of yard-long rolls, of twenty other kinds of provisions.

Beyond the kitchen a second door opened out into the *cour*, where buckets clanked, a tap splashed, and the whistling of a knife-cleaning machine could be heard. By yet another door Marie and Rosalie were bringing in chairs collected from bedrooms, attics, landings, and any other corner.

"May we both come in?" Miss Walsh asked timidly.

Madame Leroux turned.

"Ah! Enter always, Mademoiselle. It is not to all the world that I permit it—but for the little demoiselle of M. the Professor, but yes, but yes—To help? But certainly, if that gives her pleasure. One would have said that she would have preferred to spend the fine morning with M. le Capitaine in the forest, he with the one arm who admires her already—" Madame's glance was as swift as the dart of a chameleon's tongue after a fly.

She was already dressed for the day, her dark hair dragged up to the top of her head in a fist-shaped knob, secured with combs, and her front locks *frisés* above her mercilessly intelligent face. Over her tightly-fitted gown of black *broché* and *passementerie*, showing a fat white V of neck, a velvet band and a pendant, she had passed an enormous apron of blue-and-white check.

She was looking over her well-covered shoulder with eyes that were everywhere at once, and giving orders in a voice that was as shrill as a whipsaw and as quick as a mill-race.

"Hold! Prop that door open, Rosalie, instead of bumping it each time with the good chair, little careless one; one would say a swing!" (She took breath in a gasp.)

"And those oysters from Monsieur Paul; are they not yet arrived? Do not open them immediately, as last time; and even so, see that you open me but half of them in order that they may keep. And thou,

Marcel, take me that mat into the yard instead of brushing me the dust over the vegetables!" (Gasps.) "*Bon dieu*, one would need twenty eyes—As for these knives, Etienne, have you the intention to grind them to powder rather than find other work? It is then not necessary that they serve us for another day?" (Gasp.) "My faith! . . . Ah, Mees Ouall she—Agathe—but no, it is not necessary that you help. Go, go and make yourself beautiful for after the *déjeuner*, when you are presented to the friends. Make yourself beautiful for Pierre, who shall mount up afterwards to beg you to descend for a little half-hour, like a princess!" (Gasp.) "*Eh bien*, if you hold to assisting me now, but not in the kitchen, no, no; if you will have the goodness to dispose on the table within the *serviettes* that I have already placed in a heap. Also the glasses; they are in those cupboards there; no, not there, Mademoiselle, here, here, here. Arrange them all precisely as in England, at your *château*, yes? It is that! It is perfect!" (Gasp.) "And the little demoiselle of the Professor shall set out the cards with the names—But no, no, no, no, no; she does not know the names nor where they sit. Better to place these pots of cyclamen on the window-sill, Mademoiselle, if you please. One would say real flowers, would one not? But two francs." (Gasp.) "Fifty! It is true! *Ah, pas ça*—" seeing Agatha Walsh, entirely at a loss, picking up from the sofa-corner and unrolling a tricolor flag. "Not that. It should have been interlaced with the other. I was desolated, but one could not obtain in time, the Union Jacques. Flowers only, therefore. *Tiens*, I have not placed a cloth over the safe—"

She spread over the iron cash-safe a cloth edged and inserted with the lovely pillow-made lace of the neighbourhood, while her nimble French tongue ran ceaselessly on.

Her niece-by-marriage-to-be, helped by Olwen, set to work with all the good will in the world to lay the large round table. From the cupboard drawers indicated by Madame's plump hands they brought a tablecloth, an ornately embroidered table-centre, and napkins of the finest linen, all wedded to that beautiful lace; from the cupboards they took old and exquisite glass, and silver that could not have been bettered at the Grange of Miss Walsh's youth. Olwen noticed that the old-fashioned carved bread-cradle that swung from the ceiling had already been filled with blossomed and berried boughs of the arbutus, patron plant of the place. She thought as Mrs. Cartwright had thought, "I shall always think of arbutus—and here."

The chairs, some of them rush-bottomed, others of carved gilt, were ranged about the table; then Olwen and Agatha Walsh sped out into the yard and returned with the knives that Etienne, the boy in the green drugget apron, had at last polished to his satisfaction.

In the middle of the red-tiled kitchen Madame Leroux still stormed as shrilly as though she alone of all excellent housewives possessed worthless servants.

"Is it not enough that I myself must arise at half-past four today, and it is that I must do *all* myself, me, as well as to entertain the friends and the relations of Monsieur, they who are eating their blood with jealousy because he marries himself with an English lady of the high nobility? And why are the boards not placed over the bowls of soup? My faith, it is then that *I* must work, *I* must arrange, *I* must plan, *I* must have the eyes everywhere, everywhere, everywhere, while you let the fire die down, female idle ones who do nothing but regard with open mouths and talk in corners and try to eat me the *glacés* fruits out of the dishes?" (Gasp for breath.) "Take you these immediately, Marie Claire—" she waved towards a score of trussed chickens that looked like a frieze of poultry—"and set them in the pans. And pose you those lids so that the pottage may simmer as it must." She pointed to the vast arched fireplace with the grid running from one end to the other. "*Mon Dieu*, if this boy here had as many legs as an octopus he could not more expressly place them in my way. That he does at each moment! Is it that I have sent my own children out to receive *les amis* even at Arcachon, to be encumbered by thee? The children? They will feast out here in the yard with the children of the notary and the little cousins; I do not wish that they are the whole time with the grown ones when one talks—"

And she bustled out into the *cour* to look to the long trestled table there which had been surrounded by a still further variety of chairs.

It was here that Miss Walsh in her halting French asked where was Gustave, where was Monsieur Leroux?

"The men?" Madame gabbled. "Ah, for that, where would they be? Invisibles, so long as there is work to be done," with a half-indulgent laugh. "You will see also, in good time, you English ladies, that which the *service militaire* does for the men! They make their service. They return. They put themselves at their ease. Behold, they are required to do nothing further for the rest of their life. It is we, Mesdemoiselles, we who are accustomed to it; we other French wives. You also, you will see! Ah, hold, the oysters! Now, Etienne, you will dust me once again the seats of all these chairs, I say to you, and with a dry duster, I pray you, not a wet one; dry, dry, dry, dry, dry—"

In this exalting hubbub did Olwen pass the whole morning with her friend until the sallow little Italian waiter came down to announce that *déjeuner* was served.

They went up. How cool and quiet, it struck them, were those upper reaches of the hotel. . .

But as they were seeking their places a quick "Oh, come and look!" from Miss Walsh brought Olwen running to the side window. "Oh, here are the people—"

The procession of the French *invités* was coming down the road from the little tramway terminus. It was solemnly headed by the three little pigtailed Leroux girls, each holding by the hand another child, bare from mid-thigh to ankle, and wearing an adaptation of the sailor suit. After them, in a broken line of twos and ones and threes, came the grown-up people.

First and most resplendent of them appeared the individual whom Olwen rightly guessed to be the *notaire* from Bordeaux. He wore a white bowler hat, a white waistcoat, and he carried in his hands, which he held well out in front of him, a large bouquet tied with tricolour streamers and the Union Jacques which Madame Leroux had desired, and he overshadowed even his rotund *endimanchée* wife in her purple costume and forward raking hat, who bobbed in his wake. She was escorted by Monsieur Leroux. Next came Monsieur Popinot, the clerk from the passports office, all in black, but carrying Madame Popinot's pink parasol. She, a plump and pretty little woman, carried a year-old baby in a corolla of lace.

Then came a sister of Madame Leroux, as dark, as mercilessly intelligent as the manageress herself, talking eagerly to Pierre Tronchet, effective in his blue and red.

Another *artilleriste* on leave, evidently a comrade from the regiment, walked a pace or so behind them, between two silent young girls; then a trio of stout, bearded old men gesticulating freely, then a lady in another forward raking hat, then a party wearing deepest mourning, but wreathed in smiles, then others. . . then again others. . . Tronchets, Leroux, ramifications of both families, relatives, friends, and those whom it was intended to dazzle. . .

Olwen, gazing upon this *cortège*, suppressed a wish to think aloud of a rhyme of her childhood:

> *"The animals went in four by four,*
> *Hurray, Hurray!*
> *The animals went in four by four*
> *And the big hippopotamus stuck in the door."*

This last line, she considered, might almost have applied to several of the *invités*!

All of them, as they approached the hotel, stiffened, pulled themselves together as if they were going past the saluting point of a review, assumed photographically unnatural expressions, and walked delicately; then they seemed to deflate and hurry as they slipped past the corner to the back entrance to the premises.

"Oh, I'm not a bit hungry," sighed the agitated Miss Walsh as she turned from the window and sat down next to Olwen at the long table. The *déjeuner* was as perfectly cooked and served as if no subterranean banquet had been in preparation. "Oh, fancy having to be 'shown' to a host of people! Oh, I can't help feeling almost glad that Gustave's father and mother aren't alive! If they had been, you know, he would have had to ask their consent to marry me, even though he is thirty-eight. Oh, it is such a mercy that Madame didn't want me to sit through the whole of lunch."

"Much the best plan!" agreed Mrs. Cartwright from her side of the table.

"Oh, yes; I don't appear till they have to drink my health—oh, but I am so nervous! And do you think I look all right in this, Mrs. Cartwright? . . . honestly?"

She wore an expensive new dress of prune-coloured *glacé* silk, ornamented with a kind of lace bib and with rows and rows of little crimson buttons that fastened nothing. Both Mrs. Cartwright and Olwen fibbed valiantly, and had their reward. The loveliest frock in Paris could not have been more becoming to Agatha Walsh than her flush of pleasure.

That *déjeuner* downstairs was supposed to be *intime* and private; but the distant sounds of it were already becoming audible to the more public part of the hotel.

First a soft but thunderous drumming as of applause upon the table-top was heard.

Then a skirl of laughter, the piercingness of which, near to, could only be guessed at.

Then, booming fragments of a voice that rose above others just as an occasional column of foam spouted higher than those other Biscay rollers on the reef. Then an uninterrupted booming. . . Apparently a speech was in progress.

An involuntary and smiling silence seemed to fall upon the luncheon parties in the *salle* above, almost as if they would have felt it impolite to talk through what was going on below. Truly, Miss Walsh was making the hotel one that day—the hotel to which she had only come because of that hat-pin stuck in a guide-book and pricking at random a name on a page!

Then suddenly, the door of the *salle à manger* opened. The blue-and-red apparition of Sergeant Tronchet stood to attention just inside it: darkly flushed, beaming, silent.

(It may here be said that none of the visitors ever had known this swarthy well-set-up French soldier anything but silent. All that most of them had ever heard of his voice had been the murmured "Madame. . . Mademoiselle. . . Messieurs. . ." that accompanied his heel-clicking bows. Only Miss Walsh had ever had any conversation with him. But had not this been to some purpose?)

"Oh, he's come to fetch me," she exclaimed now in a voice that failed. "Good-bye, Olwen dear," she added, as if she never expected to come back alive. "I shall see you and Mrs. Cartwright and the Professor at tea-time—you are all coming to *my* tea, aren't you?" she finished appealingly.

Then she disappeared, with her peacock-proud *fiancé*.

"THE DAY HAS ONLY JUST begun, my dear child!" declared Mrs. Cartwright to Olwen, rising. "Come to my room and take a rest before *we* come on in the next act. Run up, will you? I'll follow."

Olwen ran up; glad of a breathing space.

That party, three floors and five or six rooms away, did still dominate the whole hotel! She was glad to lie back in Mrs. Cartwright's basket-chair and to draw a long breath. She had nothing to do that afternoon, she thanked goodness. . .

But Mrs. Cartwright, as soon as she came in, drew a chair up to her writing-table and began to make notes, chuckling from time to time.

"Tell me when the people begin to go," she begged Olwen. "I had to make an errand about the tea, and take a peep in just now, I couldn't miss it. . . My dear! The heat! And the din down there! Poor Miss Walsh!

How Madame crammed them all in I don't know. . . And Monsieur Leroux with his black domino beard and his pouchy eyes, *and* all those women exactly the same height whether they sit down or stand up. . ."

She was scribbling sketches of them all to send to her boys. . .

The noise downstairs rose to sounds of confused singing—*Le Chanson des Baisers*, then fell at last.

"I think they're all going away now," said Olwen from the balconied window, and Mrs. Cartwright ran to join her and to watch the homeward-faring procession filing by.

First the notary, his white bowler hat a little dinted, appeared round the corner of the hotel. He was arm in arm with Monsieur Popinot, who still carried his wife's pink parasol, and who seemed to have an idea of putting it up over the pair of them as they went by the windows, but was restrained by a gesture, suppressed but fierce, from the notary. His purple-clad wife hustled the children ahead of her; the party in mourning were giggling joyously together, then assumed a gravity.

With the same effect of pompously pulling themselves together with which they had passed the front of the hotel, they all repassed it now.

Even as they turned their backs upon it, the strain was seen to relax again. Up went the pink parasol in the distance.

"Ah, there; there goes Gustave's comrade the *artilleriste*," commented Mrs. Cartwright. "First at the fight—and last at the feast; yes, he's the last."

The *artilleriste* swaggered delightfully, turning to wave a farewell, and obviously caring little whether it were to the front of the hotel or the back. . .

And then, about seventy yards behind the last of these revellers there went by two other figures.

They were those of Captain Ross and Mr. Awdas, who had been making themselves scarce for the day.

And perhaps it was because Olwen was busy with her own effort not to look at one of them that she did not notice Mrs. Cartwright's swift glance at the other; the flying boy.

As if he felt that glance upon him, Jack Awdas looked up and put a hand to his cap; a smile rippling all over his face.

Olwen would not have read the purpose behind the smile.

XII

Moonlight and the Charm

"O, swear not by the moon, the inconstant moon,
That monthly changes in her circled orb,
Lest thy love prove likewise variable."

—Shakespeare

Now let us take the roof off, as is done in fairy stories about other charms.

Let us steal a peep, that is, inside various rooms of that hotel, where this story is laid.

In the basement, first of all, let us cast a glance at the *appartement* that had echoed to the feasting of that luncheon party, and had been later the scene of a sedate and ultra-English tea. Nobody there now, except the hotel manageress and her husband. Monsieur Leroux with that black domino beard of his, is dozing in the most capacious chair; Madame is poring over her accounts. Every now and then her eye lights up with a spark from the smouldering fire of pride within her; for who but she has such a right of feeling proud at the end of that day of meals and acclamations (and washing-up?). She thinks of her nephew Gustave's brilliant *partie*, and of the bedazzling of all her friends, most especially of the notary's wife, here in this very room. The little close room seems to her once more a-glitter with the glass and the silver and the display. . . Only the prune-coloured velvet curtains are tightly drawn before the pots of imitation cyclamen, and there enters no gleam of the light that is bathing the forest and the sea without—light of the waning moon, melting and cool at once, at once disdainful and seductive.

Upstairs in the *salle à manger* the engaged couple have been dining as guests of the guests. Mrs. Cartwright and the Professor had suggested this, and their proposal was cordially received. The health of the *fiancés* had been drunk, and the old French gentleman with the red button-hole has added the toast to the next betrothed from that party there present tonight.

And now Gustave Tronchet and his bride-elect are still moving from group to group in the *salon*, and the diffident, old-maidish Englishwoman is transfigured. It astonishes her to think that she could ever have felt that violent shyness so early in the day. She has forgotten how her knees trembled as she faced that perfect zoo of foreigners, all beards and bosoms, come to inspect Mees Ouallshe.

She feels now that she carried it off admirably. She has been amplifying to herself since the ten words of French that she had managed to stammer out then, and by now they appear to her a classic oration. She feels she was born to this kind of thing. On her *fiancé's* stout arm she moves about the room like a spoon that is keeping on the stir a pan of hot and incredibly sweet social jam. As Mrs. Cartwright says to herself, "No ordinary English engagement to a man out of her own world could ever have brought the dear good creature these triumphs; let her enjoy them,"—and everybody enjoys seeing Miss Agatha Walsh radiant, while she even more enjoys being so seen.

As for Sergeant Gustave Tronchet, if he were not enjoying it, also, who should be? Accepted, *rangé*, adored!

He marshals her about from *salle* to *salon* and lounge, drawing her back as she peeps through the chink of the big hall door at the beckoning moonlight without.

"No, Agathe! You will *inrhume* yourself—"

She turns to beam brighter than the moon itself at the comely dark face of the only man who has ever protested whether she took cold or not. He, too, has been studying a speech in the language of the country into which he is marrying.

He brings it out, and the ears of love are quick to understand even his English, even his accent.

"I oueelle trai to you rendaire 'appee, Agathe!"

"Oh," she breathed, with a little clutch to the blue-sleeved arm. "Oh, but you do, you *have*!"

They return to the *salle*. . .

But the assembled visitors cannot spend the whole evening in contemplating the happiness of Miss Walsh and of Gustave Tronchet, *serjent d'artillerie*.

Other groups begin to make their own arrangements; in one of the bedrooms the Madonna-like French mother and the Brittany nurse are putting to bed Lucien, the little damson-dark boy, who was also at

Miss Walsh's tea; he is repeating, with the correct pronunciation of a child to whom all language is new, a little prayer that she has taught him:

> *"I see the moon and the moon sees me,*
> *God bless the moon and God bless me!"*

In another bedroom Olwen Howel-Jones has just run up to get into her big driving-coat; she thinks of going out for a breath of fresh air and of moonlight. Why not? Mrs. Cartwright will probably come if she's asked.

ROOF ON AGAIN HERE, PLEASE. For at this point of the story Mrs. Cartwright was standing just outside the *salle* windows beside the dark spiky shape of a cactus; she had put on a pale-hued wrap, and in the puzzling light and shade she appeared gleaming and straight as the flowering rod of the plant. Just as she was looking out to where a few riding lights showed in the *Baissin*, Jack Awdas strode up beside her.

"Come for a turn down on the sands," he suggested, cheerfully. "It's not cold; it is one perfectly good night for a walk."

Now it is almost easier to take the roof off an hotel and to look down unchecked into its various rooms than it is to unveil and take stock of the contents of a woman's mind with its strata upon strata of confusing elements.

So, for what Mrs. Cartwright was feeling, we will take her word as she told herself that she felt relieved and settled about the *affaire* Jack Awdas.

She was glad it was all over. The boy had imagined himself in love with her.

A great mercy that he had not, after the manner of some men, allowed himself to dangle and sigh and create an atmosphere in which one did not quite know where one was. He had voiced his absurd and youthful passion at once. He had actually proposed to her—to her who might be his mother. So much the better, as it happened; because *now* she had been able to say "No" definitely. It had all been definitely settled and tidied up in that wood on the way from the oyster park.

Now, it was finished.

Now, it was quite safe again.

It would be silly to avoid the boy since both of them knew where they were.

Besides, he had had that horrible nightmare. He would have to go flying again. Not even yet were his jangled nerves quite healed, poor child! He ought, he really ought to have some one to look after him, to give a thought to his welfare now and again. . . some nice, sensible woman. . .

Mrs. Cartwright, in thus describing herself to herself, did not for one moment admit that if the boy had already proposed to her in the sunlight, he simply couldn't help himself in the moonlight.

So she answered him lightly and conventionally; she fell into step beside him. They walked.

She was too old for him, as she'd told him. A generation too old! But she was still not too old to walk with him, to listen to him. And. . . When is a woman too old to wish she were young enough?

It was brusquely enough that Jack Awdas broke into speech.

"I say," he began, "how old should I have to be, then, before you'd want to marry me?"

She had been looking away across the *Baissin* with its twinkling lights, its guardian jewel flashing from white to red. She turned abruptly, dismayed, as one is dismayed when some trouble, dimly foreseen (and defied) descends upon one's head.

Oh dear. . . Oh dear. . . It was not quite at an end then? She had not yet definitely put a stop to this very young man's folly?

"Oh," she returned. "Oh, but we had agreed, I think, not to talk about. . . *that*, any more. . ."

"Had we?" he retorted. "You had 'agreed,' perhaps. I hadn't."

"But—Please! There must be no more of it."

"What?" He threw up his head. "We must have it out, you know. We are going to."

"No, no—"

"Yes, I say. Yes. As I was saying—How old should I have to be before you'd want to marry me?"

Mrs. Cartwright gave a little hopeless sort of laugh to herself as she threw upon him that quick glance that seemed to be not looking.

He put on his coat (at her orders), his flyer's coat with the wide collar that made his head seem even smaller and the oval of his face more perfect as it rested against the fur. That young, young face topping the athlete's body that towered above her own, that spring and lilt of his walk had never before made such appeal to the sense of physical beauty that was in her.

Claudia Cartwright thought that in this faculty she brought up the arrears of the countless members of her own sex who would seem to be entirely without it. A woman had once said to her, "*I don't find any man much under forty-five worth considering. Youth doesn't appeal to me. I never can see the attraction!*" and to Mrs. Cartwright this was exactly as though her friend had boasted, "*I am colour-blind! I can't tell one tune from another, either! Also, I never care for flowers.*"

The boy at her side was beautiful, in the diffused and shifting light, as a young marble Hermes dressed in the trappings of today and come to life to court her. The next twenty years might teach him many, many things—but they must strip from him one by one the charms of which he was all unconscious, as he demanded of her how old he must be to please her.

She should stop him there, she knew. Since he had not seen that it had been the end, she should put the definite end to it; go in.

She should not dally or coquet with this thing.

Instincts that she had thought long dead were lifting their heads within her; too strong to be beaten down at once. For the life of her the woman could not help dallying with that passing moment to which every woman alive cries out within herself, "Oh *stay! Thou art so fair*—"

Aloud she said (truthfully enough, but in a sense that he did not follow), "I might not want to marry you if you *were* older."

"Why not? Why not? The other day in the wood you said it was my age that you barred," he went on, persistently. "It isn't that you don't like *me*, is it? *Is* it? If you just happened to be my own age, then, you'd take me, wouldn't you?"

Would she? Ah, wouldn't she, she thought, vainly. And again for the life of her she could not keep that subtlest, faintest trace of coquetry out of her voice as she replied, "You seem very sure of that."

"Mustn't I be? Tell me at least. *Tell* me what you think of me!"

She seemed to catch herself back just in time from uttering follies. "I think you are a dear boy; one of the dearest that I have seen," she said, evenly. "But I know that you're wasting your time with an ageing woman like me."

"A what?" he almost snorted.

She repeated it all the more firmly, perhaps, because she knew that she was looking her youngest in that soft light of the waning moon.

"An ageing woman like me. For I am that. Just think of it, quite sensibly, for a moment. In a little while you would see me getting to be just the same as friends of your mother's, that you're specially nice to and talk to because they are old. Yes! Listen! It's coming. Before you have a line on your face or a grey thread in your hair."

"I shall get as bald as a coot. All flyers will; it's the tight leather caps, here—"

"Nonsense! Ages before that, my hair will be growing grey all over."

"It's quite grey now; absolutely white in the moonlight—silver! And it looks top-hole," he assured her, laughing down at her. "Why, you look wonderful. You always do. You can't talk about the usual sort of women getting old, and pretend you're going to be like that, because you aren't. How could you ever be? You're different."

"Only to you," she sighed, "and only for the moment."

"Moment! I swear *I* shouldn't ever alter—"

"No? Let's turn." They retraced on the sands the lines of their own footprints; his boot-marks making a contrast with the slim, light prints of the woman's shoes.

"What have you got on your feet?" he asked her presently, almost roughly, stopping to look down. "I never saw anything like the things women go out in. Haven't you got *any* sensible boots? . . . You aren't fit to take care of yourself, as a matter of fact. You've got to let me take care of you."

"My dear boy," she smiled, shaking the head on which the moonlight was spinning those prophetic webs of silver, "all nice men at your age begin to feel that need of taking care of something. A young girl, that's what you ought to be seeing to the shoes of, and looking for wraps for, and all that. Not me, not me. A young girl."

"What young girl?" he demanded mutinously.

Mrs. Cartwright was silent as they passed into the darkness under the wooden jetty. Out into the light again they came, and up the beach, back, in the direction of the hotel piazza, and of the old cannon that stood on its stone plinth at the foot of the stone steps. They reached the cannon, and still she had not spoken.

She was thinking, hard.

A young girl, she had said; and she could think without "minding" it in the least, that the best thing this lad of twenty-two could do would be to fall in love with a young girl. She had thought so several times lately. It was odd, however, that she always thought of this solution as "a" young girl, not any particular one. Not little Olwen Howel-Jones, for instance; oh, no! Nor her (Mrs. Cartwright's) young niece Stella, not any of the Mabels or Ethels or Dorothys that she knew at home, and to whom she might have introduced the boy. None of these could she think of for one instant in connection with Jack Awdas. Yet, one of these days, some lucky girl must be responsible for the happiness of all his days (not just of one glamorous afternoon in the forest) and all his nights (not just of one night when the power of darkness had been kept at bay, and when he had fallen at last asleep "as one whom his mother comforteth"). Yes, later on, there must be "a" young girl for him. . .

He stopped by the cannon.

"Don't go in. Just a little minute," he coaxed, softly. "I can't talk to you in there."

"It's no use talking," murmured Mrs. Cartwright.

But she did pause.

And, as he sat down on the body of that obsolete gun, and then, unfastening his thick coat, spread a flap of it out, she did yield so far as to sit down, in her pale wrap, on that corner of his coat beside him.

He leant an arm on the cannon behind her. Both looked in silence over the lagoon, towards the reef.

White, red; white, red—flashed the warning light.

She felt herself at the beginning of a conflict that must tear her this way and that; but his mind was single and set. He was just blind, obstinate, and keen.

He said, "I told you that night when you sat up with me what I thought of girls. I don't want 'em. I want *you*, and you're all I want; or ever shall. I can swear to that. Oh, I know myself! I can swear to it."

The arm behind her trembled a little with his earnestness.

For one mad moment Mrs. Cartwright admitted to herself that if she could be twenty-two again for one year, she would buy that year with the rest of the time that she had to live. Ah, to be twenty-two! To let that hard boyish arm close round her, clasp her, crush her! To turn, with lips and eyes aglow, to turn to him as she felt herself drawn to do—drawn, driven—

But because she felt thus she kept around herself that invisible, intangible armour of refusal which is every woman's at need and which no outside power can pierce. She did not need to move one half-inch away from that corner of his coat on which she sat. Yet. . . Yet she could hardly believe that he did not guess at the growing disturbance in the heart that beat not so far, after all, from his own.

Appealingly he broke out. "*You* must marry me. I don't know why on earth you want to talk about other girls to me!"

"'*Other*' girls—!"

"Yes. You're just a girl to me. You *are* a girl, yourself. I can't see you as anything but a girl!"

She made a little gesture with her long arms, lithe and elastic still as when she was a schoolgirl, only more rounding in modelling; she pressed a hand to her hair, still brown and thickly growing. She turned away the face that showed lines brought by years of worry, of concentration upon her work; ah, they were there even in the moonlight and even though she tended her skin as prettier women often neglect to do. She could feel that in every inch and ounce of him this boy was alert and conscious of her nearness, of her suppleness of body, of that faint scent of rose, kuss-kuss and orris that clung about her.

It couldn't be. It mustn't be.

Lightly as little Olwen could have sprung up, Mrs. Cartwright sprang up from her seat upon the muzzled cannon and said quickly, "I am going in."

As she set her foot upon the first step of the piazza, she turned to young Jack Awdas with what she told herself would be, definitely, her last word upon the subject. Her little laugh was whimsical and mirthless as she said it.

"You think you see me as a girl? Ah! Wait until you see me beside a *real* girl!"

XIII

WILD-FIRE AND THE CHARM

"A light that shifts, a glare that drifts,
Rekindling thus and thus."

—Kipling

A little earlier, on that same evening, the disturbing Charm had set to work in other directions.

Little Mr. Brown, who had taken his dinner as usual at the hotel, was lingering on the terrace on the other side of the building from the piazza. He was smoking a cigarette, which the "*Défense*" notices would forbid him at every turn on the forest; but, apart from this, it was not to be wondered at that the gregarious little Londoner was in no hurry to get back to that sylvan shanty of his. The contrast, after that evening, would have been as great as that between a chandeliered ballroom and a cave.

Oh, the loneliness of that hut at night! His cheerful urban soul got fairly fed-up, as he would express it, with all that wind-sighing-in-the-pine-tops business. Of course, as he'd have told you, the little old hut was good enough for lolling outside of with a book, or for writing his letters in of a morning. If only they'd allow him to smoke there he would be quite fond of the dashed little dug-out by now, but he didn't pretend to find it a very attractive spot of an evening.

Even of an evening, perhaps, it wouldn't have been so dusty if he'd had somebody with him. With his cigarette between his teeth he found himself humming a song of seven years back:

"It's all right if there's a girl there,
That's the place where I'd like—"

At that moment Olwen Howel-Jones, her slim shape buried in a big driving-coat, appeared upon the terrace.

He approached her joyously.

"Going for a little stroll round the houses, Miss Olwen?"

Olwen shrank within herself. She did not want any more of the obvious admiration of this quite nice boy; it had dismayed her to find that in shooting at a star (Captain Ross) she had hit a blackberry-bush (little Mr. Brown). After that declaration of his in the wood she had felt almost inclined to tear that misleading Charm she wore from its ribbon and to toss it down the wind into the *Baissin*! However, she could not be rude to him just because he didn't happen to be somebody else. Hesitatingly she replied that she had thought of going for a little walk with Mrs. Cartwright, who seemed to have disappeared.

(She, as we know, was at the moment pacing the sands beside Jack Awdas.)

"Ah, you're at a loose end, then, are you," returned Mr. Brown, cheerfully. "Well, if I might have the pleasure—?"

Before Olwen could either grant or refuse "the pleasure," there stepped out on to the terrace Captain Ross, who with a note of some purpose in his "good evening," took up his position on the other side of the girl.

Now, all through that thrilling day, something (heard quite at the beginning of it) had been humming in Olwen's heart like a wind-harp that responds to every passing breath. It was that something let fall by Madame Leroux, and it had tossed Olwen far too high up into the rosy clouds to take more than a quite superficial notice of the subsequent events of that rousing day. She had helped Miss Walsh, had listened and watched with Mrs. Cartwright, had drunk healths—but all the time she had been secretly hearing, over and over again, one lightly-uttered remark.

"Monsieur le Capitaine, he with one arm, who admires Mademoiselle already—"

Madame had thought that! There must be truth in it. The Charm was working and not only in the wrong direction. It was true that Captain Ross had talked to Olwen as if she were a little girl; he had avoided her in the forest when he was carrying that table-top for Mr. Brown, and he had blackened this evening for her by taking not the smallest notice of her at dinner; he hadn't even come up to touch his glass to hers when the toast had been proposed to the next engaged person for that hotel. To set off against all this, Madame Leroux (that piercingly acute Frenchwoman) had given it as her opinion that he admired Mademoiselle.

Now he joined her and Mr. Brown on the terrace.

His coming had a curious effect. Olwen became filled with apparent animation and delight in the company of little Mr. Brown. This was not deliberate coquetry, but pure instinct. The kindest-hearted girl in the world, the most kernel-sweet maid never hesitates before one form of feminine cruelty—*to make use of the admirer for whom she does not care in order to spur the man she loves*. It is not an admirable instinct. But it is a form of self-preservation in Woman, for which Man alone is responsible. . .

Perhaps it is not fair to allege that every man in his heart is a dog in the manger, hating to see his fellow-men smiled upon by a pretty girl? Perhaps it's not true that his interest in the girl is awakened when he sees her interested in another? No! Perhaps it's a libellous old theory that simply doesn't hold water as a rule.

Only, what myriads of exceptions it does take to prove that rule!

In her happiest voice Olwen, standing between the two men, began talking to Mr. Brown. "I do think that hut of yours must be a delightful place to live in! No cleaning! No sweeping! and you've only to put out your hand to get those lovely blackberries for breakfast—"

Captain Ross, leaning on the balustrade, was seen to hump his back a little.

"Can't say I fancy blackberries as a breakfast myself, but I daresay it'll come to that," grumbled Mr. Brown, cheerily. "Blackberries, and 'bright *water is my drink from the crystal spring*.' Can you make anything out of this tangle about allowances, Ross?"

Captain Ross was apparently *not* the finest judge of pay-warrants in Europe. A short "nope" came from over his humped shoulder. Olwen noticed that his one hand was resting on his left-side-jacket-pocket, that appeared to be bulging with something he had slipped into it.

"Dashed if I can make 'em out," said Mr. Brown, pleasantly. "According to my reckoning, Miss Olwen, there was my regimental pay for July, rations and lodgings for August, and they'll be in arrears for September—and no hospital stoppages. . . Cox's do make mistakes; ask anybody. Anybody!"

Olwen agreed that Cox's did make mistakes. Honeyed sympathy informed her tone as she said so.

"Well, that's just that," Mr. Brown concluded, beaming upon her. "But, as I was just asking you, what about a turn on the prom. in the moonlight?"

Here the hump of Captain Ross's square shoulders suddenly straightened out.

He took his hand away from the packet in his pocket, gave a hitch to his belt, then, turning to Olwen, and in the most matter-of-fact voice imaginable, he told the fib that took her breath away.

"I guess Miss Howel-Jones is engaged to me for this dance. Isn't that so, Miss Howel-Jones?"

"Dance? But—" gasped little Olwen, stupefied. "Nobody is dancing!"

"Then I guess we'll have to sit it out together on the old cannon or somewhairrr," said Captain Ross, coolly. "Shall you be all right without anything on your head?"

Now if Captain Ross expected that upon this hint Mr. Brown would retire in good order to his hut, there to brood upon allowances for the rest of the evening, he was no very fine judge of subalterns in the London Rifle Brigade.

Mr. Brown, M.C., stood firm. "Look here, Ross—" he was beginning, when another voice, a deep, genial, elderly voice, was heard behind the shutters of the window through which Captain Ross had come out upon the terrace.

The voice enquired, "Has anybody seen my niece?"

Little Olwen jumped.

"Oh, it's my Uncle. Do open the shutters, Uncle! I'm out here, with Mr. Brown and Captain Ross," explained Olwen, hurriedly. "It's—it's ever so early, you know! We were all just thinking of going for a little walk—"

"No; I've got it," put in the unquenchable Mr. Brown. "What about a pull on the lagoon, to look at the phosphorescence? You too, Ross," he added, hospitably; guessing that Professor Howel-Jones was of an age that might allow its young nieces to go for moonlight rows in boats on lakes with two young men, but scarcely with one. "I saw a skiff drawn up by the jetty. You don't mind, Professor, do you?"

"At this hour?" demurred the Professor, looking out into the light that made of his massive old head the summit of Mynedd Mawr in a snowy December. "For you to take your death of cold, Olwen *fach*, in the night air?"

Little Olwen, pulling up her storm-collar, murmured appealingly above it. "Oh, *darling*! I shall be as warm as warm! Do let me go."

She did not know that in her coaxing she was helped by a girl long dead. It was to a certain note in the voice that she had from her mother that the Professor ceded now.

With a little nod he said, "Very well," and all but added "Mary." "Very well, Olwen *fach*. I trust you gentlemen not to keep her out long. I wish you a pleasant row; good night to you, good night!" And he went in.

"Come on; let's make a dash for it," said young Brown.

He led the way; followed by Olwen and Captain Ross, the latter in a worse temper than he had been in since he left the hospital.

"Jump in," said Mr. Brown, as they came up to the little empty skiff moored at the foot of the jetty.

In the skiff little Mr. Brown, cheerfully resigned to doing all the work, took both oars; as he would naïvely have said, he rather fancied himself in a boat. He pushed his shirt-sleeves up above a pair of short but neatly-turned forearms, and as he rowed on that foreign lagoon margined by that French sea-wall, his cheerful chatter was all of the Thames above Richmond, of sunny Sundays and of parties on Eel-Pie Island. The two in the stern sat rather silently, letting him talk; Captain Ross sulking as he would never have admitted he sulked, Olwen uttering now and again a little "Ah" of delight at the phosphorescence on the water.

For it was wonderful, that sea that flamed as they pushed out into it. The boat's keel cut into the shimmer of pale green as into a field of glow-worms; it lighted up to left and right, blazing, dying down, rekindling fitfully as love itself; raining in spangles from the oars, dripping in jewels from Olwen's fingers as she dipped them over the side of the boat.

"Trim, Miss Olwen," said Mr. Brown, jerking his bullet head. "A bit nearer to Ross, if you don't mind."

Olwen moved; in the softly rocking boat overbalancing a trifle, she bumped against something hard and angular on the seat close to her companion. It felt like a camera or a book.

"Oh," she said, "did I knock you, Captain Ross?"

"No—" he said—and then he brought out of his jacket-pocket that which she had seen bulging it into that square shape on the terrace. It was a box covered with coloured satin and tied with gay ribbons.

"Candy," explained Captain Ross, somewhat curtly. He lifted the lid and offered the chocolates to Olwen, then perforce to Mr. Brown, who stopped rowing and leant forward, opening his mouth as he had done to the blackberries.

"Pop one in, Miss Olwen, please," he laughed, hands on the oars; but it was Captain Ross who leant forward in the boat and stuffed the sweet into his mouth.

"Thanks," said little Mr. Brown, with his mouth full. "Very pretty attention of yours, Ross, I must say, bringing out chocs for me when I like 'em."

Captain Ross planted the box on Olwen's lap.

"Don't," she laughed shyly. "I shall eat them all up."

"I guess you're meant to," he said shortly. "I got them for you in Bordeaux."

"For *me*?"

"Sure. I wanted to see if you'd eat candies, after what you said the other day to me in the lounge."

Through the soft noises of the water Olwen's soft voice took up "What I said?"

"Yes—when you said, 'Who wants candy?'"

"Oh, that," said Olwen, looking down at the green lambent water of which the rippling light beat up, soft and magical upon a face whose young curves could have dared a harsher radiance. She then looked back across the lagoon towards the big block of the hotel, picked out against the pale sky. She also glanced to her right, at the sand dunes that barricaded the waters of the *Baissin* from those of Biscay Bay, and at the lighthouse, winking white and red. She looked, in fact, anywhere but at Captain Ross, sitting so close beside her in that boat.

She was bathed in such a rapturous dream of moonlight and phosphorescence and rosy clouds and proximity that she was afraid to look at him. Fear lest he might read a confession in her eyes did for her what wisdom itself might have prompted.

A sophisticated woman in Simla, for example, had once told Mrs. Cartwright that she found no variation of the Glad Eye more successful with some men than the glance withheld. How dogmatically would this have been combated by Captain Ross! More than once had this expert in Woman's Ways affirmed, "*If there's a woman on this airrrrth that I've no use for, it's the woman who looks away when I'm speaking to her. I don't dawdle talking to a woman who doesn't look at ME all the time—*"

His impulse at that moment was to catch this little chit beside him by her slender shoulders and shake her good and hard. If he'd had two arms, he thought savagely, that's what he'd have wanted to do with 'em. He'd have loved to do that, then and there, and be hanged to that young butter-in of a Brown! Young Brown could be ignored, anyway. Let him get the boat along; the only pity was that he couldn't row with his back to the stern.

Captain Ross, turned a little sideways on the cushions of the skiff, attempted, by looking the girl full in the face, to make the girl look straight back at him. Not a successful method. Olwen's soft bright glance slid away from him even as the phosphorescence slid away from the oars.

Curtly he demanded, "You *do* like candy, after all?"

"I don't call it 'candy.' That's American, or Canadian," Olwen said with that indifference which was her only idea of Love's camouflage. "I say, 'chocolate,' or 'sweets.'"

"Is that so?"

"Yes," said Olwen, looking now at the box that was, as she knew, to become her most precious and inseparable treasure, her first gift—from Him!

As she sat holding it, backed by luminous sky and luminous sea, the little slim Pandora with her casket, he too looked at it between her hands; touched the bow of it.

"That'll do for a hair-ribbon for you, I guess," he remarked.

All that Olwen could think of to say was "I don't ever wear any ribbons."

"Is that so?" retorted Captain Ross maliciously. "Then what's that little pink tie-thing you've gotten coming out over your coat-collar at the back?"

Precipitately, Olwen's hand went up to the ribbon that was sewn to her Charm, and that, according to the mysterious and osmotic nature of ribbons, had let an end work up and out again. She tucked it in, with the eyes of the two young men upon her little dark, ducking head, and the small hand white in the moonlight.

That moonlight flashed too on the line of Captain Ross's fine teeth. A great alteration had suddenly come over his dour mood. He had two reasons for laughing good-humouredly. One, because he had just given a welcome present (event that always adds to one's good will towards the receiver), and two, because he had scored off the little chit now, with her ribbon! Ha!

His bad temper had vanished as her pretty confusion appeared. Again she dipped her fingers into that gleaming wake; she shook them, dried them against the thick skirt of her coat.

"You've gotten your hands cold now," said Captain Ross, in a pleased tone, and his left hand caught hold of the fingers of her little chilled right hand as if to verify the fact.

His own was a short and rather stumpy hand, Olwen had often noticed, with beautifully kept nails and with the cushions of the palm developed and muscular from the double share of work that was put upon it; generally she had seen it held half-closed above the watch-bracelet on a sturdy wrist. She had never shaken hands with him. . .

She thought he meant only to touch her fingers and to let them go. But he held them. He held the little soft fingers, in the shadow of her loose cuff and under a fold of her thick coat. They lay, firmly tucked into that clever magnetic left hand of the soldier who had only that one hand to do everything with.

Olwen, a prisoner enraptured with her chain, sat silent and still. She thought, "I suppose I ought to take my hand away. Oh, need I? No; I can't. He's only holding it to warm it, perhaps. And then if I took it away he might think I thought he thought he was *really* holding it!"

She sat in the boat that glided through that fairy mere of lambert waves, shimmering with green. Little shivers seemed to start in her elapsed hand and to run up her arm quick as wildfire, and spreading like wildfire through the whole of her slight frame. Yet she was now, as she had promised the Professor that she would be, "as warm as warm." Once she moved her hand a little in its prison, but that was only as a bird might stir and nestle in its cosy haunt. The man's clasp tightened a trifle, but she had made no effort to take away the hand that he was describing to himself as "a little bit of velvet."

As she assured herself some time afterwards, "Well, how *could* I? How can you possibly take your hand away from a man's who's only got one arm to hold you with?"

The boat sped on. . . and the thrills that trembled through the girl did not, surely, leave the man unstirred.

"Well, what about it, Ross?" broke in the making-the-best-of-it voice of little Mr. Brown, resting at last on his oars. "What about another of those chocolates?"

With one of his quickest movements Captain Ross's hand left the shadow of Olwen's cuff and grabbed the biggest chocolate walnut out of the box. He crammed it into the other young man's mouth as if it were a gag.

Then, unseen, his hand sought the girl's again, found it, held it close. The boat sped on through the whispering wildfire. . .

XIV

Clouds Upon the Charm

"The burden of bright colours. Thou shalt see
Gold tarnished, and the grey above the green."

—Swinburne

After an evening of ecstasy such as Olwen had lived through upon those iridescent waves, what could the girl expect?

It is one of Fate's harshest rules that in one way or another we pay for our ecstasies. The more golden the moment the more dull and clouded must seem the hours that follow: and that is just because we have seen that magic green shimmer on the breaker's crest that the grey of these smooth waters looks to us so leaden. Ah, better to know the sadness of this than never to have set keel in any but the quiet waters! To have no reckoning to pay because no ecstasy has been ours to enjoy is surely the bitterest price that can be demanded of us. . . But Olwen was too young to recognize this.

So, when the next day she emerged bit by bit from her dream, she was sore and resentful to find all life at its flattest.

To begin with (and, indeed, to go on with; for this was the whole leaven of discontent), Captain Ross encountered her as if there had been no magic voyage, no hand clasped in hand, no wildfire, no silent thrills between them. "Ah, good morrrrning, Miss Howel-Jones. Another beautiful day—"

Beautiful, indeed. . . Olwen felt as if by rights the sun should have gone out and the rains should have come to weep over the lagoon. As a matter of fact the weather remained radiant. Her idol's easy, friendly manner had dealt her a blow that stunned her into a torper of low spirits, and there seemed nobody to give her a helping hand out of it.

Mrs. Cartwright, usually so sympathetic and interesting, talked to her (Olwen) as if her thoughts were far, far away: with her serial-people, the girl supposed vexedly, or with those boys of hers at school.

Young Mr. Awdas—well, he never talked to Olwen. An apathetic young man, she considered him. All flyers were interesting from their very job—otherwise *how* uninteresting was Mr. Awdas! Nobody but Mrs. Cartwright (who was so kind), would bother to draw him out, Olwen thought.

Then Agatha Walsh—impossible to talk to *her* today: her Sergeant Gustave Tronchet's leave was up, and he was to depart to join his battery that evening. They could not be married until his next leave. Poor Agatha was paying too for her golden moments.

Mr. Brown—well, as for Mr. Brown (who had, after all, done all the work in that boat the night before), Olwen felt that she could have slapped him. Upon Mr. Brown's well-meaning bullet head she felt herself pouring the resentment that she might have reserved for Captain Ross and his forgetfulness, his insensibility. Silly little Mr. Brown! Why on earth couldn't he run away and attract somebody (hadn't Olwen given him a talisman for that very purpose?) instead of hanging about trying to talk to somebody who was already distracted enough as it was, because her own talisman seemed sometimes so potent, sometimes so useless? That it should have allured Mr. Brown into being sentimental about her seemed the last straw! (to Olwen.)

But it wasn't. For it was Professor Howel-Jones, it was her Uncle himself who contributed to his niece's burden, on this day of depression, what was really the last straw.

It happened as Olwen brought to him, with a little air of triumph, the typed copy and the duplicate of the last section of the last chapter of his book on "Agarics."

"So that's finished," she said.

"That's finished," agreed the Professor, his brown gaze running over the sheets. "Olwen, I've done well here. This has been an excellent place for work; excellent." He laid the copy down on that chaotic work-table of his, and added, with cheerfulness, "Well! There's nothing to keep us here any longer, now."

This Olwen did not take in at once. "Nothing to keep us, Uncle?"

"Only the passports to be *viséd* and made out for Paris," returned the old man. "I want to stay a night or so in Paris before I go on to London."

A great blankness fell upon Olwen's small face. "The passports," she repeated. "Paris!!! You mean you want us to leave quite soon?"

The Professor's head was bent over his work-table. "A couple of days, my dear, I suppose. You can be packed up and all that by then. You are broken in by now, aren't you, to your packing up and getting on without much warning?"

But this had taken Olwen without any warning, it appeared.

She stood there as if frozen, and said, "Away from here!" and in her heart exclaimed, "Away from *him*!" She stood aghast, an image of all the maids in love who have ever been sentenced to banishment from the presence of the beloved. She had put away from her up to now all thought of such a dreadful thing happening. Simply, she could not have imagined it. Going away from the hotel in the pine forest, while he still was left in it! Going away, before he had ever said to her a word that counted? Going away—with that Charm unproved?

It was time the Charm required; Olwen was agitatedly certain of that now. Time.

It had taken so many days before he had even held her hand; given so many other days, and what might not happen? But she was not to know. Those days were not to be allowed to her. She clenched into her palm the nails of those little fingers that Captain Ross had held in that warmly-caressing clasp. She was to go. . . never to see him any more. . .

She cleared her throat, pulled herself together, and asked, "And after Paris, Uncle, where do we go; London, you said?"

Now, this was a gleam of hope; London!

For she had once heard Captain Ross, in talking to Mrs. Cartwright, tell the writer that when his sick leave was up and after he had been boarded, he had prospects of an office job in town. If he were in London, and if her Uncle and she were also in London. . . well, then the outlook would not be entirely so black. It would not be the every day and several times a day encountering of this French hotel; but there surely might be meetings, if they were together, in London?

But the Professor, eyes still upon his papers, said, "London for a week or so, but I'm always glad enough to get out of the place. I shall be going down to Wales, then; I can leave you at your Auntie Margaret's, dear, before I go on to Liverpool. My plans will be unsettled—"

"You're not going to have me with you, then Uncle?"

"No, Olwen *fach*. For the present, not," he told her above the rustling of the papers. "I shan't require you for the work in hand for the next— Let me see, four or six months, perhaps. You will be able to go home; have a nice rest from work; help your Auntie in the house, see a little bit of your sisters and of your old friends."

Olwen felt precisely as if the genial-voiced old man were condemning her to penal servitude for the rest of her natural life.

"Uncle!" she exclaimed in horror.

It was met by a mildly surprised glance from the old man.

"What's the matter, small lass? Aren't you glad to be seeing your home again?"

"No," blurted out Olwen. "I don't want to go. Oh, I don't. Uncle! I'd rather be with you. Much. But if you can't have me, I—I—I won't go back—"

She put up her little head, shaking it violently as if in the face of a vision of the home in which she'd been brought up. Comfortable, old-fashioned, rambling place that it was, set in wild beauty, and echoing with gay voices, it repelled her; it seemed to her a prison from which there would be no further escaping towards the Heart's Desire. At work as her Uncle's secretary, there still seemed chances of movement in her life, there still seemed possibilities. . . But as a girl at home, she felt she would be chained and bound by a thousand chances against.

She told herself rebelliously, "Down there, I should never see him again! I won't go!"

Unconsciously her hands clasped themselves upon her breast, upon that slender talisman that she was wearing.

The old man regarded her, at a loss why the child should be agitated, she who had always seemed happy enough with her sisters at home.

"But, Olwen *fach*, if you don't go back, what do you want to do?"

"I want to stay on in London, Uncle!"

"In London—dear me—curious taste! Why? What could you do there?"

"I could do War work, like lots and lots—like every other girl!"

"Tut," retorted the Professor. Being a Welshman, he pronounced this word to rhyme with "foot." Being a man of his generation, he still disliked to think of any girl at work except domestically or for him.

"What d'you want to do that for, Olwen *fach*?"

To this question Olwen could hardly answer with the whole truth.

How many girls insist upon working in London because there, also, is working their particular Captain Ross?

Olwen's mind was set upon a plan.

She would think out the "hows" as soon as she left this place.

Only a couple more days in which the Charm might work for her, here!

XV

The Losing of the Charm

"Farewell, thou latter Spring! Farewell, All-hallown summer!"

—Shakespeare

I t's perfectly easy to have a good time in this world without any men," declared Mrs. Cartwright, smiling. "In fact, as easy as it is with them. In many ways, easier!"

Her listeners looked at her without conviction. For they were Miss Walsh and Olwen Howel-Jones. Poor Miss Walsh, having passed thirty-four years of her life in a manless world, having been then caught up into a Paradise for two, and, further, having been banished from it again with the departure of her Gustave, felt that nothing could be more untrue than this remark of the writer's.

As for Olwen—well, this was on the morning after her Uncle had sprung upon her the news that all *her* "good time" was to end in two days' time. And one whole precious day of that remaining two was to be wasted; *wasted*!

A somewhat mysterious message had come from Bordeaux, asking all three of the British officers then sojourning at Les Pins to go over and spend the day with their comrades-in-arms at a base about which none of these soldiers would answer any questions. They had gone, all three of them; Captain Ross, Mr. Awdas, and little Mr. Brown. They wouldn't be back all day. Not all day would Olwen have a glimpse of him whom presently she might never be seeing at all—and still Mrs. Cartwright affirmed that it would be possible to have a good time!

Probably Mrs. Cartwright guessed at the young girl's frame of mind as easily as at the less disguised feelings of Sergeant Tronchet's betrothed; it had not been for long that the writer had wondered "Who that child's so desperately in love with?" But brooding was a thing that Claudia Cartwright considered a wasteful and useless proceeding on the part of any young girl. She determined to put a stop to it, if possible, and that was why she went on gaily, "I often think of how Eve would have got on if she had been made first; probably she'd have thoroughly enjoyed having the whole of that Garden to herself, whereas Adam—! Bored to tears, of course. Not good for man to be alone. . . Well, since all the men have gone from here, why shouldn't we have a party of our own?"

"A party!" echoed Miss Walsh, lugubriously. "Oh, Mrs. Cartwright!"

"Why not? I am sure Sergeant Gustave doesn't want you to shut yourself up because he's gone back to the front; come and see something to put into your lovely long letters to him. And since those other three young men have gone off on a stag party to Bordeaux, we'll organize a dove lunch, as the American girls call it, and go off to Cap Ferret. It's perfectly lovely there. Olwen, where's the Professor? I'm going to beg leave for you. Come along, Miss Walsh—"

There was about Mrs. Cartwright that day an almost schoolgirlish flow of vitality that the other two found it impossible to resist; their own being at a low ebb, they let themselves drift with the current of hers. The corners of Miss Walsh's mouth ceased to turn quite so definitely downward, and the clouds in Olwen's bright eyes seemed about to disperse. In half an hour they were all ready, and setting out for this trip to Cap Ferret, which lay beyond the *Baissin*, the dunes, and the lighthouse.

In the bright autumn sunlight the little motor-boat buzzed with them across the lagoon that had set such a fairy scene, that night. . . But there was a gay wind blowing now, sending the big white clouds rolling across the sky in towering columns like those of the Biscay waves, seen from afar.

"We'll go right down to Biscay, after lunch," planned Mrs. Cartwright, as they landed at the small iron pier above the oyster parks. Then she guided them through the belt of pine woods that lay between the two borders of sandhills, past the lighthouse which they saw every day as a warning finger, but with which they now made acquaintance as the huge tower it was; she led them to the inn where they were to lunch. This was a long white building, its corners rounded and scoured by the flying sands borne on the gales of winter.

"Outside is the best dining-room," said Mrs. Cartwright. "I daresay Madame will think us mad—but it's an Indian summer day today. The Professor told me that you Welsh people call it '*the little summer of the Angels*.' Come along!"

And having given her order to the smiling French landlady (who wore a black shawl, a bright blue apron, and a brighter blue glass comb in her black hair), she led the others to a table in the sunny yard, under the wooden veranda. Its green paint had flaked off beneath those noisy gales, but the latticework was over-grown with passion-flower vines and other vines, richly clustered with bunches of sweet white grapes.

"Our dessert," said Mrs. Cartwright, nodding towards the fruit. "Madame will come and cut the bunches while we are eating the Biscay sole."

Lunch was brought; before she began upon the sole Mrs. Cartwright threw off the loose brown coat that she had worn for the crossing in the motor-boat, and appeared in a frock that Olwen had never seen before. Yesterday, the girl had noticed, a carton-box had arrived for the writer at the hotel; doubtless this was the dress that it had contained. . .

It was of rough sky-blue crêpy stuff with touches of creamy edging and of dull pink stitchery, very simple, for all Mrs. Cartwright's clothes were simply cut. This was something more than simple, though, almost. . . trivial, was it? A frock for a more insignificant person? Olwen could not have told you why she shouldn't quite like that frock. It wasn't altogether that it seemed too young; and it did fit her, perfectly. Perhaps the fact that Olwen noticed it at all showed how well the elder woman's clothes generally did suit her.

Today—not only her frock was different, but her mood was different. It puzzled little Olwen entirely. . .

As the sole and the potatoes in their jackets gave place to an admirably-cooked ham omelette, Mrs. Cartwright was saying almost audacious things, that passed as swiftly as the shadows of the gulls swooped over the sands. And she seemed conscious that she was "being different. . ." Why? It was almost as though she were playing at some game; she thought feverishly. As if half of her sat apart, watching the play, criticizing, exchanging notes with people who were not Miss Walsh, not Olwen.

The girl, having never before looked upon her friend as a riddle, sat wondering at her. . . In that sheltered corner the savoury scents of the meal mingled with the inevitable pine scent and the tang of sea while the sun flung blue shadows upon the bright table and the plates; dancing delicate silhouettes of vine leaves and tendrils and passion flowers. There drifted to them from the woods the sound of the cow bells; "tonkle—tankle—tonkle—" and from the shore the distant roar of breakers.

Suddenly, as the inn servant removed and brought coffee, Mrs. Cartwright broke out, apparently à propos of nothing.

"Ah, well!

> "'Better an omelette *aux fines herbes* where Love is, than the
> Carlton and a chaperon therewith.'

Forgive my quoting my own works, but I was thinking of one of those books of mine that I—that we never write. Plenty of other things in Life like that. Men we didn't marry, their babies that we've never had—"

Then she laughed.

"I wonder what people would have thought if I'd ever written that book. It's the one I threatened your friend Captain Ross with, Olwen, the other night. Would you like to hear a bit of it, girls?"

And without waiting to hear whether they would or not, she went on in that deep, whimsical attractive voice of hers:

> "'Don't tell your mother beforehand that I am a lady.
> Possibly I'm not. You won't know. But she will.'

I remember thinking of that when a great friend of mine in the navy told me about his engagement. He made a joke at the time about sailors and their *culte* for *mésalliances*. . . Here's another bit:

> "'Always write to me when you're away. Never mind if you've
> nothing to say. It doesn't matter if you don't say anything.
> Only write!'

I can see the young man now that I said that to," said Mrs. Cartwright, and the expression in her eyes was of one who looks down from a hill-top upon the landmarks passed, far back. "He'd only been married a month to a school chum of mine, and was suddenly ordered off. He couldn't take her. I told him that even if the mail only went out twice a week there was no reason that it should not take three letters each time—"

Here Miss Walsh, who did not seem to be listening, broke in. "I think that's very true." She fingered in her bag an envelope with the printed label, "Controle Postale Militaire," and looked cheered.

"This young man numbered his letters after that. Then I remember a girl friend—ah! she's a grand-mamma now—married before I did. I remember her once saying something that I should have stolen from her.

"'Do you mind not giving me these useful solid, durable
presents of leather, which you men love and which are
hideous in our eyes? Why not something charming that won't
last; scent, powder, or chocolates in a pretty box?'

And this, which is the last that I shall inflict upon you, dear yawners, nobody at all told me. I made it up, unaided, and by my little self." She looked away above her coffee-cup as she quoted it, and her eyes were the eyes of all the girls that be, appealing to all the plighted lovers:

"'Remember that nine out of ten women in the world will
never know what Love can be, and that *six out of those nine
are married women*. Please won't you try to make me the
happy Tenth?'

And now, when all the people have said Amen, what about a walk down to Biscay?—No, Miss Walsh! Please. This is my *day*. I proposed this, and I know you won't grudge me this little pleasure."

She paid the *addition* and drew on her loose white gloves.

Through the woods they went, and over the sandhills planted with grass in lines to keep that barrier together.

Olwen, in her red woolly coat, walked between Mrs. Cartwright, whose short blue skirts flapped like a wind-blown succory flower above her ankles, and Miss Walsh, who was holding on to her hat. Little Olwen thought irrelevantly—"and, fancy! we're all three wearing that Charm!"

They descended from the dunes, passed the loose shuffling upper sands, and came on to the stretch of other sands, smooth, hard, and firm as a ballroom floor set down in the widest landscape that any of them had trodden yet. Soaring skies, illimitable beach, and oh, how empty seemed the sea far, far behind the breakers of Biscay Bay!

At the sight of those breakers, whose sound had been growing in her ears, Olwen gave an involuntary "Oh! *Look* at them!"

From the hotel windows they seemed nothing more than a crawling white line. Here they were rushing monsters that seemed to shake the shore where they broke. They broke and spouted not more than fifty yards away, then swirled and seethed almost to the feet of the women in surf, in the lines that would be taken by boiling milk.

Olwen stood nearest with spray on her cheeks, thunder in her ears, and a storm of unimagined whiteness before her eyes, finding it all riotously beautiful. But the last thing in the world that she expected was what Mrs. Cartwright then said:

"I say! Let's bathe. It would be too gorgeous in there!"

Miss Walsh, behind her, looked as if she could not believe her ears.

"In *October*, dear Mrs. Cartwright?"

Dear Mrs. Cartwright laughed as she threw out her arm towards the waters, soaring to crash, soaring again to crash. . . "*That*," she cried, "was going on before the months had names!"

"Oh, but I never knew any one dreamed of bathing after August," murmured Miss Walsh, still clutching her hat, "and, besides!" (as if that settled it), "you haven't brought your things with you."

"That's just what I meant," declared Mrs. Cartwright, taking a deep breath. "I'm going in."

"Oh, please don't!" protested Olwen. "I can swim quite well, but any one can see *that's* dangerous. Supposing you were caught in and swept away. Oh, I wouldn't."

"I shouldn't dream of letting you, child," cried Mrs. Cartwright gaily. "I'm going in," and she stooped to unlace the brown thongs of her sandalettes.

"Oh! I'll go on and gather shells, then," said Agatha Walsh (hurriedly turning her back as if she dreaded to let her eyes fall upon some repellent sight, reflected Mrs. Cartwright, with amusement).

The elder woman was of the type that, under such circumstances, makes no more ado about getting out of her clothes than she would about taking off her hat. She was of that type—and of that build.

They dropped from about her, the flapper's frock of succory blue and the silken under-garments, and with them she seemed to cast off as well that rather feverish sprightliness of the last hour. It was a genuinely girlish delight that shone from her eyes as she ran, lightly and free-limbed, over the sand and into the surf that flung itself towards her body of a slender statue, white as those crests. She revelled in that hour that was hers, Claudia Cartwright's—hers and that girl's who had been Claudia Crane's.

"Not too far in!" warned Olwen from higher up the beach.

BERTA RUCK

"Right!" called her friend's voice from out of the dazzling sunlight spray; the sound of it lost in the crash of the breakers and the scream of the gulls that wheeled and dived like a flight of white-winged aeroplanes above her.

She sprang and dipped; threw herself forward, breasted the waves, and tried to swim, always frustrated by those tossing waters that made of her a plaything, all panting and aglow with joyous life.

Olwen watched; anxious. But Claudia Cartwright was not to be caught in and swept away; not she. It was something else that was to be so lost; unseen by Olwen, unthought about at all.

From where the bather's garments lay in a soft heap under a smooth heavy stone that she had set down to keep them from blowing away, there disentangled itself a ribbon that she had worn about her neck and that she had untied, carelessly, just before she ran down to plunge into the sea.

It blew along the sands above the scatter of shells.

It blew along, fast and faster, the pink thread holding that feather-light Charm that the wind had swept away.

XVI

The Counter-Charm

*"Too old, by Heaven; let still the woman take
An elder than herself; so wears she to him,
So sways she level in her husband's heart."*

—Shakespeare

The two parties (those of the stag gathering and the dove lunch) returned to the hotel at almost the same moment, just before dinner-time.

"*We've* had a ripping time!" Mrs. Cartwright said gaily, in answer to an enquiry from Captain Ross; young Jack Awdas, hearing, gave her a reproachful glance. But there was no time for reproaches. Madame had announced "*On va servir!*" and there was a rush for rooms. But not before Awdas, at the door that was next to his own, had murmured urgently, "I want to talk to you afterwards, there's something that I *must* say to you. Come down quickly, won't you?"

The others tore through their dressing. Miss Walsh wanted to retire to Madame's sitting-room, there to have a soul-satisfying "mourn" with Madame over the departure of Gustave, and to pick out of Madame's stream of reminiscences a pearl or so to remember of the boyhood of that excellent nephew. Little Olwen, who had overheard Mr. Brown saying, "Look here, Ross, none of your shoving me out of my place at table—even if I do sleep out, there's no reason why I should be made to sit with the back of my head towards everybody I want to look at, dashed if there is," was eager to run down to the *salle*, and with a glance or a greeting make an excuse for the right young man to be sitting facing her.

Only Mrs. Cartwright took her time and was rather late for dinner. As she redressed her hair, still damp from her bathe, and slipped into her tawny-golden tea-gown, the writer's face was intent. She was thinking, thinking hard. Even in moving about her room she kept glancing at a couple of pig-skin bags stowed into a corner. One of them bore the name of Captain Keith Cartwright, and of his regiment; what service it had seen since it had first gone out with them to India. She knew what she ought to be doing with those bags at this moment.

Packing them up, to go.

Yes, she ought to be folding her skirts and wrapping up her boots and shoes and sorting her manuscripts. One word to Madame, and a *fiacre* could be obtained that same evening to take the bags, and herself with them, to the hotel at the Ville d'Hiver, where she had already spent a night on her way here. There she could stay until her passport was made out for England, and then she could go back to her rooms in town, back to be near her boys at school, and right away from this place of conflict and too sweet disturbance—away from Jack Awdas, who wanted to say something to her after dinner.

She knew well what it was. Ever since that moonlight walk he had been besieging her—not with words again, but with every glance of his blue eyes, every turn of his head towards her, every husky, beseeching note of his voice.

Now for a third time he was going to put it into words. She did not know how to check him. It was because she wished—she so wished that she need not.

Again and again already, by night, when she was tossing sleeplessly, by day, when she was talking of other things, she had gone over the question.

Marriage—with that boy.

He was not the first, he would not be the last who had adored a woman old enough to be his mother. And she herself was not the first woman who, past what is considered the age for Love, had received, offered to her as a bouquet, the gathered share of love that could have sufficed a score of young girls.

Had this been always a wrong and an unlovely thing?

As she slipped on her bangles after washing, Mrs. Cartwright found herself thinking, with a half-mutinous, half-deprecating little smile, of some of the greatest love affairs of the world. They stood out in the history of human kind just as the lighthouse yonder towered above the low-rising dunes. Their passions blazed white-hot and rosy-red through the night of centuries; but were they stories of the loves of immature women?

Antony's Cleopatra—how old was she when she romped in the public street to show her defiance of Age and Conventions generally?

How old was Ninon, beloved of lads not one, but two generations after her girlhood?

"I'd never wish for *that*," thought Claudia Cartwright, "but what about Diane de Poictiers?"

She mused a moment upon that story, upon those sweetest of love-letters written by a young and ardent king to "*Madame ma Mie.*" They bore the dates of many years, those letters signed by the cypher which was the "*Lac d'Amour*" for Henri and his Diane—the first Frenchwoman, Mrs. Cartwright reminded herself, to go in for the exotic practice of the cold tub. And she was forty—*forty* when that affair was in blossom! Her statue as Diana, the bather, Mrs. Cartwright had seen in pictures, and the tall slim Englishwoman's vanity had recognized a familiar pose.

"I *am* like her," she thought now.

But in the middle of her thought she pulled herself together, tossing aside the towel as she laughed without amusement.

What was the use of it; what? Why dwell on the outstanding Exceptions, of whom the very fame went to prove the relentless rule that a waning woman and a boy may not find lasting happiness together? These stories of Cleopatra, Ninon, and Diane were lamentably beside the mark. But the stories of matrons of today who had married their sons' contemporaries hadn't drifted across the writer's experience.

Stories of mistakes recognized almost at once, but too late. Of passion that died quickly down on the one side, leaving on the other side an unrequited and consuming flame. Of sad-faced, elderly, neglected wives at home. Of desperate efforts to retain fading attractions; of grotesque make-up, of golden hair and gaiety, both false. Of the interests of separated generations, their claims, their mental outlook, always at war! Of youth, fettered and fuming, straining towards his kind. . .

At best they were pathetic, these stories.

At worst they were ugly enough. They justified the contempt in the term "Baby-snatcher!" They established the principle, "A middle-aged woman who will *marry* a young boy is no sportswoman."

Now Mrs. Cartwright had always hoped that, with all her faults, she could never be accused of being unsportsmanlike. Still confident of this, she ran downstairs to dinner.

Her lateness only postponed by a little the hour of reckoning.

The flying boy, rather pale but with a smile in his eyes, told her that he had ordered coffee for her and himself to be brought into the lounge, since all the other people seemed to be drifting into the *salon* after dinner. In the further corner of that lounge, under an artificial-looking palm, he drew up for her a wicker-chair.

"Sit down there!" he ordered her with a new masterfulness in his husky charming voice. "And listen to me. You'll sit there until you've given me the answer that I want."

She sat, leaning back, lax and graceful.

He fastened his eyes upon her.

She could not meet them, but she was aware of every line of his face, printed upon her heart. She loved him. She did not deny to herself that she had come to love every look and every tone of him; and the facts that their mental outlook must be different and that her own experience, her wider knowledge must yawn as a gulf between them did not lessen his attraction for her, as it might have done for another woman. Claudia Cartwright had often smiled when she heard certain prattlers of her own sex avow their demand to have "their mentality fed, and their need of being in perfect intellectual sympathy" with the men (sometimes elderly men) whom they married.

In Mrs. Cartwright, as we know, the sense of physical perfection was better developed. . . the worse for her, all the worse for her now.

Jack Awdas, standing over her, was saying, "I can't go on like this, you know. You've got to have me, or I've got to get away. It's come to that."

Her heart, it seemed to her, seemed to miss a beat at this, then to beat faster as she sat there. She shook her head, almost abstractedly, for her thoughts were racing ahead of the words she would have tried to frame. They were slipping from her, those wise and too true arguments to which she had submitted, alone in her own room and without his eyes upon her, disarming her of all her wisdom. Instinct within her clamoured, "But I love him so! I want him!"

She ought to be upstairs now, she knew, packing those bags for dear life.

She ground the heel of her slender slipper into the floor of the lounge before her as she thought of this, and she thought, "Ah, if marriage were for a year, say! *Then!* . . . If I could marry him and die before he began to tire—even his mother would not hate me then." Then came the breath-taking thought, "He will be flying again presently. He may crash again. . . Ah! . . ." This was unendurable. She thrust it from her to think, "*For a time* I could make him gloriously happy! Happier than any girl alive has power to do—"

And she thought wildly that there were plenty of girls in their early twenties who were older than she; as well as colder, with less gift for Passion. Girls who were narrower in their outlook, girls who were less generous, less sympathetic, less adaptable than she, as his wife, could be. There were girls with petty minds and tongues that could say little, jealous, spiteful things about other women. These had nothing but their ignorant youth; did that outweigh all that she had to give? Ah, she could point to girls still in their teens who were already nearer the end of their powers than she was, even nearer the end of their looks. Was it really better for him to choose a girl? It was her, Claudia, the woman, that he wanted. . .

She could surely make of herself another exception to the unpitying rule that Youth must mate with Youth.

"Say 'yes' to me; say 'yes,'" urged Jack Awdas, and he let himself down, softly, to sit on the wide wicker arm of the chair. She felt that if it were to save her life, her lips could not now frame the word "no."

There was a short and agonizing pause in which both listened, without hearing it, to the sound of the wheels of a *fiacre*, drawing up outside the door of the hotel.

"Say 'yes,'" repeated young Awdas, more urgently, "or I clear right out."

"*Better*," she forced herself to murmur.

"Better?—And if I go, I won't remember what you did for me that night. I shall try to forget it; d'you hear? I shall try—"

"Don't," she said, very low. "I couldn't forget it if I tried."

"*Ah!*" It broke from him exultantly. "Then you do care! I knew you would, I knew I could make you! The other was rot; I knew you did."

She threw her head back and aside; she made a last struggle. She would have risen.

"No, you don't," he triumphed. "Now say 'yes,' and then perhaps you may get up, darling; *darling*—!"

At the delight of hearing it from his lips she shut her eyes even as a sweetheart of little Olwen's age might have done. It was her moment of ecstasy, poignant and ageless and pure. . .

A moment only.

There broke into it footsteps and a girl's voice, a charming voice, but of an inflection most un-English.

"Why, yes! Wasn't I expected? I wrote the hotel anyway. . . *J'ai écrit*. . . Miss Golden van Huysen. . . Oh, pardon me—"

Mrs. Cartwright's eyes had opened upon something that seemed like a sunburst breaking in upon the dim and formal, Frenchily-furnished lounge. A vision it was of gold and colour. Radiance seemed to emanate from it—from her. . . For it was just a girl, a blonde and generously-built girl, whose coat, thrown open, showed a crisp light uniform with the Red Cross. Her head, proudly carried, was backed by the hanging lamp that made a glory around it, and Miss Golden van Huysen, self-introduced, might have stood for a symbolical figure of Young America breaking into the War, descending upon the Old Continent with help in her hands.

She moved, and the light fell directly on her face. It had the contours and the bloom of a peach, and under her slouch hat her eyes, large and wonderfully wide apart, shone out with candour and young eagerness for life. Yes, youth, youth! That was the keynote of her. That, and the sweetness of honey, coloured like her hair; the kindliness of milk, white as her skin.

Mrs. Cartwright, with doom at her heart, looked at this young girl. So did Jack Awdas, who had sprung to his feet and off the wicker chair-arm. The girl frankly returned the glances of the lady sitting back there, and of the boyish English officer who was (as she ingenuously put it to herself) "the loveliest looking young man she'd ever seen."

Jack Awdas did not know that he was staring almost rudely. . . Mrs. Cartwright knew. She also knew what a kiss had been interrupted by that look at another.

And when the bustle of this arrival and of Madame and the *chasseur* and the "grips" and the Franco-American explanations had died away to the first landing, it was Mrs. Cartwright, standing, who spoke.

She spoke quite lightly and with a smile on her lips. She came of soldier people.

"Dear Jack, there's nothing more to be said. I know I'm right. But *you* needn't go. I'm going instead. I must get back to my boys for half-term. I shall be off early in the morning, so this is good-bye."

"But—" he protested, in a voice that was not quite that of five minutes before.

"No. That's all. I hope—No, don't come with me. Good night!"

Before he knew, she was gone.

XVII

Drop-Scene

"There is no man that imparteth his griefs to his friend but he grieveth the less."

—Bacon

Mrs. Cartwright went up to her room, but she did not pack those bags of hers at once.

Instead, she put on her coat, tied a scarf over her head, changed her shoes, and went for a walk.

She knew that she must tire herself out. She had thought she was rather tired already from her tussle with the waves that afternoon, but that wasn't enough. She must be more exhausted before she could sleep for a few hours. She would order them to call her very early in the morning, so that she could be packed and off before any of the other visitors had left their rooms.

She set out, and she couldn't have told anybody in what direction. A path was soft—probably with pine-needles—beneath her feet. Before her eyes there was a striping of light on darkness; still a moon between the trees.

She walked. She could not have said off-hand what she thought about as she swung along. Not many definite thoughts filled her mind. Only a very definite picture of young Awdas's fair eaglet face, looking with startled and pleased surprise into the face of that beautiful girl. One look; the boy had just been taken aback at the sight of a stranger, and such an unusually pretty one. Then and there Claudia Cartwright didn't herself know *why* she knew that this, the look that did not seem to mean anything, meant. . . everything.

It meant that she, the woman at her last love affair who had been within an inch of accepting the proposal of that boy, must begin to pay, already, for her one moment of ecstasy.

The coming of that girl had stopped not one, but all kisses for her.

She knew what was coming between that boy, all awakened and malleable from his first passion, and that girl. They were heritors of an age in which Love has quickened his pace to keep up with the double-march of war.

She was resigned. She had foreseen it. Hadn't she said to him, "Wait until you see me beside a real young girl"? It had come upon her rather abruptly, that was all, but she need not really allow herself to suffer. . .

She whistled a little tune between her teeth as she swung along. She was thinking of nothing, she was just moving quickly and regularly, as a mechanical toy that has been wound up to go for a certain time before the machinery runs down.

So mechanically, so fast she covered the ground. Suddenly a voice called out, "Halt! Who's there? Mrs. Cartwright?"

With a start, she found that she was in the forest, approaching the clearing and the woodcutter's hut. The sturdy, square-set figure that, coming away from the hut, had encountered her on the moon-dappled path, was that of Captain Ross.

"Hullo!" she returned, brightly. "Have you been cat-calling on Mr. Brown? Isn't it perfectly lovely? After all, this is the time of day to go for walks, I find."

"Is that so? I thought this was the time of day you sat writing your great worrrks."

"Sometimes; but how did you know?"

"You told me you were sitting up working that last time Awdas had that infairrrnal dream of his," said the Staff-officer. "That was how."

But at this the machinery that had kept Mrs.

Cartwright going so steadily for the last hour or more, broke down without warning. Without warning, she blurted out in a low, unnatural voice, "Oh, Captain Ross! I am—in such trouble."

Her limbs failed her and she would have fallen.

The next moment she found that she was sitting upon a pine-log, with her head upon the solid support of Captain Ross's shoulder, and with his arm thrown very comfortingly about her. She wept, copiously and silently, all her tears; the only tears a man had ever seen Claudia Cartwright shed.

This man, to his eternal honour, made no attempt to check them or to enquire into them. He sat there, supporting her, clasping her with the arm of a brother—this man whom she had not before regarded as any particular friend of hers. She wept, taking his handkerchief, large and scented with cigarettes, that he presently stuffed into her hands. She knew that she must be making him feel miserably uncomfortable and upset; she cried on, unashamed in the silence of the wood, telling herself that it would be for the one and only time that she would give herself this relief. Presently she sobbed out, "I loved him—"

Captain Ross's "Is that so?" was entirely unstartled and matter-of-fact.

Actually he had been too pole-axed with amazement to do anything but the natural thing; but a finer judge of women might have been less of a comfort to her. He sat holding her stolidly until she gave the long-drawn breath and the apology that mark the ebbing of the storm.

"Thank you so much," she was able to say presently, almost as lightly as if he had put a coffee-cup down for it. "You'll forget it, I know. I must just tell you that it was in my own hands. I refused him. I shall be glad, presently. But—"

She paused, and the man muttered awkwardly something about wishing there were anything he could do—

She spoke softly but gravely now. "Captain Ross! Be very gentle, won't you, with that little, young girl?"

Captain Ross did not ask what young girl she meant.

PART II

I

The Charm Neglected

"Few people realize that Love is a hybernating animal."

—Extract from Private Letter

Olwen Howel-jones sat at her War work in room 0369 on the sixth floor of some Government offices called—

We will call them The Honeycomb.

The entrance to this hive of activity was near Charing Cross, and its courtyard was one continual procession of cars, cyclists, motor-cyclists, dispatch cycles with little side-car mail vans, also of men in every conceivable uniform; most of them (as befitted a swarm of such bees!) were decorated with wings. . . Goodness knows how many telephone extensions The Honeycomb possessed! Lifts carried you up to floor after floor. Each floor was packed with cells that had been bedrooms and private sitting-rooms, each cell with workers making Victory-honey (and perhaps with odd drones watching them do it). The whole place with its come-and-go of clerks, messengers, telephone girls, civilians, typists, switchboard girls, and their khakied male superiors, was in a never-ending buzz.

The small cell marked 0369 had big windows that looked up and down the Strand: it held three workers.

Olwen's roll-top desk stood back to back with another; the two backs screening off her colleague of the other desk. This other desk had an unusual feature. From behind it there came a stream of comments in different voices, so that it seemed as if several unseen people were sitting there. These voices were:

> First Voice—A natural girlish treble that slightly rolled its R's; being the voice of one Mrs. Newton, in charge of cell 0369, who possessed the gift of mimicry.

> Second Voice—A masculine drawl that died away of sheer superiority in the roof of the mouth, after the fashion of one Major Leefe of that Department.

THIRD VOICE—Rollicking and boyish, intersected by loud "Ha's" and "Bai Jove's" in the manner of Lieutenant Harold Ellerton, also of The Honeycomb.

Mingling with the click of the typewriter, at which the third girl sat in a further corner, came the sound of one or other of these voices. Thus:

FIRST VOICE—"Miss Howel-Jones, what is the French for 'land'?
Aeroplanes, I mean?"

A murmured "*atterrir*" came from Olwen, immersed in her work, which meant dividing the morning's correspondence into four batches: A, B, C, and D.

SECOND VOICE (after a moment of paper-rustling)—"Er—yeh. . . yeh! Wha' have we heah? Letters to be translay' into Fren'. Yeh. Mrs. Newton, will you atten' to thi' too?"

THIRD VOICE (after more rustling)—"*Damn* this nib. Oh, sorry, Mrs. Newton; didn't mean to say damn before you."

FIRST VOICE—"Not at all, Mr. Ellerton; I am a married woman myself."

FOURTH VOICE (A Scots-Canadian accent)—"Is that so? What I demand of a woman is that she shall be a rrreliable worrrrkerr. I don't assk what she does affterr hours, I—"

Here all the voices ceased.

For a quarter of an hour no sound came from behind that desk, but that of papers being turned, regularly and methodically. Then the busy Mrs. Newton, not the mimic, spoke.

"Just turn up the Q. M. G. file for last month and see if there's a letter with this reference."

She gave the reference, and Olwen, after a minute's search in a manilla "jacket," handed over the letter, leaving a slip of paper sticking out of the jacket in its place. Having written "Mrs. Newton" and the date upon that slip, she turned again to her letter-trays. The rustling of papers was resumed. Then the voices again:

Second Voice—"Claim for missing kit, wha'? How do f'las manage to be always losing kit? Do *I* lose kit? Haven't *I* always goh' millions pairs bags all beau'fly press'? 'Sides, isn't even in ah sec.' Room Two—Fi'—Fi'."

Third Voice—"Ha! Reference A. B., stroke two bracket nine oh one two two dated two twelve seventeen. Do they, bai Jove!"

First Voice—"Aren't there any more 'C's,' Miss Howel-Jones?"

"Not this morning." Olwen's little black head was bent over the "D" correspondence, which she dealt with herself. "A" letters were handed to the typist, who carried them into cell 0368, next door. "B's" and "C's" were to be thrust into the basket that stood on the top of that desk-screen, from behind which a hand came up ever and anon to take letters.

With real enjoyment the Welsh girl worked on.

How amazingly she had altered, in all these weeks, from the one ideaed, feverish little emotionalist she'd been in the autumn!

Yes. Change of scene and of daily work had laid potent hands upon the plastic, fundamentally sound nature of this young girl. Routine had hypnotized her with its rhythmic monotony. She felt the peculiar attraction of being a tiny cog in all this huge machine of War work. New thoughts, new feelings, new interests packed her life; new friends, too, were a revelation to her.

Now came Mrs. Newton's more frivolous voice.

"*Arlette*, *Bubbly*, and *Cheep*, that's my record so far *this* week; and tonight I'm going to *Pamela* for the second time; all thanks to one very young youth getting four days' leave from the Front!"

Olwen laughed. The solemn little typist, however, rose to take the letters with a look that practically said, "Some people may be heads of rooms, but they don't seem to realize there's a war on!" and as she took the sheaf of papers to be signed in cell 0368 she all but slammed the door behind her.

"Seventeen; *not* the best phase of English maidenhood, neither washed nor kissed," went on the voice of the unseen Mrs. Newton. "Ah! It's nearly lunch time."

"I shan't be able to lunch with you today, Mrs. Newton," Olwen said rather quickly. "My Aunt that I stay with is shopping in town today, so—"

"Say no more," returned Mrs. Newton's voice. "I've got Aunts myself. I mean I had before I was married. By the way, I told Fascinating Fergus that I can hear him telephoning his dinner engagements in the next room. He said, with that aggressive face of his, that there was nothing prrivatt in those. I said, "Then why drop your voice when you're doing it?" And why does he, I ask you, insist on being a Tower of Silence in here, when he *longs* to be considered a perfect Devil outside? Keeping his girl friends *well* round the corner, nobody ever having seen *one*! . . . Swank!"

"Oh, he's not as bad as all that," murmured Olwen.

"He's all right at heart perhaps," came from the other side, "but I *should* like to take a scraper to him!"

And herewith there merged from behind the desk the source of all the voices that had been holding forth, in the person of Mrs. Newton.

Her Nile-green silken sports coat alone had cost more than her month's salary could have paid; her hair was arranged as carefully as though there was no thought but of her own extremely pretty looks beneath the broad velvet band that snooded her, but for all that, she was efficient. Clever, too, at darting the arrows of a bright mind at chiefs and colleagues alike. She "took in" most things, not in any disguised fashion, but by turning full upon whatever it was she wished to observe a pair of large, pale grey and pretty eyes, amused and passionless as those of a sea-maid. Their stare was even emphasized at times by the gesture of a slender forefinger and by the clearly-audible "Ah" of that treble voice.

Olwen enjoyed her thoroughly; her appreciation mingling with a wonder why she did not sometimes bitterly resent Mrs. Newton and her remarks.

Yes, two months of War work on The Honeycomb had taught Olwen already more than the A, B, C, and D of her job. Self-possession, serenity and poise, all newly acquired, were to be noticed now about the young girl as she sorted her letters (very different from the leisured correspondence of her Uncle), and smiled, partly at some thought that she was holding in reserve, and partly at her fellow-worker.

Mrs. Newton began again, "Do you know what I think is the keynote of F. F.'s character?"

"Fascination, you seem to make out," suggested Olwen, that divided smile deepening upon her lips. She sometimes thought that Mrs. Newton dwelt upon the subject of their chief for her (Olwen's) benefit, and she was prepared for it.

"Ah! But I mean the *real* keynote. It's *jealousy*," declared the young married woman. "He's a *jealous* thing. Hates any other man to have a show at all. Must have everybody doing their best work, just for his *beaux yeux* (not that he's got any, except those teeth). Yes; our Fergus must be It in this Honeycomb. He must be *The* Great Captain—"

She stopped abruptly as the door of cell 0369 opened to frame the black head, square shoulders, red tabs, and empty sleeve of the man of whom she'd been speaking; the chief of their section, Captain Fergus Ross himself.

"Mrs. Newton," he said, in the tone of business unalloyed, "have they sent up to you a letter that was taken in error to room 0720? A letter from A G 6, dated the 22nd?"

"It's here, Captain Ross," replied the head of the room in her demurest treble. "Miss Howel-Jones was attending to it. . . Here it is."

"Right. Thank you," said Captain Ross.

His bright dark glance took in the letter that Mrs. Newton handed him; it passed over the filed stack of other letters; it swept over the two desks, the typing-table, Miss Lennon's back, the calendar, the pinned-up Matania drawing on the wall, the green electric-light shades, the glass on the mantelpiece holding freesias, the chairs, the waste-paper basket—in short, over every object in the room but one.

For Olwen Howel-Jones, bending absorbed over her work, Captain Ross did not spare a fraction of his glance.

"Mrs. Newton, I am going out to lunch now," he announced. "Should there be any enquiries, I shall be back before two-thirty."

"Very well, Captain Ross."

(Exit Captain Ross.)

Then Mrs. Newton in Major Leefe's voice, "Wha'? Old Ferg' gone t' lunch? *Bet* you he's taking out some gir', Miss Howel-Jo'."

Olwen smiled undisturbed as she went to put on her her hat.

Twenty minutes later she was sitting at a table for two in a Soho restaurant, opposite to Captain Ross.

This meeting was not due to any arrangement.

What had happened was that some weeks before, Olwen, having explored all lunch-time haunts within a mile of the Honeycomb, had found this tiny, Continentally-appointed restaurant that she chose to call "The Aunt in Town." This had been on a fishday, and the fish had been deliciously cooked, as Olwen had reported afterwards. Perhaps Captain Ross did not overhear her mentioning the restaurant's real name to Major Leefe. Anyhow, there is no reason to suppose that it was not by chance that Captain Ross happened upon "The Aunt in Town" upon the very next Friday. As he saw Miss Howel-Jones sitting at a little table by herself, wasn't it natural that he should join her? He knew the girl, apart from the office, knew her Uncle. Absurd if he hadn't come up. But, as you see, there was a vast difference between his just taking the chair opposite to her, and his having planned to meet her. He did not attempt to pay for the chit's lunch. So that was that.

Certainly the fish-curry was excellent.

Captain Ross had already announced that he was fond of fish for lunch.

Consequently he took to haunting that restaurant on Fridays. Why shun it, merely because Miss Howel-Jones lunched there on that day?

As he would have told you, however, he made a definite rule of never "going out to lunch" with any woman working on The Honeycomb. With other girls, from other Government offices—well, that was another story. There was, for instance, a fair-haired Miss Somebody (who rang him up, Mrs. Newton had declared, three times a day), but she worked at the institution we will call The Rabbit Warren. There was also a pretty little friend of his on The Ant Hill. But from The Honeycomb itself—nope. Work and social relations must be kept strictly apart.

Olwen had been made to realize that from the first time she had set foot in the courtyard under those arches and that clock. She had been first astounded, then hurt, then finally she actually wanted to laugh at the different Captain Ross he now was from the one she had met at Les Pins.

The change had been sudden as the cut of a knife.

Over there on leave he had idled about the pine-woods and the *plage*; he had teased her as if she were no more than a pretty child; once he had given her chocolates; once—ah, that once!—he had held her hand. . .

Here, idleness was the last thing of which he could be accused. He no longer teased her with laughter and allusions to "*most* little girls." He had given her no more chocolates. As for hand-holding, why! She might not have had any hands. To be a fellow-worker with him on The

Honeycomb seemed enough to transform any young woman into teak or granite as far as Captain Ross was concerned.

He had his code.

"I guess no girl friend of mine would ask me for a job where I work, twice," he'd told Olwen when they had first met in London at her Uncle's hotel. The Professor's niece, greatly daring, had retorted, "Do you mean she'd get it the first time of asking?"

"She'd get 'it,' sure thing. In the neck," the young Staff-officer had explained grimly. "She'd know better than to ask the second time."

So, exactly as he was not taking her out to lunch, Captain Ross had not secured for her this post on The Honeycomb. He had told Jack Awdas to get it for her, through his friend Major Leefe. A very different thing.

Olwen had "given up" the subtle reasonings of the sex.

Today he was obviously in a bad temper. Why? After he had ordered his own lunch, he turned to her with an edgy politeness.

"I hope you enjoyed the show last night, Miss Howel-Jones."

"Show—?" said Olwen, forgetting for a second that she had been taken to the theatre by Mr. Ellerton, the young R.N.A.S. officer.

"Yes; you were too occupied to notice who else was in the house, I guess. I was in the dress-sairrcle. I looked right down upon you in the stalls."

Now, Olwen was losing her habit of the vivid blush that used to scorch her. She merely coloured up slightly but prettily as she returned, "Oh, were you?" and proceeded to eat her fish and to discuss the play— which had been *Romance*. She had thought it lovely.

Captain Ross informed her definitely that he himself had no use for such sentimental balderdash; and then told her he guessed it made her pretty late, going back all the way to Wembley Park (where her Aunt lived) after the theatre. He hoped that at least young Ellerton took her all the way home.

"Yes, thank you; he did."

"M'm. Last train from Baker Street, I presume. And then you've a long trail from the station to your house. In the drive, isn't it?"

"Yes, but we didn't go by train at all," the girl explained. "Mr. Ellerton managed to get a taxi to take us all the way back from town."

"In war-time?" Captain Ross's black-cat-like face was a study in righteous indignation. Then he took a lighter tone, tilting his chin contemptuously. "Well! If Mr. Ellerton's got money to burn that way it's no concairrrn of mine. Taxis out to Wembley Park with a girl who's employed in the same office as he is. That's Ellerton's lookout. Not the kind of thing I'd care to be seen doing myself. (No, I won't have anything to drink. A ginger-ale, waiter.) Still, if he thinks that's all right in war-time and for folks on War work together, I've nothing to say."

The ghost of a smile hovered about Olwen's red mouth as Captain Ross went on saying this "nothing."

"Sweet as honey to any girl he takes out, no doubt. The regular naval flirt. He held your hand in the theatre, or some foolishness of that sort, I daresay."

"He didn't!" retorted little Olwen, quickly, and then a message seemed to come to her, whispered, perhaps by the generations of girls in love who still survived in her blood. Upon that instinct she added, "He did *not* hold my hand—in the theatre."

The finest judge of women in Europe rose swiftly enough to this. "Is that so? You mean he only held it in the taxi going home. A much better scheme altogether."

Olwen, still refusing to meet the aggressive brown eyes that challenged her over the jar of mimosa on the table, retorted, "I didn't say so."

"It was so, though. Wasn't it?"

"I shan't tell you," said the girl, whose hand had not been held by anyone since that magic evening in a boat. "Why should I?"

"Don't trouble to tell me. I know."

"Then why d'you ask me?" she returned with a little ripple of laughter. "Besides, why should you mind?"

"*Mind?*" retorted Captain Ross, laughing in his turn, but louder. "If I'd nothing worse than that to 'mind' about, I shouldn't be the busy man I am."

He turned to the menu; and Olwen, going on with her lunch, remembered Mrs. Newton's verdict, "He's a *jealous* thing!"

She ought to have been wildly delighted. . .

Curious! She was only flattered; amused.

She felt oddly conscious today, that (to parody a superannuated song), she was *not* the only girl in the world, and he was not the only boy. That little restaurant alone was crowded with girl workers, busy as she was, being taken out to lunch by khaki of every grade and age; and, by the way, there was something to be noticed about all these girls and young women from Government offices. Once, a girl worker found it hard to hit the mean between being fluffily unsuitable or unbecomingly severe. Today these girls were approximating to a new type; pretty but *durable*. The London day that began in the office and ended in restaurant and theatre with an "on-leaver" without the possibility of going home to change, had done way with fripperies, but had brought decorativeness into the worker's kit. *That* was why skirts were short, coats impertinently neat, and hair done so that it stayed done.

"Sensible" shoes, too, were now made in pretty styles; and since taxis were problematical on wet days, rain-coats and rain-hats were at last becoming things. This mixture of utility and attractiveness was a gift of war-time to British girlhood.

Olwen gained by it. She also gained by the consciousness that there was male companionship in the world besides that of Captain Ross. Further, she knew him so much better, now! Possibly, she was not left uninfluenced by the daily sallies of Mrs. Newton at the young officer's expense (for who knows the power of the comment that shows friend or lover from another's point of view?). No longer was she lacerated by the thoughts of those other girl friends "kept well around the corner." Altogether Olwen realized that it was a good thing she no longer imagined herself desperately in love with Captain Ross, since he, though interested in all girls, was not "seriously" attracted by her. (Otherwise, she concluded, he would have said so by this time.) She was cured; she no longer wore a Charm to win him. . .

That Charm! One night at Wembley Park the ribbon that held it had come unsewn. She hadn't had time to stitch it. It hung over her mirror. One day, perhaps, she would attend to it; but she was always busy now. It didn't seem to matter. . .

Captain Ross rose to go. Olwen could picture the expression with which he'd presently look into cell 0369 to "see" if the workers had all returned.

She was generally just five minutes behind him.

Today he paused, and said abruptly, "Speaking of theatres—there's a concert or show of some sort on at the Phoenix Hut, that American place, next Monday. Awdas rang me up about it. He'd be very pleased if you'd go."

Mischief danced in Olwen's averted glance. "How jolly! But how funny of Mr. Awdas not to ask me himself! What time is this concert, Captain Ross?"

In a wooden voice Captain Ross said, "It starts at eight. If you'd dinner, say, at seven o'clock here, I could take you along afterwards."

"*You* could? But you never take girls out from The Honeycomb."

"That's so," agreed Captain Ross, with firmness. "But this is Awdas's show. You'll be with him. So shall I. Good-bye."

He put on his red-banded hat, thrust his stick and gloves for a moment into the cross of his belt as he saluted woodenly, and turned.

Olwen burst into a merry laugh. "Captain Ross!"

He turned again.

"It's all right; I was going to that concert anyhow," she told him.

"I'm going with the girl who sings; you know Miss van Huysen!"

Miss Golden van Huysen was now one of Olwen's best friends.

II

The Last Allies

"They have looked each other between the eyes, and there
they have found no fault,
They have taken the Oath of the Brother-in-Blood on
leavened bread and salt."

—Kipling

The War-missioner on the platform paused for a moment to look at his watch.

Then he resumed, in the rich deep voice that spoke English not as the English speak it, the voice that had done so much to bring the help of his great country into the War.

"But you'd rather be hearing Miss van Huysen sing; and if you wouldn't, I would. So I'll just say this one thing to you men and women at the Phoenix Hut tonight. I want you to look at this flag." He pointed to the right-hand one of the two flags that backed him where he stood; the Stars and Stripes.

"And now—I want to think of another flag. Our stars only stand for stars that are older still."

The orator's fine grey head was lifted as if he could see those stars above the many-pointed roof of the hut; stars of the night sky.

"Those stars don't change. They're rising all the while, right round the world. They were there, those stars, before you or I were heard of. They will be there when we are gone. I see them as the stars of Love and Home. And I'll tell you, friends, what I see in those stripes, too. I see the whole world turning round to Daybreak, and those stripes are the rays of the Dawn."

Measured as the roll of distant drums, as soft, as stirring, the War-missionary's voice sounded through a silence which could be felt.

"The Dawn seems a long time in coming, but that it is coming is sure; sure as our men are on the ocean now! That's all I have to say. It wouldn't be any truer if I said it twenty times, and it wouldn't be any less true if I never said it at all. . . So now—Mr. Reynolds?"

The orator smiled to the dark, clean-shaven official with the high khaki collar and stepped quickly down off the platform. Just as he did so he looked back at the Stars and Stripes. "Not 'Old Glory' now," he added as if the thought had just come to him. "'New Glory,' joined with the Old," and his smile was for the Union Jack.

His talk, as homely as the gossip of a camp, yet somehow as high as the stars to which it pointed, was not of the kind that provokes violent applause. The whole assembly in that big hall felt that it was not mere applause that the orator and his kind were out to win. Quiet brooded for a moment over the meeting, over the mingling of Allies in khaki; and over the rows of big-framed, bold-featured Americans in uniforms of brown and blue, all clean-shaven as were those Normans of whom King Harold said, "*Those priests will make good soldiers.*"

Then the spell was relaxed; there was a little sputtering of matches as pipes were relighted. Men began to talk. And little Olwen Howel-Jones, who was one of the visitors occupying the two front rows of chairs settled herself for the singing.

On her lap was a great soft heap of leopard-skin furs. They belonged to Miss van Huysen (the girl who was going to sing as soon as she could be fetched from saying good-bye to a party of sailors who were taking their leave in the billiard-room). Miss van Huysen's seat, next to Olwen, had just been slid into by Captain Ross, who would have to leave it as soon as the singer had finished; Olwen thought he must have something to say to her, but apparently he hadn't. On her other side sat Mrs. Cartwright, serene and smiling, with her hand lying in that of the very young man who accompanied her. This very young man, aged fifteen, was Keith, her elder son, now in London with his mother on account of measles at his school. In the row behind them, his long legs rather cramped, sat Jack Awdas, the flyer, with the rest of the party from The Honeycomb; Leefe, Ellerton, little Mrs. Newton, and one or two other R.F.C. officers.

Since Captain Ross did not seem to have anything to say to her, Olwen found time to glance about this great hall which was only one room of the Phoenix Hut.

The keynote to the whole place—with its spaciousness of comfort, its shields of Harvard, Yale, and the other colleges, its flags, its palms, its theatrical posters, and its three glowing fireplaces, might be found in the great pedestalled image of the American Eagle, carved in grey stone and set up in the middle of the hall. Stately he stood with outstretched wings, poised and ready to strike; and from one of those wings dangled the blue jacket of some American sailor, while upon the huge bird's head there was perched an American soldier's cowboy hat.

It seemed so typical, that mixture of dignity and gaiety!

Suddenly a rustle and a buzz went round the hall, then the applause broke out in a storm as of summer rain.

Miss Golden van Huysen, the singer, had come quickly through the doors that led from the billiard-room smiling an apology for her absence. Olwen's glance flew back to the platform as her friend stepped forward up to it.

There she stood facing all eyes, a vision of white and gold. There she shone, in front of all the illuminating lights. Into that place, already bright, she brought an added radiance as of the June sun on a field of buttercups. Golden was her name; golden her hair, golden the girdle that clipped her, its long ends falling to the hem of her skirt. Olwen looked at the glorious young form, symbolical as that of a goddess on a golden coin.

"Isn't she beautiful tonight!" she breathed.

Every man in the hall must have agreed with her, and the blue eyes of at least one Englishman there said as much.

They were the eyes of Jack Awdas.

III

Recovery of the Charm

"One sudden gleam of a face, and my cherished Ideal is real!
There moved my miracle, there passed my Fate whom to see is to love."

—Brunton Stephens

Those eyes of Jack Awdas's had known their business from the start. Wise Mrs. Cartwright, to have known what would happen, even as she sat in that basket-chair in that hotel lounge at Les Pins, all those weeks ago!

It had happened instantaneously. The electric flash had not been quicker than the glance that had passed from young eyes to young eyes. Those months ago! . . .

Mrs. Cartwright had left the French hotel the morning after—had left Les Pins and the man she had refused. Her place at table next to Jack Awdas had been given (as she guessed it would be given) to her successor.

That goddess-built young American had made friends with everybody, easily and at once. The French families had regarded her as if she'd been a visitant from another planet. Olwen Howel-Jones had been subjugated on the spot. But Jack Awdas from the very first *déjeuner* had scarcely for a moment left her side.

Never before had he seen a girl so frank, yet so apart, so boyish in her unaffected good-fellowship, yet so womanly.

Unchaperoned she had travelled from the States to join her father in London, where he was attached to the Embassy, and where she meant to continue her special War work. But upon landing at Bordeaux she had found a cable from him stating that he would be out town for some days. She'd had no use for an empty house. So she had decided to stay in France and by the sea for those few days.

To young Jack Awdas they were a gift from Destiny!

Some people consider that the truest and most human touch in the world's greatest love drama is that which pitches the young man already infatuated with one woman into the purest passion for another.

There is no hiatus of feeling between the gloomy "*I am done*" of Romeo sighing for Rosaline, and his quick "*What lady's that?*" when Juliet appears; there is no thought of that first lady afterwards.

Yet who shall measure what Juliet owes to Rosaline?—what rough ways made smooth, what cold young crudities softened and warmed, what kindling of susceptibility, what speeding-up of passion?

And, for all this, what thanks may Rosaline expect? "*Oh, she was just someone he used to think he cared for.*" Or, "*I'm sure she couldn't have been a very nice woman.*" Or even "*Horrid! Robbing the cradle, I call it; I don't know how any woman can!*"

But none of these verdicts would ever be passed by Golden van Huysen, either upon Claudia Cartwright or upon any other woman. She had read of the theory that women are "catty" to their own sex; smilingly she disbelieved it. Like attracts like. Just as her own heart had never known an ungenerous prompting, so her own lips had never uttered a spiteful remark. She therefore never heard one. If she had, she would probably have widened her blue eyes and exclaimed with a little air of discovery, "Why, that's not *kind*!"

And this big and innocent creature was the very type which (if she'd had her choice) Mrs. Cartwright would have chosen for the man whom she herself was too old to choose.

He didn't ask Golden van Huysen to marry him on the first day of their acquaintance. No! He had waited until the third day.

"Mustn't rush things," he'd told himself, as if those three days had been three years' duteous service of a knight of old. So he had merely made himself into this young girl's shadow.

To her it was no novelty to be attended and worshipped. Wasn't every girl that she cared to know accustomed to this setting of masculine worship? Golden took as naturally as she took air and food the existence of a train of such young knights.

Only. . . from the first she realized vaguely that this one was somehow different from the others she had known and liked. This tall young man with the small crested head set on his sweeping, wing-like shoulders, who had drawn her first quick glance in the lounge. She admitted it quite frankly to herself this young flying-man *fascinated* her.

Why was it?

She had met plenty of flying-men before. Hadn't she talked to them in the aerodromes of her own country—which was also the birthplace of that very marvel, flying? Hadn't she been introduced to her aviators who had broken records for altitude, distance, and time? Hadn't she danced at balls with some of the very first pilots who'd ever looped? Flying and flyers had been no new proposition to her, but *this* flyer. . .

Presently the young American girl began to realize what it was that was new and special about "this flyer."

It was symbolized in the little gold stripe on the cuff of his flying-jacket. He was the very first *fighting* flyer who had crossed her path. The first she'd met who had already given battle to men in the air, the first she'd known who had been shot down in fighting for the cause which was now her country's too.

Never before had she seen a man who had actually used her country's invention of flying as the instrument of battle.

She, with her whole country, had wished to use this invention as a beneficent gift.

Her country had seen that *before this gift could be so used*, stern work lay before the men of the air. She saw it, too. . . As that War-missioner had said. Her country was looking with other eyes upon her Allies.

For Golden these new friends were typified in the young Briton who wore the wound stripe as well as the wings.

She told herself wonderingly, "Now isn't it queer that I should ever come to like one of the English so well. This Bird-boy is quite nice enough to be an American. . ."

Neither of the young people remembered afterwards at what exact moment of that second day she had called him "Bird-boy." Though he took it with a hidden lift of the heart, he did not use any name at all to her until the third day.

On the morning of that day she announced to him that it would be her last day at Les Pins.

"What? Going?" he cried aghast, as if the idea that she must one day go had never occurred to him.

"Why, yes! I'd never meant to stay here at all. It was just because of father, and now he cables me he'll be back in London before I shall."

"Well, but I say!" Jack Awdas broke in in consternation. "Shan't I see you any more?" It seemed unspeakable.

"Didn't you tell me you were coming back to London at the end of the fall, to a Board or something? My father would be pleased if you came and saw us then."

"But that's not for ages!" he cried, his face blank. "I'm not due back in town for another month! When are you going? Tonight? Tomorrow?"

"TOMORROW MORNING EARLY, TO BORDEAUX; then on to Paris, then London."

"All by yourself?" exclaimed the young Englishman stupefied.

She laughed. "Why, certainly, 'all by myself.' That's funny! Why, I've made all the travelling arrangements for father and myself since I was twelve! I'm a lot more useful than he is, that way. I've been most all over the world. 'All by myself.' Why, yes! You're shocked? Now isn't that real old-fashioned, and English? It's the way they talk in those novels with the sweet little heroine in book-muslin, whatever that is, in the days of Queen Victoria. Haven't you got past that, in this War? If you haven't it's time America did come in and teach you a few things! I guess I'm as capable as you are of looking after myself, Bird-boy!"

"You certainly aren't," he declared resolutely. "I shouldn't let you, if— if I were anything to do with you." He pulled himself together and added, "Well, there's all today, anyhow. Look here, can't you let me take you somewhere jolly all by myself, just for today?"

He could never have made this suggestion to a young woman of the traditions and upbringing of, say Miss Agatha Walsh. But already he knew that SHE would take it as it was meant.

"Why, yes, if you like," she said.

So they'd gone off to Cap Ferret. Midday had found this tall girl and boy upon Biscay shore where four days before Mrs. Cartwright's dove-lunch party had walked, watching those rollers. Soaring to crash, gathering and soaring once again to crash, those great waves boomed the chorus that had sounded across wide sea and wide shore long "before the months had names." It would go on sounding long after the names of those two on the seashore had ceased to be music to those who loved them.

But this was the moment when the waves sang for them, only for them.

Golden van Huysen had said something about surf-riding. The young aviator, his eyes turning for a moment from her to the tumultuous waters, had muttered, "Dangerous game for a girl!"

She laughed. "What a lot of things there are that you English think a girl can't do! It would do you lots of good to get to know some American girls. Then you'd see!"

He made no reply. His eyes were again upon her.

She wore what he had come to know were (out of uniform) her only colours; white and gold. Her dress of some creamy white stuff, perfectly cut, and over it she had slipped a knitted coat of yellowy silk. Crisp as a gardenia-petal, her skirt blew out above her ankles, and her feet, not small, but shapely as those of a sandalled Hermes. No hat hid her hair, which glinted like a casque in the sun as they turned away from the sea towards the dunes.

Here Jack Awdas took the plunge.

"See some American girls, you say? You're all the girl I want to see," he declared, not knowing that he spoke with the boyish vehemence that had so lately taken Claudia Cartwright's breath. The persistence with which he'd wooed that first love he now turned upon this—this only love of his.

"You're all the girls in the world to me," said he. "D'you understand?"

She did, and she did not. She stared at him: her uncovered gold head almost on a level with his own fair head, crested by that flyer's cap.

"Yes, rather!" continued the lad, definitely. "Now, what about it?"

He held out a hand to help her up the dunes, but she climbed as lightly as he.

"What about it, please?" he repeated. "What about your belonging to me for keeps, I mean?"

The girl had a curious little gesture as she looked at him, then away.

Surprise was in it, and protest, and a virginal dignity; also amusement, unpreparedness, and wonder. . .

She repeated his words. "'Belong' to you? To you? Oh! No, I—"

"Don't you like me?" he shot out.

"Oh! I like you very well," she answered quickly, almost hurt herself by the thought that she might have hurt him. "I like you so well! I like to be with you. I like to talk to you. I—yes, I like to look at you," and she turned one of her frank and friendly glances upon that handsome figure striding by her side, that fresh face, all pink in the sea-breezes. "But I guess I'd never want to 'belong' to any man!"

He smiled into the sweet bewildered eyes. It was the smiling side of his obstinacy; obstinate and keen again, in love as in war!

"I say—How old are you?" he asked.

"Twenty-one," she told him.

"Well, then! You don't mind my asking, do you? Hasn't any man ever wanted you to belong to him before?"

"You mean asked me to marry them?"

"Yes."

"Why, yes," she admitted with her crystal straightness. "Men, proposed to me? Why, stacks of them! But they didn't do it that way."

She looked back and out to sea, as though she could see on the other side of that severing Atlantic the half-score of her splendid young countrymen who had offered her marriage as tribute is offered to a young queen.

"You are—queer people over here," she said softly.

"Queer?"

"The way you talk of 'belonging.'"

"Queer, if it's the right man and the girl he wants?" Jack Awdas asked.

"But," she said, sweet and stately, "I should always want to belong to myself."

Then he understood. He said quickly, "Of course I'd always want that for you, too. But—oh, look here! Would the other stop that? As I see it, it might help it."

The puzzled wonder grew in her look. All this was strange to her; she had read of it, heard of it. All this was unexpectedly different from books, from college, from life until now. The old was so unexplored to the new, embodied in its modern Diana. At twenty she had seen half the capitals of two hemispheres, yet she was in his eyes more backward in some ways than a girl who had never left her native village.

Mrs. Cartwright could have told her that it is by "belonging" that a woman forms her individuality, and that it is only by giving that she can either gain or keep what she has.

He went on softly talking. Presently he said, "I know now what people mean by being made for each other. You were, for me. Yes, but I was for you. Oh, yes. Oh, yes! . . . You can't tell me you honestly don't think so. . . You don't want to send me away; you don't want not to see me again."

"Oh, *no*," she agreed, quickly, looking away from him as if to face a situation. She was of the type that faces, losing no time in wondering what she ought to think. And this was the very first time she had ever wondered *what* she thought.

She did like him. How it had grown, that first "fascination," born from a look! But—At last she seemed to find the words that summed it up.

"This is a big thing," she said, gravely. "It might be the biggest thing that's happened to me; but, Bird-boy, there's no hurry about it."

"No hurry?" He seemed to think that "hurry" was now the main point.

She shook her head. "We don't have to settle anything about it, right here and right now. Now *do* we?"

"Yes. *Yes!*" urged the boy.

"No," denied the girl's wise young voice. "See here; I'll be in London, and you will be there in a month. There's plenty of time. You'll come over then. . . Then we can think of it. . . Then maybe we'll talk of it again. . ."

"Oh, will we," muttered Jack Awdas in a voice of utter expressionlessness. For the moment he was ready to say nothing more.

Silence fell between them.

Each full of thought, they ascended and descended the belt of softly-rolling dunes and came to where the sand had drifted half-way up the trunks of the growing pines.

Suddenly Golden gave a little exclamation. "Oh, look; what's this?"

"What's what?" he asked, stopping beside her.

"I thought it was a cute little flower that was growing up the tree," said the girl with down-bent head, "but look, it's sown on to a ribbon, and it's got itself wound way round the branch—"

She was disentangling the object that had taken her eye; a couple of lengths of ribbon, faded to white by the sea breeze and stitched to a little padded square of satin, once mauve, now pale as the sand.

"What is it?" she wondered.

Half-absently Jack Awdas caught hold of the other ribbon as he looked at the thing.

And there was nothing to tell them what it was, the sachet of the Disturbing Charm that had hung about Mrs. Cartwright's neck just before she had plunged into the waters of Biscay Bay; the Charm that the wind had caught and whirled away across the sands until at last it had been in that pine branch from which a girl's hand unwound it.

"Something from a wreck?" mused Golden.

The Charm dangled between them.

He was scarcely thinking of what he was doing as he twisted that ribbon over his own fingers.

He was set, so that he would not have realized, now, that he had set before. This was a universe away from that. *She* knew that, the other one. . . She'd been kind. . . It wasn't that she hadn't liked him, he believed. She *had* begun to like him near her, she *had* liked it when he said "darling." Ah, to think that he had ever wanted to say "darling" to any woman before! Here was his darling, and she must be made to see it, not later, not in London, but "right here and now."

As he twisted the ribbon, he spoke in the tone that had caused that other woman to shut her eyes; for it was the note of the mating call.

"I say, darling—"

Again the girl shook her head, but—was there now the least quiver of indecision in her gesture?

"I say, if nobody else has ever been allowed to call you that—"

"Oh, no!" she cried, sincerity itself.

He was mechanically twisting up that ribbon between them; another inch he took, another.

"Then if there's nobody else you liked well enough for that, there's a chance for me," persisted the soft husky voice of her lover above the faint distant crashing of those breakers behind them.

"Shall I tell you what?"

"What—?" she asked, slowly, no longer looking at him. A kind of arrogance seemed to shine up in him. Somewhere deep down in his heart he was cheering himself on by the reminder that he knew more than she. He seemed vaguely conscious of some force upon his side. . . He would not have believed anyone who had told him that a woman's strongest love, poured out upon him, had lent him magnetism, charged him. He fastened his blue eyes upon this girl, as upon some doggedly desired objective seen from his battle 'plane as he drove through the blue, but he did not reply. He smiled, with all that is far-away in those searching eyes of his.

He had twisted up the last inch of that ribbon. Now he caught hold of the Charm that hung between the two ties, then came to the twin ribbon that she held. Before she knew what he would do with it, he wound that ribbon about her fingers and palm, binding her hand to his own with the Charm in it.

Close, close and warm his pulses beat to hers.

"I've caught you," he ventured, very softly, eyes intent upon her. He smiled more broadly at the first faint dawning of lovely trouble in her face. "Yes! This is what they'd call marriage-by-capture, I suppose?"

She didn't speak. She didn't move as he caught hold of her free hand as well. He held his crested head gaily as he said to her, "Of course I'm

English and old-fashioned, and I know American girls are independent, and I ought to see the things they could teach me! But there's something I could teach one of them. Let me try?"

Softly he muttered the word which was to mean everything as his own name for her. "Girl! *Girl!* . . . I say, let's learn from each other?"

Still she didn't speak. How find words, when at a nearness, a name, a touch, some spell seems snapped and the meanings of all words thereafter seem entirely to have altered? This stranger who had become her friend so soon had even more quickly changed to—

"*What?*"

Her lover nodded, saying below his breath, "It will be all right."

Then, loosing one of her hands, he deftly unwound the ribbon that was about the other. As he was stuffing the Charm with its ribbons inside the breast of his flyer's coat, words came at last to his love.

Laughing tremulously, she asked, "Why, what are you doing that for?"

"Putting it by, safely," he smiled at her as he stood just a step away from her on the sand. "It'll never leave me now, not that ribbon that— that tied our hands together for me. I say, I shall fasten it to my 'bus later on, to bring me luck, Girl. It's started already, what?" He jerked his belt straight. "Hasn't it?"

And with the words he took that one step nearer that brought her into his arms.

"Ah, please," he said, more softly than ever. "Please. . ."

He drew down to his shoulder the face so full of sweet disturbance, he folded her close, close to the wide breast beneath the white-embroidered wings. As if swayed by a Charm, she drew a long breath, then smiled in wonder, nestled, and yielded to his kisses—the first for both of them. . .

"What about America coming in now, Girl? She will, won't she? . . . Yes, but say yes; you *must*! Say it!"

"No, Bird-boy! I just won't *say* it," was her last touch of mutiny. "And—and I guess we'll see about that 'belonging' later on."

"Yes," triumphed Jack Awdas. "I 'guess' so too!"

That was all those months ago.

IV

THE VOICE OF THE CHARMER

"She is singing an air that is known to me;
A passionate ballad gallant and gay,
A martial song like a trumpet's call."

—Tennyson

All that had been in November. It was now January—which brings me back to the Phoenix Hut, where Golden van Huysen was preparing to sing.

Advancing to the edge of the platform, she said, smiling, but as quietly as if she'd been proposing a game in a room full of children:

"What'll I sing you, boys?"

An instantaneous chorus of men's voices answered her, and she laughed. Evidently she had heard, though Olwen hadn't caught a word of which song it was they all wanted.

It was "the" sentimental song of the moment, that song whose name varies from season to season. As I write, it is called differently from what it will be called by the time you read. Once it was "Until," once "Roses of Picardy." The soul of it remains the same. "Cheap and common," smile the superior. Yes! Cheap as the air we breathe. Common as sunlight.

Golden van Huysen pronounced its present name to the accompanist, who struck four cords on the piano. Then, into a dead silence, her voice stole out.

It might have been the gushing of honey from a suddenly broken comb. Already her speaking voice could set Olwen's heartstrings vibrating in response to the sound, but Golden's singing voice (a rich mezzo-soprano) was almost more than her little Welsh friend could endure for pleasure. It cleft the middle of the note, the middle of the heart. Olwen sat, her hands clenched under those furs, listening, listening. She could not have told you what the words were about. She only knew that when the immortal nightingale sang to his rose, it must be in some such song as this. . . The two verses of the song ended, and the applause that followed them was as much a murmur of deep voices as it was a clapping of hands from Americans, British tars, Canadian, kilties. . . Without a pause, the singer whispered to her accompanist. The wonderful voice rose in a second song, of which the words might have been trivial, but which were music because of their singer. Not a man or woman in that hut made a movement. . . In all she sang three songs.

Just before her last song she took a couple of steps backward, and stood, tall and resplendent, between the two flags with a hand upon each.

She had not sung three notes before the audience had risen to their feet, with every soldier and sailor in the hall standing to attention. For it was "The Star-Spangled Banner" that Golden van Huysen was singing now.

There are some songs that never age. Of these are those a mother sings to her child; of these, too, are those a Motherland sings to her absent sons. This one—Well, all in that hall had heard it a thousand times before, yet this might have been the first time. Golden sang it as once Sims Reeves sang "Maud," as Patti sang "Home, Sweet Home"— in the perfection of simplicity.

At the end she neither bowed nor smiled. She just backed out, as before some Royalty of emotion, between the English and the American flags.

With a deep breath the audience felt that it was as though a light had been put out. . .

It was this radiant personality of hers, as well as her power of holding her hearers spellbound in hut, hospital, theatre, and soldiers' club, that had gained her the name by which half London knew her now—"that wonderful American they call the Sunburst Girl."

V

THE BEST GIRL-FRIEND

"She was Sweet of Heart."

—Epitaph on the Tomb of an Egyptian Princess, 700 B.C.

Olwen, with Golden's furs, hurried through the billiard-room to the outer hall with the "Enquiries" counter, the long bar, and the rows of refreshment-tables crowded by soldiers and sailors.

One table was empty, reserved for Mr. Awdas's party, but the young flying officer had been called away on duty just after his *fiancée's* second song. Olwen was sorry for him, but his loss was her chance; and she saw so little of this friend of hers.

As she handed over the great leopard-skin muff, she said, rather appealingly, "Are you staying, Golden?"

"Why, aren't you?" Golden said, glancing towards the group who were ordering coffee. "It's quite early."

"Yes; and I felt like a walk," said the other girl, wistfully, "and I thought if we got out of this crush I might see you to speak to—"

Golden laughed. "Very well," she agreed. "I'll come with you; wait while I shake hands with Mrs. Cartwright. . ."

The two young girls bade a quick good night to the party, and before it was quite realized that they were leaving, they had passed through the hall, descended the wooden staircase, and reached the entrance to the Strand.

It was a clear and sparkling night above the murky lamp-glasses, with a touch of frost. Away to the west the spoke of a single searchlight could be seen creeping this way and that like a snail's horn.

The tall girl and the little one turned to take the quieter streets in the direction of Baker Street, Olwen's terminus.

Already they had walked many a mile together, those oddly contrasted girl-friends, during that growth of this quick, firm friendship. Several times the Welsh girl had been invited to the big house near Grosvenor Gardens, which was Golden's home; the little house at Wembley Park had in its turn welcomed the American. There had been appointments for matinées together, and for lunch. Olwen, in fact, would have wished to claim the Sunburst girl whenever Jack Awdas was out of town, bound for France with a new machine. Taking aeroplanes across the Channel was now his job. Little Olwen had been the first of her girl friends to whom Golden had confided the pact on Biscay Beach that had made of her Bird-boy the happiest man flying.

But as Golden was not of the type that lets any Third (however dear) into details that concern a happy two, Olwen had never heard of the part played in that scene by a trifle of pink ribbon and satin in which her own hand had bestowed a Charm. . .

If she had known of it, it might have been better for her. It might have startled her out of the lines that her own life was taking; humdrum lines, she knew—she scarcely realized that they were also growing towards the lines of disillusionment, even of cynicism. Being gloriously in love was a thing for the few, she thought. Certainly a bright fixed star seemed to shine over this girl by her side and over the Jack she appeared to adore. But what gleam of it touched the life of Olwen? She had now reached twenty, and the phase when a girl believes herself to have outgrown everything she ever used to feel. Certainly she had gained, by that casting off of some of her feverish emotionalism and credulities, but was there nothing this young girl was in danger of losing?

It was as they were turning into Cranbourne Street that Golden van Huysen, who had been swinging along without speaking, did startle her by a sudden remark:

"Olwen! I didn't know you could be so cruel."

Quickly Olwen's little head went up. "Cruel, Golden? What can you mean?"

"I mean just plain cruel. What made you say good night in the way you said it, as if you didn't care if it were good night, or good-bye, or good riddance?"

"'Good night' to whom? I spoke to Mrs. Cartwright; she was the one who mattered," Olwen said a little defensively. "All those other people from the Honeycomb—well, I wanted to get away with you, and I see *them* every day."

"And are '*they*' all the same to you?"

"Of course," said Olwen in a resigned voice, "you *mean* Captain Ross."

"Certainly I didn't mean your little Major Leefe, who talks as if it hurt him, not your young sailor-boy, who loves to laugh."

"Well, I see Captain Ross every day, and I expect he thinks that's far too much."

Golden's reply was a soft laugh. "Oh, you British, you are the funniest things! Either you want to grab a thing before you take another breath, or else you wait staring at it until you can't see it!—Why, Olwen, that man's crazy about you."

"Not he!" returned Olwen, decidedly, and with another sort of laugh—a slightly bitter one.

For she had just remembered that this was the second time some one had thought this thing. She heard again the mercilessly shrewd voice of that French manageress at Les Pins.

"Monsieur le Capitaine, he with the one arm, who admires Mademoiselle."

She, Olwen, had actually been silly enough to believe it, then. She didn't believe it now; how could she? Did she have any reason? Those Fridays were the only time she saw him to speak to, and even those, as he'd practically pointed out to her, were the purest accident.

The rest of the time—she laughed again.

"My *dear* Golden, if you could *only* see him at the Honeycomb!"

And there seemed to resound in her mind echoes of Captain Ross's voice at the Honeycomb—or were they echoes of Mrs. Newton's mimicries of Captain Ross?

"Hullo—yes?" curtly down the telephone in his office where Olwen had come for instructions. "Yes; Miss Howel-Jones *is* working on the Honeycomb. You will find her number in room 0369—" Then, in an iron tone to Olwen, "Miss Howel-Jones, I should be glad if you would give your *correct* telephone number to any friends whom you wish to ring you up. . ."

And so on. Was that the manner of a man who cares?

More echoes were broken in upon by the gentler voice of Golden.

"I don't need to see him at any Honeycomb. I saw it in one, at the Eagle Hut. If he's different in the office, why, that's his fine sense of duty, and you ought to like him for that. . . Jack thinks a deal of Captain Ross. So does Mrs. Cartwright, and she's a real, intelligent woman. Why, do you know, just before Captain Ross came on to the meeting tonight, your little friend Mrs. Newton said something about him; I think she likes to make fun of him a little. Mrs. Cartwright said, quite quietly, *'I have a great affection for Captain Ross!'*

"I guess she wouldn't have said that without some reason for liking him. Jack thinks he's fine," young Awdas's sweetheart concluded her plea for the absent. "Don't you like him, Olwen?"

There was a silence as the two girls walked up Tottenham Court Road, comparatively empty at this time of the evening.

Then Olwen drew a quick little breath, turned up her face to her friend's, and let out an emphatic "I did like him." Then in a soft hurry of words, "I liked him all that time in France. Yes. Awfully! I thought of him and thought of him, Golden. It seemed to make everything. . . beautiful to me." Then a little ashamed laugh, "I was—silly, then!"

"Silly?" repeated her friend gently. "That's not the way it seems to me. That's a lovely thing in a girl's life." She lifted her chin over the leopard-skin stole and looked ahead to the stars above the murky lamps, to the skies in which lay her own lover's pathless way. "Make everything beautiful; that's what love should do. I *know*," said Golden, shyly, but proudly. "I didn't know for certain, until Jack showed me. I'm so pleased you know too. . ."

"Oh, but—that's not new," Olwen protested quickly. "That's over."

"Over? Then—if you don't mind telling me, what do you feel about Captain Ross now? What does he mean in your life?"

Little Olwen had asked herself this very same question until she'd given it up, and now she scarcely knew whether to laugh or to shrug her shoulders.

"I'll tell you," she said lightly, after a moment, "exactly how I feel about Captain Ross. I would have told you before, if you'd asked me. To start with, I work all day at the Honeycomb, where there are hundreds of other girls, and men. Some of these people amuse me, and some don't, so—"

"But—'*amuse*'—" repeated Golden, blankly. "Does that stand for anything big?"

The soft Welsh voice of the other girl retorted, "It does, when you are working, and—and there isn't anything else. Isn't it natural that one likes the amusing people best? Mrs. Newton is amusing. Major Leefe doesn't mean to be, but he is. Mr. Ellerton is nice to go about with—"

Again Golden broke in gently. "Olwen! I don't like to hear you talk that way."

"Why not? Les Pins is over. And when a thing's over," pronounced this sage of twenty, "sensible people don't waste any more time on it."

"When you say that, it seems to me to be belittling a very—" Golden made the characteristic American pause after the adverb—"beautiful thing."

"It's different for you who have one man meaning the whole world to you. As I haven't. Well, I want to be amused, Golden."

More gently still Golden repeated, "I don't like to hear you talk that way, Olwen. Don't you feel any more that Captain Ross is different from the others?"

"I feel he's less amusing," declared the girl, walking beside her.

"And how," asked Golden, "does that young Mr. Ellerton 'amuse' you, then?"

"Well, he gives me a good time. I like being with him. He rattles away all the time. *He* doesn't snap my head off—"

For half a minute there was silence as they walked along. Then Golden stopped by one of those dimly-gleaming lamps and peered down into her friend's small, mutinous face; her voice dropped a whole note as she said slowly:

"Olwen! You wouldn't do such a thing as play Mr. Ellerton off against Captain Ross to make Captain Ross jealous?"

"Oh, no," Olwen said quite honestly; forgetting something as entirely as a change of mood can cause one to forget. She had mischievously enough, allowed Captain Ross to go on thinking that the young R.N.A.S. officer had held her hand. . . She didn't even care enough to remember it. . .

But at her answer the American girl heaved quite a sigh of relief. "Forgive me," she begged. "Forget I said that. I ought to have known it wasn't like you."

And here Olwen really felt herself humbled by the standards of the straight young goddess at her side. For the first time the younger, less womanly but more feminine and complex girl suffered a pang of remorse on account of a certain little Mr. Brown. Him she had certainly made use of at Les Pins to annoy Captain Ross. The blackberry time was not intentional; but that time on the terrace? Would Golden ever have talked to a young man "at" another young man? It would be better, she knew, if every girl could think and act like Golden. . . it would be better. . . But to every girl her problems.

Golden went on, "You've done it without wanting to, then. He was scared tonight that Mr. Ellerton would sit by you. You aren't out to make him jealous, but have you wondered if he thinks that's what you're doing? I've told you that he watched every look of yours!"

"But I don't believe it," persisted Olwen, feeling somehow more disturbed, less contented with life as it was then she had been that day. "Why should I?" and into her voice there crept another note.

It was a note of unspoken irritation, exasperation, and appeal. In how many soft girl voices does it not sound, telling of budding emotions nipped by the frost of silence—of hopes that had grown tired of raising their heads—of womanly impulse turned back upon itself—of influences that might have made the sunshine of two lives, but that dies of forbiddance because some man has shown himself so near to speaking—and has not spoken!

"He cares," said Golden with the conviction of some young great-eyed oracle.

A passer-by separated the two girls for the moment. As they came together again Olwen retorted, "Then why can't he say so? Men do, when they like a girl well enough. Your Jack did, in a minute."

Golden gave a happy little laugh. "But, as I say most every day, you British are so queer! You're so different! Some of your men want to propose before they even say 'Pleased to meet you.' Others seem to have this habit of waiting and waiting until some cows of their own come home, I guess."

"It's the second sort that I don't understand," sighed the Welsh girl. "If a man is fond of a girl, why doesn't he want to say so at once?"

Golden shook her head. "Now that is something that I can't tell you."

Presently Olwen said, as if getting rid of something that had been a little on her mind, "I read in a book of essays about engagements and things, that Mrs. Newton lent me, that *a Proposal was one-half the Engineering of Some Girl, and one-half the False Pretences of Some Man*. . . but I hope that's not quite true. . ."

"It is not true," said the American girl serenely. "It's ugly."

With this profoundly simple remark, uttered as if it were some creed, she turned with Olwen down Warren Street; and they were half-way to Baker Street station before either of them spoke again.

Then said the Sunburst Girl, "I wouldn't have missed this walk. I think you needed to talk to somebody who knows Love's lovely."

"Somebody who seems to upset things I thought were *settled*," grumbled Olwen, affectionately.

"That's why I'm glad I came with you. I just hate to see you in a hurry to settle all the wrong things!"

BERTA RUCK

Olwen persisted. "For the umpteenth time, as Mr. Ellerton would say, that man doesn't care two-pence about me, Golden."

"Just because he hasn't proposed?" smiled Golden as she took the last word. "But he will. Watch out for it. Good night, dear."

The heavy furs lifted to her gesture as she turned, then swung away under the stars towards the South.

VI

The Charm Remembered

"A is happy, oh, so happy!
A is happy, B is not."

—Gilbert

The words of Golden remained with her friend all the way back to Wembley Park, down the Drive of little red-roofed villas, and up the short-flagged path between the standard rose-bushes that led to her Aunt's front door.

Olwen took her latch-key from her bag and let herself in; as she did so she heard the voice of the Aunt from the sitting-room, "Is that you, dear?"

"Yes! I'll be down in a minute," she called back, and ran straight upstairs to the bedroom with the pink-curtained window that overlooked the back lawn.

She wanted to be alone for a moment or so. She had just told the Sunburst Girl that what she wanted was amusement, but what she would have liked now would have been solitude.

Why had Golden unsettled her again like this, when she had been getting along so cheerfully?

She sat down on the edge of the springy brass-railed bed drawn up against the window. It was open, and the breeze stirred in the curtain behind her head, full of uneasy thought... As she drew the hat-pins from her head she glanced restlessly about her room, bright, girlishly pink-and-white, with the atmosphere of a room that had been lived in happily enough. Mechanically Olwen's eyes fell upon the dressing-table, upon the crystal powder-box, upon the signed photograph of Professor Howel-Jones—about the frame of which there was twisted a long piece of pink ribbon, sewn to—

Why, it was that half-forgotten Charm of her days in France!

Half scornfully she smiled now at the memories that it brought to her.

It seemed another Olwen that she remembered, poring over typewritten directions for the use of that Charm... Fancy an Olwen who believed in that! What a simple way out of the problems of Love, to wear a mascot and to have everything happen that one could wish!

This did happen to some people, Olwen mused. To Golden van Huysen it had come without the help of any talisman. Golden possessed within her all that quality of Charm of which that "inventor" claimed to have found the secret. She was one of the lucky people who hold that secret without knowing what it is. . .

But as for materializing it into something that might be annexed and worn—well, thought the new and more sophisticated Olwen, what had been the success of that, so far? Half laughing now, she considered it.

That other, romantic little Olwen had (in her first enthusiasm!) written to that newspaper address for more of the Charm.

No answer had been vouchsafed to her.

Therefore her experiments had been limited to four. She had planted out her Charm upon four people: Miss Agatha Walsh, Mrs. Cartwright, little Mr. Brown, and herself.

With what results?

This older, wiser Olwen ticked them off now on her fingers.

One, Agatha Walsh—successful. She had become engaged to her Gustave and was perfectly happy.

Two, Mrs. Cartwright—unsuccessful. Absolutely nothing had happened, thought Olwen, vexedly; her friend the writer had received not one word of added attention from her Uncle, and had remained unclaimed except by that work and those boys of hers.

Three, little Mr. Brown—more than unsuccessful. Not only had he failed to attract anybody on his own account, but he had shown symptoms of becoming attracted to a girl who didn't want him.

Four, Herself—unsuccessful again. No results at all. You can't count as "results" two attacks of masculine dog-in-the-mangerishness, one box of chocolates, a few ragging remarks, and an evening of having one's hand held in a boat. No results. . .

That left one out of four cases in which the Charm had worked. *Only one out of four people lucky in Love!* Was it so the world over? One in four meant a quarter of the people in the world! . . . Well, perhaps that wasn't such a very poor percentage, Olwen told herself more briskly as she gave herself a little shake out of her meditations and ran downstairs to the sitting-room, where a cup of cocoa and a plate of those neutral objects known as War-biscuits had been set ready for her by the Aunt.

This Aunt was Professor Howel-Jones's youngest sister, a small demure woman of forty-five, with the air of constantly saying, "Of course *I* am the failure of the family." She had been left a widow very young, and it was her pose to give out that she had never been asked to marry again. But her pretty eyes laughed, most disconcertingly, while the rest of her face remained prim. She smoked, sang Clarice Mayne's songs and forbade Olwen to call her "Aunt" anything.

"Thank you, Lizzie," said her niece, as this lady handed her over a letter that had arrived by the last post. Then, glancing at the signature, Olwen gave a little exclamation of surprise. It was over the well-known type of coincidence that brings a letter from some one almost immediately following one's own thoughts of that some one.

For the letter was signed, "Yours affectionately, AGATHA WALSH."

Miss Walsh wrote from Paris, where she had just been having "Oh, such a lovely time shopping with Madame Leroux, who had taken a month away from the hotel, and had been looking up some of the relations—"

Followed an account of these relations who had evidently taken the English *fiancée* to their bosoms; Agatha, who had been English and provincial, was rapidly becoming a good French *bourgeoise*.

She went on, "Oh, and there is such news, Olwen. Figure to yourself that Gustave is coming to London with General Chose next week! Coming as his orderly! Just think how lovely for me! Of course I shall come over at once. I have not been in England since September! We must all meet, we and you and the Professor and dear Mrs. Cartwright, if she is in town! And won't it be like old times again! and oh, Olwen, I may even be getting married—"

This last word was so heavily underlined that Olwen had to laugh, and the Aunt asked her what she was so pleased at.

"Oh, only that there *are* some very happy people in the world even now," said Olwen.

"'Some' pessimist", murmured the Aunt, whose vocabulary was not of her epoch. "Never mind, Olwen; I have just remembered something. An admirer rang you up on the telephone this afternoon, and would you ring him up at the Regent Palace Hotel as soon as you came in—?"

"What?" said Olwen, astonished. "What was his name, and why d'you think he was an admirer, Lizzie?"

"I think he admired you by the tone of his voice, in which he said, 'Miss Olwen,'" said the demure Aunt, who had a private and vicarious delight in watching all the activities of her young niece. "As for his name—what was it now? Something rather out of the way."

"I don't know," wondered Olwen. "Was it Mr. Ellerton?"

"Oh, no; not our young Naval man who finished our last drop of whisky, by the way—no, I thought at once of him, dear, but it wasn't. It was—oh, yes! He said, *'Ask her to ring up Lieutenant Brown.'"*

"What? *Not* Little Mr. Brown?"

"I couldn't tell you what height he was," murmured the Aunt, but already Olwen, amused, had run out into the hall and had taken up the telephone.

(Coincidence, then, had been busying itself with another of the Les Pins party!)

After some little delay the Regent Palace found Mr. Brown.

"Hul-*lo!*" the familiar boy's voice sounded over the wires as cheerily as it had sounded over the waves and through the pine woods. "That you, Miss Olwen? . . . That's great. How are you? . . . That's top-hole. . . Me? Oh, I'm fine, thanks. Yes; I'm up for a Board. I say, Miss Olwen, when can we for-gather? . . . Can I see you tomorrow? . . . Dinner? What are you doing?"

Olwen said, "I'm going to a party at Mrs. Cartwright's—"

"No! By Jove, are you? I say, I'm glad you mentioned it. I nearly forgot. I'm booked for Mrs. C. too. Rang her up and she asked me to roll up at seven. Can I take you along? Miss Olwen, can't I have tea with you in town somewhere first?"

"Er—" began Olwen, doubtfully. Truth to tell she had not wanted to see very much of little Mr. Brown; she had not wished to encourage his boyish sentimentality for her.

He took up quickly, "Won't you have tea with me, here, tomorrow? I've got something very particular to say to you, Miss Olwen."

"Oh? What is it?"

"Give you three guesses. I say, you know that mascot you gave me?"

"Yes?"

"Well! It's brought me luck, I reckon."

"Oh, has it? Well, what is it?"

"That's what I want to talk about tomorrow," came with a joyous giggle from the other end of the wires; evidently the speaker could scarcely wait until tomorrow's talk. "I say, can't you guess, Miss Olwen? Master's got off, this time."

"Got *what?*"

"*Off!*"

"I can't quite hear what you say," called Olwen, puzzled. "Who has got what?"

"Oh, spare my blushes," begged the voice of Mr. Brown, and then brought out the announcement, "I'm engaged to be married, Miss Olwen, that's what!"

"Oh—*oh!*" gasped Olwen. "I'm so glad—"

"Thanks! Thought you would be! You wait till you hear all about it though. You prepare for a shock, Miss O. Tea tomorrow. Four o'clock. That suit you? I'll meet you at the door—you know, in the hall just in front of the big place where all the animals feed. Right! So long! Chin-chin!"

"Good night!" called Olwen, and rang off. Then she stood gazing at the telephone almost as if it were the small figure in khaki coming towards her out of the forest.

Engaged—Little Mr. Brown!

The Charm had worked with him, then, after all?

That made two out of four. . .

Well, that was a better percentage than she had thought she might hope for, thought Olwen as she turned away.

Did it mean that after all *half* the people in the world were lucky in love?

VII

Petrol and the Charm

"For your own ladies, and pale-visaged maids,
Like Amazons, come tripping after drums;
Their thimbles into armed gauntlets change,
Their needles to lances."

—Shakespeare

I've got a table in the corner over here," said little Mr. Brown to Olwen through the buzz of talk that drowned all but the louder strains of the band in the tea-room of the Regent Palace Hotel.

It was, as ever on a Sunday afternoon, a welter of khaki and girls. The wicker chairs could not be seen for shrubberies of furs, coloured forest of millinery; there was scarcely a space on the floor clear of muffs, vanity bags, and feet; big feet in brown boots, little feet in high-heeled coloured shoes; swathed feet in hospital wrappings. It took Mr. Brown and Olwen minutes to steer their way through this labyrinth to the further corner by a window that the little campaigner had marked down and engaged just after lunch.

"Now, that's better," he said. "Nobody will come and walk over us here, and nobody can hear what I say through this racket, not that I care if they do. . . Well, it's nice to see you again, Miss Olwen. I've been fairly bursting to have a good old mag with you, ever since all this happened. . . What? Yes, two teas, please, Miss, if you can call 'em teas. Spelling it with an E at the end is nearer the mark nowadays; sort of reminding you of what once was tea. I've got some sugar here; pinched some out of HER cupboard yesterday—good start, wasn't it? Are you one of those people who miss lump sugar with every breath they draw, Miss Olwen?"

Olwen smiled into the pink, pug-dog face that looked pinker, more pertinacious than ever; the boy held his head even more assuredly in the air, but his blue, prominent eyes were humble as well as joyous, and the whole of him radiated amazement at Fortune as well as delight.

"Tell me about 'all this,'" Olwen begged, and little Mr. Brown zestfully drawing in his chair and letting a pleased grin crumple his cheeks, broke into his story. . .

Here and there Olwen interposed a question, a "Really," a "Why," a "What did she say to that?" but for the rest she listened mutely as a woman must, with the widening of her eyes, with a nod, a turn of the attentive head, while the cheerful boy's voice—a thread in that closely woven pattern of other voices all about them—ran on and on.

"It was only last Saturday it started. Imagine that! Seems ages ago to me now, so much happening. . . However, to begin at the beginning. I'd been to my Board in the morning, and the silly old blighters had given me another three weeks' leave before putting me on light duty. I was in a taxi, coming away from them, because I was in a hurry, promised to meet a fellow I knew for lunch at the Troc. . .

"By Jove, I never even rang him up after! I've only just thought of that fellow who used to be in the Lace Department at that old show of mine, and I hadn't seen him since '14. Too bad. I'll have to write him. Anyhow I can't help it; absolutely everything seems to have gone straight out of my head.

"Well, I was going to lunch with this fellow, and then I thought after that I'd ring you up, Miss Olwen, and see what you were doing, and if you'd perhaps care to come with me to the Alhambra or something. If I couldn't get hold of you I was going to look up Ross, I thought, and Mrs. Cartwright. . . This was where I was mapping out things that came rather different, as it happened!

"We were coming along Piccadilly towards the Circus when my taxi-man (an absolutely dud driver, as I'd noticed) barged straight into a motor-cycle and side-car that were going along at no end of a lick for Knightsbridge. He only pulled up in the very nick of time; the cycle and the rider were over and into the mud; a filthy day it was, p'raps you'll remember—drizzling and the streets like a soap-slide.

"Out I nipped, before the crowd had even begun to collect, and picked up the motor-cyclist with one hand, and started saying what I thought of the taxi-driver with the other—he was swearing away like a trooper at 'these here so and so and so and so side-cars'; and the little nipper who had been upset was cursing him to blazes, an octave higher. The voice took me by surprise, of course. . . The little thing was so covered in mud that I couldn't have told you off-hand if it were a boy or girl or a retriever dog.

"A girl; yes, it was a girl, of course.

"One of those lady dispatch-riders, they call them. Cap like mine, trench-coat down to her knees, top-boots, riding-breeches. . . laughing all over her little splashed face. . .

"Well, in about two twos I'd pushed his fare at the taxi-driver and sent him off and was assessing the damages to that motor-cycle of hers—nothing wrong at all luckily! while she wiped her face on a huge khaki handkerchief and put her cap straight. Short hair, of course, rather sticking out, curly. . . I always thought I loathed short hair on a girl. Suits her A1, and it's most awfully soft and jolly to run your fingers through. . .

"What? Oh, no, not *then*. Give us a chance. I wasn't allowed a chance to touch her hair for ages—you'll see.

"All this time I was being all over myself with apologies, and she laughing and saying it was all part of the day's work, only the taxi-man had put her back up; taxi-drivers did always seem to be women haters! She told me (standing there by the kerb) that she was just coming off anyway before her three days' leave that she gets in a month, and that she was dashing up to Harrod's before they closed, because she was on duty from eight to six ordinarily, and never got any time to do any shopping for herself.

"(Mind you, that's the only grouse she seems to have at all after doing a man's job day in, day out; no time to get her shopping done!)

"I thought to myself at once, the way one does, 'H'm, here's a nice little bit of skirt, if you could see it for mud.' Not that it *wore* a skirt, but still. So I said, pretending to be rather fed, 'I don't suppose there's another taxi to be had for love or butter now, so I'll just push on to Harrods' on my flat feet.'

"'Oh,' she says, 'were you going to Harrods'?'

"'I am,' said I, determined to now, anyway.

"'And you're wounded, too, aren't you,' says she. 'I'll give you a lift. Hop in.'

"In I hopped into that side-car; and off we buzzed to Harrods', and we were just in time before they closed for her to buy half a dozen pair of the best quality brown silk stockings for herself. (I'd seen she was a lady, you know, and all that.) She said she hadn't a stocking left to her foot—Tiny feet she's got, Miss Olwen! Reminded me of yours, honest, they did. Same sort of hands, too. Coming out of her great gauntlets like snowdrops, growing in a drift of brown leaves—No, I didn't make that up, that's what she told me some ass of an old Colonel that she used to drive the cars for said to her once. I think it's neck, the way some of those old Johnnies with one foot in the grave go on giving the Glad to any pretty young girl that's near them. . .

"Well, after Harrods' shut, we went on to some place where she could get a wash and brush up, and we had a spot of lunch together. She was a real jolly little thing to go about with, I thought. We sat talking—you know the way ones does—until it was nearly tea-time.

"Tea we had out, too. She would stand me tea, said it was her shout, and because I was wounded. Seemed to think that because a fellow had been pipped once he was helpless for evermore. Generally I loathe women fussing over one for that, but she was different. . . Struck one as so comic, you know, that tiny little thing with those hands and feet to be got up like any old mechanic, and to do all that hefty work in all weathers—and for her to get frightened that I might be tired!

"Well, so we went to Rumplemayer's.

"Afterwards I went with her to take her bike back to the Park. You know she's attached to the Royal Flying Corps there; yes, that's what she does now. Carries their letters and messages for them all over the show, to your people at the Honeycomb too, sometimes. Sometimes she drives out officers to the various training schools for flying, all about. Has to clean her own bike, too! Wouldn't let me give her a hand, said it didn't look well. Extraordinary, the lot she gets through! . . . And I used to hate girls being 'independent,' too.

"I asked her what put it into her head to do all this, and she said it was because one had to do one's bit somehow, and the harder the better, so that it sent one to bed tired enough to sleep.

"Dashed sporting little girl I thought her.

"It was dinner-time before I knew, and I asked her if she'd come out. (I had got just one pound note left on me!)

"She said, as naturally as if we always fed together, 'Shall I go up to my rooms and get into respectable clothes, or d'you mind if I came in my uniform?'

"I said, 'Oh, come along!' And we went off to a quiet little place at the back of the Palace.

"By that time, d'you know, I felt as if I'd known that little girl for years and years and years.

"She seemed just like the best little pal a man could have. We talked—oh, about any old thing. I sort of felt at home with her. So she did with me. She told me so. But it was me that did most of the talking. Only, what d'you think? We never bothered to ask each other's names. That was the funny part. I'd told her all about me being in a shop before the War—Lace, forward—and how I thought of having a shot at in Canada, p'raps, and all that sort of rot. Miles I'd yapped to her; even about my mother dying when I was a nipper. . .

"I wonder the girl wasn't bored stiff. I can't make out now why she wasn't. However, as I say, they might never have named this child N or M for all she was given to hear about *that*.

"Fact was, I clean forgot about names until I took her home—she's got two rooms in one of those big old-fashioned houses in a street off Baker Street. Then, as I said good night to her on the doorstep, I said, 'Oh, by the way, who do I ask for tomorrow?'

"She said, 'Coming tomorrow?'

"I said, 'Well, you told me it was your three days' leave, and I thought p'raps you'd come for a walk'—thinking to myself that I might be able to raise another quid or so for meals from some man at the Regent Palace, which I was.

"'Oh,' she said, with a little sort of laugh. 'Rightoh. And I haven't told you, of course, my name's Robinson,' she said as she went into the house; big dark hall, it seemed to swallow her up.

"I said, 'Brown's mine,' and off I went—and I couldn't simply get the little thing out of my head all night, and what a jolly little chum she was. Don't laugh at me, Miss Olwen; no, I know you're not really laughing, but I am, I can tell you. 'They laugh last who laugh laughs,' as that chap says at the Hippodrome.

"Next morning I was round at that house so early that I hadn't the nerve to ring the bell. I had to patrol the street for another half an hour before I rang.

"'Miss Robinson?' says I to the old girl who opened the door, but before she could answer I could hear the little girl herself singing out over the banisters, 'Hullo, I think I know that voice! Come up, Mr. Brown—'

"I legged it up to the first floor. Her sitting-room door was open; well, in I went, and there I got a nasty one."

Here Mr. Brown stopped to draw a breath, to finish his cooling tea, and to offer a cigarette to Olwen, listening with all her ears. There is no audience to a love-story so intent and so satisfactory as the girl to whom one has been attracted. Curiosity as to her supplanter burns in the breast of the woman whether or no she had been attracted to the man; curiosity made of varied elements—sympathy is one, and competition is one, and the undying yearning to compare notes is another. . .

Little Mr. Brown went on.

"Well, it was a pretty room, full of sun in the morning. Pretty coloured curtains and cushions about; and lots of flowers and that yellow bobbly thingummybob scented stuff—mimosa. And then. . . Her in the middle of it all—*all different*. . .

"I stopped dead and stared at her, never even saying good morning. Miss Olwen, I can tell you it was a shock to me.

"Last night, you see, I'd left her looking like a saucy little tomboy in that khaki working kit of hers with a cap the same as my own on her head and a black-and-white badge of the R. F. C. on her shoulder, and those brown riding bags. . .

"This morning here she stood all in a dead-black frock, with a widow's hat on and a long black veil streaming away from her little face.

"I stared, I tell you. I saw the situation absobloominglutely changed, in one.

"'Good Lord,' I said, 'you've been married?'

"She opened her eyes at me and said, 'Why shouldn't I?'

"I looked at her, such a little woman in her girl's clothes, but taller than she seemed in t'other rig-out, and I said, 'I didn't know you were married. I thought you were a kid of a girl. A widow. You didn't tell me.'

"'You didn't ask me,' she says. 'You might have seen I wore a wedding-ring. Men never do seem to notice rings—or anything else, I can't think why.'

"I stood there like a silly ass and said, 'I never thought of you being married. I s'pose I only looked at your face—'

"And I suppose I'd been magging so hard all yesterday about myself that I hadn't given the girl a chance to put her life history across me!

"She told me then, all quickly as I stood there, that she'd been married last year to her cousin, just before he went out. He was in the Flying Corps. He crashed in France just three months after they'd been married. Then she joined this Women's Legion. (You know they're jolly particular who they let into it, Miss Olwen: have to have no end of refs. from *padres* and lawyers and people.) She threw herself into her job. . . She'd been working like a nigger ever since. . .

"All I could think to say was 'Well, this knocks me out.'

"She laughed and asked me why it should make any difference, her being Mrs. Robinson instead of Miss? She asked me if I didn't like her in those things she'd got on? She said, 'Most people think it's rather becoming, all this black.'

"It made her little face look like a wild rose coming out of a coal-bucket, but what could I say to her? I tell you I was so flummoxed I stood there like a stuck pig—I don't know what I said next; honest, I don't.

"So then she offered me cigarettes, and I took one in a sort of dream, and felt all over myself for matches. Couldn't find any.

"Only, then—

"D'you know what I found, Miss Olwen? Blessed if I didn't stick my fingers into my belt pocket here, and feel something soft. I brought it out. It was that little mascot of yours. She asked me quickly what it was.

"'Oh,' I said, 'something a girl put there once, to bring me luck,' and I stuck it back again.

"'Oh,' she said. I saw her looking at that pocket.

"Then she said, 'What about going for that walk we've heard so much about?'

"'Right you are,' I says, pulling myself together. 'I'm ready if you are, Mrs. Robinson.'

"Then she said, 'No; I'm not quite. I shall have to keep you five minutes, not longer.'

"She popped through a door at the other end of the room and left me gazing at a big photograph in a silver frame on her table with violets in front of it. 'Yours, JIM,' on it. Him, of course. Fine-looking chap in R. F. C. uniform. I didn't wonder she'd taken him. Anyhow, he'd had a short life and a merry; a topping time! Marrying *her*, and then getting shot down in action before he knew he was for it. I was envying him when the door opened and in she came again—

"By Jove, she had done a quick change in five minutes and no mistake!

"She'd got out of the widow's weeds again and into khaki the same as yesterday, except that there was nothing on her curls, and she'd put on a short skirt and little brown brogues and a pair of those silk stockings she bought yesterday; and she came straight up to me and said quietly, 'Now, look here—why were you all upset when you came in? What's put you out? My being a widow?'

"'No,' I said, straight. 'It wasn't just that, but never mind.'

"'Yes, let's have it out,' she said, and I looked at her standing there in her khaki, but somehow I only saw her in a frock again, and I thought to myself all in a rush, 'All right, you asked to have it out, and you shall,' and so I just blurted out, 'It was seeing you, and knowing all in a minute how much I wanted you myself—and remembering.'

"'Remembering what?' she says as sharp as a needle.

"And I said, 'My dear, I haven't a *bean*.'

"And I grabbed up my hat and gloves and I think I would have said 'Good-bye' and bolted.

"But she just looked at me so that I couldn't.

"Then she looked away and said, 'If beans are all that matter—!' and then she picked a couple of violets out of the vase by that photograph, and tucked them into her jacket, and, just like a kid, said, 'Jim always loved me to have a good time. Jim would like me to have everything I liked, I *know* he would—'

"And here's where the room seemed to go round and round until it steadied down with me holding her tight. . .

"Well, then, Miss Olwen—well, then, there we were; engaged! Or practically then," amended little Mr. Brown, his pink face deepening in hue. "It was hours after that that I began to grasp how little it mattered about my not having anything but debts to ask any girl to marry me on; why, great Scott, d'you know who she is? Her Uncle, her hubby's father, is old Jack Robinson of Robinson and Mott; he's got the biggest aeroplane-body business in the Midlands, and he, this Jim of hers—well, she's got all he was to have. He arranged it so. She was to marry again if she liked, and whom she liked. And—Well, she's a girl who might have her pick; apart from the money. Then there's all her money as well; and yet—yet—"

He paused for words just as the band at the other end of the tea-room got the upper hand of the buzz of talk and sent a lilt of insistent melody through the air above the parties.

"Fancy you fancying me" was the tune.

> *"Fancy you fancying me,*
> *I can fancy anybody fancying you,*
> *But fancy you fancying me."*

"Incidental music; jolly appropriate," laughed little Mr. Brown, happily. "What that girl could possibly see in your humble beats me. I expect most people who meet us thinks she's balmy—"

But Olwen, smiling and interested and sympathetically murmuring, was thinking again (secretly) of the Charm.

VIII

Rations and the Charm

"A dinner of herbs where Love is."

—Proverbs

If there is one thing that bores a man," gave out Captain Ross, in a voice like the clashing together of Tube lift-gates—a tone that he had adopted all that evening, since nothing seemed to be going right, "if there is one thing that bores a man stiff, it's when some woman starts in to '*Love*' him."

He paused to glance across the table at Olwen, gaily chattering with Mr. Ellerton.

"It don't matter what woman," pursued the young Staff-officer inexorably. "*Any* woman. If he's keen before, that chokes him dead off. He's not out for any of this Love-with-a-capital-L business that women are such nuts on. Once he's done the chasing, he's gotten all he wants out of it, I guess. Man's a hunter, Mrs. Cartwright."

"I know," cooed his hostess. Inwardly she exclaimed, "Dear Ass! . . . But is he going on like this for the whole of my party?"

Up to then Captain Ross had only spoken to her and to the other young Scotsman whom he had brought with him. At Olwen he had simply glowered. At Miss van Huysen on the other side he had not looked.

"What's Love?" he continued, still to Mrs. Cartwright. "It's an amusement. That's what it ought to be. An Episode. It's the Women who insist on spoiling it; taking it seriously. Nothing in this world is worth taking seriously; barring a man's job. . . What's woman? The Plaything of Man. And what's Marriage?"

It was, as he pronounced it, a word of one syllable.

"Marriage," he answered his own question, "is an idea that the sensible man looks at from every angle, and then cuts right out until he can't find anything better to do. If he is really a sensible man, he invariably can find it."

"Ah," uttered Mrs. Cartwright with the little appreciative laugh of one who hears for the first time an original thought brilliantly phrased.

But she wanted to be soothing; she was fond of Captain Ross. One does not sob out one's weakness on a man's shoulder once and think of him as a stranger thereafter. She had asked him to forget. She never forgot. . .

A pity he'd come in this absurd mood, she thought.

Her party, at her flat in Westminster, had arrived at the stage of the feast when tongues were loosed and the young guests were gossiping and chirruping in merry twos and threes.

Little Mr. Brown was beamingly loquacious in spite of the absence of his khakied *fiancée*, kept out of town that evening on late duty. Between Mr. Brown and the fresh-faced naval boy, Mr. Ellerton sat little Olwen Howel-Jones, enjoying herself without disguise and looking her very best. She was a girl who had "days"; this was one of them. Never had her glossy black hair "gone up" so well, or her face lighted up so vividly; never, against her pale skin, had her laughing mouth bloomed in such a carnation-red. Never had any dress suited her so well as that flapper's frock of succory-blue with touches of cream, and dull pink. It was the frock Mrs. Cartwright had worn once on Biscay beach; she had pressed it upon Olwen as she said good-bye at Les Pins, telling her it was a young girl's colour after all. There Olwen sat in it now, laughing and being talked to by two young men at once and looking a picture in it. . .

It was from this picture that Captain Ross's dark eyes looked so pertinaciously away, as with new sardonic energy he informed Mrs. Cartwright that by the time a man had learnt to handle women he'd learnt that their place in his life was not all that important that he wanted to handle them at all.

Mrs. Cartwright passed him the Sauterne.

"Thank goodness that there is at least enough to *drink*," she reflected with a quick whimsical glance about the well-cleared dishes on her supper-table that had held:

1. Remains of chicken, with an intolerable deal of rice and curry to a very little fowl.
2. Allotment potatoes.
3. A pound of Normandy butter bought that morning in Boulogne and brought over in Sergeant Tronchet's haversack.
4. Pease-pudding.
5. Beetroot. . .
6. Green salad.

Well, they'd seemed to enjoy what there was.

"Ah!" exclaimed Mrs. Cartwright, here catching a remark from over the table. "A penny from *you*, Mr. Brown!" And she pushed over to him a money-box with the Blue Cross upon it, known as "The Fine-box."

This claimed a penny from whomsoever entering Mrs. Cartwright's abode should make any allusion to a subject which she declared was now inadmissibly boring: namely, food. One met quite intelligent people who became hopelessly tedious about "recipes," "how they managed," and so on. Rations had to be; and catering, food-cards, and substitute foods. But why intensify the Unspeakable by unnecessary speaking about it? Hence this box.

She took Mr. Brown's penny (a fine for some cheese anecdote or other), rattled the box, and glanced, as usual without seeming to do so, at her other guests.

Next to young Ellerton sat a niece of her own; a pretty girl in grey and scarlet nursing kit; the red- and blue *artilleriste* uniform of Gustave Tronchet next; delighting the eyes of his *fiancée* opposite.

Agatha Walsh had taken off years, Mrs. Cartwright thought, since they had parted at Les Pins. In place of the "old-maid" look, she was acquiring that of the young and prosperous woman—her smile seeming not yet entirely her own, and she had a new gesture or two modelled on those of Madame Leroux, her aunt-to-be. Also, her speech was altered. Some one must have rallied her on her "English" habit of beginning every sentence with "Oh"—Mrs. Cartwright missed it as she caught fragments of Miss Walsh's talk to Jack Awdas, who sat on her left.

"Now could *you* tell me, Mr. Awdas, the really best sort of man's wrist watch? . . . I want to get a really *special* one for Gustave—it is his '*fête*' on Thursday. . . not time to engrave anything, I'm afraid. . . Ah, yes, if you could come with me on Monday, you and Miss van Huysen, to help choose! That would be so amiable of you—nice, I mean. So stupid of me. I *keep* putting in the French words for things always, now!

"Ah, a bracelet-watch like yours, that would be perfect. . .

"Was there a *cadeau de fiançailles*—let's see, what do you call it in English, an engagement present?"

And she put her carefully dressed head on one side as she inspected the watch that Jack Awdas, smiling, held out towards her. Jack was silent this evening, Mrs. Cartwright had noticed already, as she noticed every detail, still, of the young flyer's looks and manner. . . He was in some happy abstraction, she saw, worlds away from the brightly-lighted table thronged with these young people chattering over their grapes and oranges. . .

There was a light behind those horizon-blue eyes of his even when they were not turned upon the sweetheart at his other side. There was an undernote of something new and joyous in the tone of his voice as he spoke to her.

("What *d'you* think about it, girl?")

From the Sunburst Girl, as ever, a radiance seemed to emanate that was more than the effulgence of her white-and-golden dress. But she, too, was quieter than usual as she sat; now giving a little friendly smile to her hostess across Captain Ross and his dogmas, now leaning to the right and putting in a word about the matter of the engagement present.

("But, Bird-boy, if Miss Walsh *wants* it in platinum—!")

Now turning her wide eyes affectionately upon the girl friend opposite to her. Olwen was not flirting with the young sailor who talked so much and had so little to say beyond his "Bai Joves" and "Ha's"; she was only blooming in what Mr. Brown had already called "the sunshine of his smile"; she was also caught in and made beautiful by some of that happiness that flowed in a current about the table under the pink inverted parasol of lights, flowed from Golden and her Jack. . .

Golden and Jack. . . What pretty lover's secrets was between them now?

Still watching them covertly, Mrs. Cartwright could only wonder why, since it was possible for young human beings to be grown so big and beautiful—why in the name of a thousand pities did Nature turn out so many samples of the stunted, the plain, the commonplace? Must this well-matched pair stand for the exception rather than the rule? She watched them, and that scene of physical perfection which had so nearly brought Claudia Cartwright to shipwreck over a boy-lover was no longer her torment, but her comfort.

She had wept all her tears; she had tossed sleeplessly through all her hours of fierce rebellion; she had gone through the most agonizing ordeal of her woman's life. But thank God it was over now. . .

It was over! and her eyes travelled now to that which is a woman's only balm for such wounds as hers had been.

He sat, the master of the house, with a school-fellow between himself and Agatha Walsh. This school-fellow was sixteen, a year older but three inches shorter than young Keith Cartwright. Keith was already well over six foot. Coltish at present, with great wrists shooting ever too quickly beyond his cuffs, and feet that seemed four sizes too large for his ankles, but wait until he began to fill out! thought Claudia proudly. Her rightness of bone, her limbs, her suppleness had gone to her boys; Reggie, on a visit in the country, was just as good, but it was her elder son who seemed the child of her soul as well as of her body. He had her tastes, her impatiences. Her own ardour would presently be breaking into flame in his heart. She felt (as even the mute-bird mothers feel) that she at least would not fail to understand him. She smiled across the table into his face, pink and free of care, with its clear eyes, thick lashes (those were from his father's side), and the fruit-like, perfect oval that does not outlast twenty-five. She, the mother, faded; but she had set in these young plants and they were budding.

Keith's voice (or rather voices, for he himself never knew in what octave his words might break forth) came roughly but affectionately across the table to his mother.

"I say, mums! What about coffee—" so far in the bass, and now a treble squeak of "if you don't mind. Harrison says he's got to get back home, and I wanted to put on these new records"—relapse into the bass, "for him first? . . . Rightoh. . ."

They had coffee before they adjourned to the sitting-room. It was a low-ceilinged, soothing place with soft brown walls, low cushiony seats, a richly-glowing Persian rug, some brass, and a few pictures. Mrs. Cartwright's standing-desk at which she worked had been wheeled away into a corner near an old oak coffer. Its place was usurped by the tall stand of a gramophone. About this the young people clustered, talking "records" . . .

"I say, have you got that topping thing of George Graves's—?"

"Not a talking one; Miss Walsh wanted something *pretty*—"

"Well, what about 'The Naughty Sporty Girl,' Miss Olwen?"

"Bai Jove, did you hear him in—?"

"Heaps of room to dance, if—"

"Look out, please," said Keith Cartwright, lugging at a heavy flat packet; and presently he put on a loud "selection" from some revue.

It was under cover of this music that Captain Ross who had been carrying on with his Scots friend a conversation that seemed to consist of variations on the letter R, suddenly left him in the middle of a question as to the "Pairrrrrrrrrrsonnel" at the Honeycomb, and came up to Awdas, who was making his way to a vacant place on the arm of the couch whereon Golden was sitting.

With some force, Captain Ross gripped him by the upper arm. In the tone of one who has been for hours storing up some accumulated grievance, he muttered, "Say, Jack. I've got to have a word with you. *Now*," he added, peremptorily, "Come out here, will you?"

IX

Champagne and the Charm

*"Here's to the Wings of Love,
May they never moult a feather."*

—Toast

Almost roughly he dragged Jack Awdas into the little entrance lobby, where, under a couple of mounted ibex heads, a carved oak chest was piled up with khaki caps, gloves, and British warms. The red silk-shaded hanging-lamp glowed down on the two young men reflected in a convex mirror on the other wall; Captain Ross's black head was therein enlarged until his figure had the proportions of a tadpole; his face showed the expression of a deeply-injured man, of one whom his friend had "let in" for something uncalled-for and gratuitous.

"See here," he began abruptly. "I've got to tell you. There's something I know that I don't know if I'm supposed to know."

Jack Awdas gave his husky boy's laugh.

"Well, dash it, there are a few things that a Captain on the staff is supposed to know after all. '*Wearing red things round his hat, he's employed at this and*—'"

"Don't rag, Jack. This thing's about *you*." Then, almost violently, "I saw you this morning."

That red light glowed on a change in the fair one of the two faces as the young flying officer looked down upon his friend, "I say, d'you mean—?"

"Yep. I saw you."

Awdas, still startled, broke into another laugh. "Sorry, Ross. I didn't mean to steal a march upon you, you know. But look here, old thing, how the devil did you see me? You weren't there. Nobody was, ex—"

"I was in my office. Saw you all right from the window there."

"The deuce you did! . . . I say, if you let it get known about the Honeycomb, that you've got a view like that, you'll have some of the Mandarins snaffling that office of yours for themselves."

Captain Ross did not smile as he returned curtly, "There must be a dozen of our windows looking, straight out on to the entrance to the Adelphi Chapel."

Then a broad grin overspread Jack Awdas's fair face. "Well, is that all, old thing?" he asked, tucking his handkerchief up his sleeve and making as though he would turn back to the door, through which there rollicked, but subdued, the strains of "Me and My Girl" put on very quickly. "Weren't you going to congratulate me, Ross?"

Ross growled, "I guess a fellow doesn't want to put his foot into it by throwing about congratulations for a secret marriage—"

"Secret? Good Lord, nothing secret about it," the other young officer took up quickly, as he sat down for a moment on the edge of that heaped-up chest. "Look here! We haven't told anybody about it because there simply hasn't been time yet. When we came here tonight we were going to tell you. We wouldn't put off Mrs. Cartwright; we were going to come as if nothing had happened, and then make a wedding party of it; tell you all, first thing. But how've I been able to get a word in? First there was our gallant ally the Sergeant that everybody had to make a fuss over in French, and then there was young Brown and his widow, *that* announcement! and then there was you—"

"*Me?*"

"Yes, you yarning away about what women were and what they weren't, and if so why not. There hasn't been time to get a word in, man. Secret?" He laughed joyously. "Why, I expect Golden's just telling Mrs. Cartwright all about it now." The bridegroom crossed his long legs and grinned up into the unresponsive face of this bachelor standing before him. "Yes; this morning! I didn't see what there was to wait for. . . here, have one of mine. Golden thought it was a bit quick, but then so she did when I wanted to be engaged to her, after three whole blooming days. Thought it was *sudden*! That's—why, it's nearly four months ago. Anyway I said to myself yesterday, 'This engagement's been dragging on long enough; looks like lasting for ever'—so I got the license right away, wired for my mother, broke it to Golden's governor, who has always been very decent, and—Well, they were the only guests as far as I knew, never guessing that you and the rest of the Honeycomb were gazing from the windows at my girl in her veil and orange-blossoms. So will you congratulate me on my marriage?"

The face of the finest judge of marriage in Europe was a study.

FOR WEEKS PAST NOW, FROM the windows of cell 0638 at the Honeycomb, Captain Fergus Ross had been accustomed to glance up from his desk and to observe through the window various taxis, cars, or broughams drive up to the door of the Adelphi Chapel.

He had seen young people and their friends alight in ceremonial kit. He had watched them go in; and he had seen young couples presently come out again, sometimes under arches of swords, sometimes under those of crutches and walking-sticks, sometimes in a simple shower of confetti. No doubt these sights had confirmed him in his misogynistic broodings.

This very morning he had attracted the attention of his colleague, Major Leefe, to the window, and, pointing down upon a hurrying young figure in khaki with a sword, had announced with a grim and pitying smile, "There goes another good man to his doom."

Even as he pronounced the last word (which he did as though it were the German for "stupid"), he observed the hurrying figure below to raise its head for a moment as it looked quickly around.

He had recognized Jack Awdas.

Five minutes afterwards he had seen Golden in all her bridal glory, step out of a taxi with Mr. van Huysen.

You could have knocked Captain Ross down with a feather.

What was everybody coming to? he had pondered irritably ever since. *All* his friends. . .

"I CONGRRRATULATE—" HE BEGAN STIFFLY, but at that very moment a clamour broke out above the music in the room they had left.

"Where is he?"

"Fetch him in—"

"Fancy bolting like that—" came the muffled cries.

The door was flung suddenly open as Brown, Ellerton, the Highlander, Sergeant Tronchet and the Master of the House burst suddenly into the lobby.

"Here he is!"

"Now, you rascal—"

"Dark horse, what?"

"Come in, you dog—"

"Ah, *farceur*! Félicita—"

"Bai Jove, trying to hush it up—"

"Mr. Awdas, I say. Mr. Awdas—"

"Ah, would you—"

"Monsieur de l'Audace!"

"Priceless!"

Among them they almost carried Jack's Herculean young form back into the sitting-room.

Captain Ross followed.

The golden head of the Sunburst Girl towered above the heads of Olwen and of Miss Walsh as they pressed upon her their enthusiastic good wishes. Laughing, flushed, sparkling, she was giving her version of that dilatory courtship of Jack's; while Mrs. Cartwright in the corner by that desk of hers, was hunting in some *cache* of hers for something (to wit, the last drop of Bubbly she possessed).

"Here's more surprises about your English ways," the American bride was laughing. "Here's this Bird-boy of mine—well, you all know the quick and sudden start of our engagement! There was father and I thinking maybe it wouldn't matter so much provided we had a sensible time to get to know one another in after say a year! Then yesterday Jack gets suddenly scared that we'll both be grey and rheumatic fossils if we aren't married half an hour from then. . . Say, Olwen? What could I say? I don't know how he does it—it's mesmerism or a charm, I guess, for when once Jack takes it into his head—"

Here the laughter and cheering of the men broke out. The Master of the House was seen to be advancing, carrying at the full length of his young arms a tray of glasses. Mrs. Cartwright rose from the chest, smilingly holding a gold-topped bottle in either hand.

"Who's going to open these?"

Already Mr. Brown had whisked a skirt of his tunic under his arm and was slipping his sapper's knife from its swivel. "Stand from under!" sang out the little second lieutenant as pop! went a cork. "Right! I'll fill 'em, Mrs. C. I'm the next starter for the matrimonial stakes, after the giddy bridegroom. Out o' the way, Ross! Don't take up the earth. . . Invited out to supper, and staying to wedding-breakfast, eh? . . . Here's yours, Miss Olwen; a bridesmaid, are you? . . . No, you don't, Ellerton; *I'm* booked for best man. . . I'm going to have one from everybody. . . *After* you've finished with my feet, Ross—"

Captain Ross, glaring above his glass at the group about that tall and resplendent bridal pair, found his bad temper of the day culminating in a very curious decision.

He was going to leave directly he'd finished this glass of champagne in which they toasted the young Awdases. And he was going to take with him, Olwen Howel-Jones. He was going to see her home. He was; not that gibbering idiot Brown, who was engaged anyway, nor that hopeless ass Ellerton, that Naval outfitter's dummy; no fear. Most certainly not. As for that fellow Jack, what the Hades did he mean by looking as if he were the only man on God's earth whose wedding-night it had ever been or ever could be? Was Jack Awdas the first young fool who'd ever managed to get himself marked down and married by a girl? . . . The whole party seemed to be one confounded whirl of tomfoolery. . . Well, he, Ross, was leaving, and taking that chit home. (It was high time.) Drive her all the way, too; because he'd got something to say to her. Straight away he'd say to her, "Now, see here, damn it, there's going to be no more of *this*, there's been enough of it, and I won't have it."

Just that was what he intended to say, and—

At this instant the Master of the House, in the treble one of his voices, called, "I say, Captain Ross, please—they're asking for *you*."

The telephone-bell had rung a moment before, and Keith had run out of the room to answer it.

The telephone was just outside; Captain Ross went to it. . .

In a minute or so he returned. He was seen to draw his hostess aside, to murmur something to her. Mrs. Cartwright nodded quickly. Then he went up for the second time that evening to catch hold, with his one remaining hand, of the arm of Jack Awdas. The young flying officer gave a jerk of his fair head; a whisper to Golden, another to his hostess. . . Before the rest of the group had realized that they were going, those two, Ross and Awdas, were out of the flat, down the one flight of steps and out into the clear moonlight above Westminster.

Then, composedly and carelessly, Mrs. Cartwright slipped her arm through Golden's, and turned to her other guests.

"I'm so sorry to be inhospitable, dear people, but I think it would be better if you went, now!" she announced, smilingly. "There's heaps of time. You see Captain Ross gets the warning from the Honeycomb half an hour before any of us, and they've just rung him up to say—"

"Raid on!" exclaimed Keith's highest squeak.

"Probably, he thinks," said his mother with a shrug. "Tiresome people these Huns are; *no* sense of fitness. Well—finish your bubbly and off with you."

There was a scurrying of the women-folk to get their wraps from Mrs. Cartwright's bedroom; a chorus of comment half exasperated, half amused. Raids were less of a terror by night than a source of deep boredom to Londoners by this time. . . They had all been in them before; they knew (with luck) just what would happen from the first whistling signals of the "Take cover" to the "All clear."

"*Bother* them," exclaimed little Olwen, disgusted. "In the middle of the party for *you*, Golden!"

The men, coated and capped, thronged the tiny lobby, waiting. . . Mr. Brown and Captain Ross's friend would escort Mrs. Cartwright's niece to her hotel. Young Mr. Ellerton was all eagerness to see Miss Howel-Jones all the way home again. Agatha's sergeant had secured a taxi to take his *fiancée* Victoria-wards; they offered a lift to Golden, imagining that the young bride would now return to her father's house in Grosvenor Gardens. But in the midst of the little bustle of departure Mrs. Cartwright had given a gentle clasp to the American girl's arm.

"Don't go," she said softly. "I am going to put you up, Golden. You are to stay with me. He told me he wanted you to stay with me tonight—"

As she finished speaking, the first warning maroon went off with a bang.

X

HER BRIDAL NIGHT

*"An airy devil hovers in the sky
And pours down mischief."*

—Shakespeare

P resently the growling of the guns began to reverberate over London. First came the far-off rumbling that is felt rather than heard; the hint whereat the mothers of households drop book or work to exclaim, "Hush! . . . It *is*! . . ."

"Don't think so, dear," return the men folk; to retract a couple of minutes later with an "Ah, yes; blast 'em. Here they are. I'll bring the kids down."

Then came the long, nerve-irritating pause.

In Mrs. Cartwright's Westminster flat there were no children to cause those anxieties with which the enemy had made himself more detested than by any legitimate act of war. Her son, as he would have wished you to note, was hardly a kid to be roused from his sleep. As he strolled back from the staircase window, hands in pockets, his manner was nonchalant in the extreme. He was no callow scout, either, to wait in a police-station for that thrilling moment when he should be allowed out to sound the bugle-call.

"Like the gramophone on again?" he suggested (luckily in the more manly of his two voices). "It would drown that boring noise for you."

"I don't think so, darling, thanks," said his mother. A pause; silence. "They may not get through after all. Won't you go to bed, Keith?"

"Oh, I don't know"—the over-grown lad was already dropping with sleep. "Wouldn't you women rather I stopped up with you?"

Golden and Mrs. Cartwright exchanged a tiny smile before the mother said, "Do you know, I don't think we'll stop up. I am going to show Mrs. Awdas to her room now. You do as you like."

The Master of the House moved from the traditional attitude, flat back against the sitting-room mantelpiece, feet wide apart on the Persian rug. "Oh, well, I don't see why I should hang about, waiting up for those wretched Huns, either," he pronounced, his pink mouth twisting sidewards as he strangled his yawns. "I'll turn in too, if you're sure you don't mind."

And he walked across the sitting-room to hold the door open for his mother and her guest to precede him.

Golden, who considered this English schoolboy "perfectly lovely," gave him a smiling good night over her shoulder.

"Good night, Precious," whispered his mother.

Very prettily the boy returned her kiss as he responded, "Good night, old Bean."

He turned out the lights behind him and betook himself to his room on the left of the corridor that skirted the flat. On the right were Reggie's room and his mother's; her old Belgian *femme de ménage* came in by the day. Her younger son's room was unoccupied tonight, but it was her own bedroom that Mrs. Cartwright gave up to Golden Awdas. Here she left her to undress, promising to come back.

She did not think that Golden would sleep at once.

She wandered back to turn up the lights again in the sitting-room, still full of cigarette smoke, and with its atmosphere still vibrant as if with young voices and laughter. And as she set chairs into their places, plumped up cushions, and, putting her hand carefully through the curtains, set a window open and wheeled her standing-desk back ready for her morning's work tomorrow, she thought smilingly of those guests of hers; all so many years behind her, in age, in emotion, in experience. She delighted in them, these young men who felt themselves masters of all wisdom, these girls on the right side of a barrier. . . The passing of it had been an agony to Claudia Cartwright.

It did not take all women in the same way, she reflected. Many went through life so entirely satisfied with inessentials; so half-awake.

Most had never been lovers or had lovers. But those who had—!

No death of a sweetheart in early youth, no cruel jilting, no bitter matrimonial experience, nothing, nothing! could compare with the poignant, crushing, rending pain of those years when Youth and Love slip away from the woman. It is a long black tunnel of misery from which she emerges (having lost much but accepted, bowed her head, folded her hands) into the grey afternoon of Life.

And then—Heaven's blessing on the maternal sense that is rich in any real woman's character, even if she never has a child at all! For it is this that comes to her aid; and she spreads it out over the girls and the men she knows; caring, helping, sympathizing with all their love emotions (or lack or them).

Henceforward everything must be vicariously felt by her. She must live in the lives of her children; in their professions and interests; she must love through her young friends. . . Little Olwen. . . Golden. . . As she thought of these Untried, their friend smiled over a tag of verse that came into her mind with the image that seemed its illustration.

"Oh, tarnish late on Wenlock Edge, Gold that I never see!
Lie long, high snowdrifts on the hedge, That will not shower on me."

Prayer, she thought, can take odd forms—well, this was hers for the happiness of her girl-friends.

Golden, she thought, would be in bed by now.

A nearer growling of guns, from the north, she judged, sounded as she tapped at the door.

"Come!" called the charming un-English voice.

Mrs. Cartwright entered her own familiar room with its known mingling of kuss-kuss, rose, and orris scent. The toilet silver, the Indian numnah on the floor, her husband's sword and sash over the bookshelf, and the enlarged photograph of him laughing under the black, semi-lune shadow of his solar-topi—these things were Claudia's background. Her eyes opened upon them each morning. Tonight they all seemed suddenly new to her. . .

It was because they were now a background to this radiant stranger in her room. Out of that cloud of loosened gold on her pillow there looked the face of a beauty as rare as any that had ever been kissed awake by a fairy prince.

"Oh, my dear," exclaimed Mrs. Cartwright, involuntarily. "How lovely you are, Golden; how lovely!"

Paradoxical enough it might seem to some women, but this woman thanked Heaven it was a girl so beautiful who had supplanted her, or rather, to whom she had relinquished that beautiful boy. She could not have endured to see Jack choose a bride unworthy in body or mind, least of all one who might be as the ordinary "nice" pretty girl often is, a bundle of mere sentiment and frigidity. To Golden she could give him. Actually she had brought them together. And now it was to his best woman-friend that the young flier confided his sweetheart.

On this, of all nights! Their bridal night!

Mrs. Cartwright could have laughed outright at the strangeness of it. Jack's wedding-night!

She remembered that other night, months ago, when in a French hotel bedroom she had outwatched the hours with a nightmare-haunted man. In the very attitude that she had taken then, she sat down now on the edge of this other bed, tucking the eider-down about her as she began chatting, quietly and cheerfully, with his bride. Through speech and pause alike the elder woman's mind was echoing with memories. It was Jack Awdas's husky voice that she heard, clearly as when it was his face upon a pillow that she watched. How feverishly he had muttered, "That's why I always shout in my dream. . . I was falling, falling, and calling out to my observer. . . We *were* pals! . . . I don't think it could ever be exactly like that with a girl."

She, Claudia, had told him, "The girl is more to you or less to you, but not the same."

And now she lay in her beauty, the girl; that worshipped "girl" of Jack's. And this—*This!*—was her bridal night.

Guns! The nearer guns were uttering now. Bark after vicious bark set windows rattling. The racket died away only to break out afresh. . .

In an interval, Golden said suddenly. "Jack told me what a really fine friend you'd always been to him. And, d'you know? I've always known I should be friends with you."

"Have you?"

"Why, yes. I said so before we left Les Pins. . . D'you remember, I saw you for a moment that very first evening, sitting with him in the lounge? But who would have thought where we should all be tonight?" mused the girl, lifting the throat that rose so pillar-wise and white above the silken edge of a night-dress of her hostess's. "In London, and me married to the Bird-boy, and an air raid going on outside. But do I have to keep you up this way? You're all dressed and everything: I'm so afraid you'll be dead tired."

"Not I. I shouldn't be able to sleep if I did undress. There'll be another hullabaloo on in another minute, I expect," said Mrs. Cartwright, cheerfully. The sound of the guns had died down for a moment. "And—well, it won't be the first time, Golden, that I've stayed up with somebody who could not sleep. . . Ah, they're starting again."

Yes, they were starting again. . .

Throughout London, nurses in hospitals set their teeth angrily over

BERTA RUCK

patients whom they had hoped to drag back to life, out of the horrors of shock. Other nurses, in maternity homes, could have wrung dismayed hands over this terror added to Nature's ordeal. And in operating rooms the white-coated surgeons cursed below their breath the hellish interruption that might cause a slip of the hand or the instrument and leave all care, all science vain. These things were the danger and the damage; not merely the bomb dropped at random; the crumbling masonry. These, and the mischief to countless little children, disturbed past soothing now, with tender nerves a-fret, heads gathered to their parents' shoulders. Little heads! They ought never to have been visited by such questions as punctuated the din in homes where baby voices asked, *"Was that a gun or a bomb, daddy?"* . . . *"Where was that firing from?"* . . . *"If a raid came right on Billy's cot, mamsie, what would you do?"*

Then there came to their ears a new sound—the gutteral, syncopated drone of twin engines—beating over the roofs.

"Ah! There's one got through, then," said Mrs. Cartwright. Following on her words came the outburst of nearer gunnery, to which the whole house seemed to shake; in twos and threes—*"Brroum—brrroum!—brrroum!—brroum!—brrrroum!"* then a more ponderous crash than all.

Then, a light tap at the door and a voice in two keys, calling with zest, "Mums! Are you all right? Is Mrs. Awdas? There's nothing to be frightened at really."

"No; all right, Keith darling. You're all right, aren't you?"

"Top-hole. I say, did you hear that last? I'm sure it was a dud shell just outside on the pavement, so—"

"Keith, you're to *promise* you won't go outside until they've gone," called his mother, starting up. "Go to your room!"

"Oh. . . all right, then. I'll nip out as soon as the all-clear goes though." The Master of the House pattered off down the corridor to his room.

"I wonder if any others will get through tonight," said Mrs. Cartwright, listening.

Golden, who had not yet lost any of her kin or seen them broken in this War, suggested that these German flyers were, anyway, brave.

"So are other beasts of prey," returned the Englishwoman.

Again the firing rolled away in the distance, following the raiders' course. . .

But a thoughtfulness seemed to have fallen upon the wakeful girl. For the first time she had given a little shiver at the sound of that receding turmoil.

"Now I hope it isn't too cowardly of me, what I'm going to say," she began, suddenly, turning on her rounded elbow. "But I can't help thinking of boys flying up there in the dark, in the teeth of guns like that. . . *He* was doing it, of course, until he crashed. My Bird-boy! . . . He's always glad when he goes up; he was grousing to me, as you call it, yesterday, because he hadn't been off the ground for a week. . . but, oh, Mrs. Cartwright! do you know, *I'm* real glad, just for tonight, that Jack can't be up."

Mrs. Cartwright smiled at her, answering her in two words that seemed ordinary enough.

"I know."

But they meant, to the elder woman, something very different from the gentle agreement that they conveyed to the girl.

Claudia Cartwright heard again the hasty whisper with which Jack had taken leave of her those hours ago. "I want *Her* to stay here," he told her. "I'd want you to take care of her."

At the time Mrs. Cartwright had been paralyzed with surprise. Golden Awdas to stay with her? Why?

Why on earth should Jack leave her—tonight of all nights? She, the bride, had seemed to see nothing stupefying in his action in going off with Captain Ross when the warning came through.

But Mrs. Cartwright knew that Captain Ross had his own duty, not anything in which Jack must help him. Jack was free, she'd heard, until ten o'clock tomorrow morning. It was not Jack's pidgin to do anything until then. . . Therefore why in the name of all that was extraordinary hadn't he taken his bride away when the others all went? Why hadn't he taken her off home with him, or to the hotel where he put up, or wherever it was?

Then, very quickly, she'd seen why.

One of the cleverest soldiers of her acquaintance had already told Claudia that, could the true history of these campaigns ever be written, it would read not merely like *another version* of the War, but like *another War*. She guessed how many things planned never happen and how many things happen that were never planned, and how few of either get into the papers. Oh, the difference between the published account and the story of the man who was there! Tomorrow would see a report of this raid, which would say nothing at all of the men whose duty. . . it had *not* been to beat back the raiders. It was *not* Jack's duty to go up that night. It was his duty not to go.

But—

Up there he was now, she knew it. Up there, in the darkness and the din! Perhaps over the house now, the joyous eaglet-boy, fighting those circling hawks. . . now, at this moment! . . .

She knew it in her heart.

And, thinking of that, she sat there smiling at the white and golden bride who was glad to think of her boy safe from this danger at least. . . There was no reason why Golden should know it too.

The woman he had loved continued to watch with the girl he loved, during her bridal night.

XI

His Bridal Night

"Tell me not, Sweet, I am unkind
That from the nunnery
Of thy chaste breast and quiet mind
To war and arms I fly.

Yet this inconstancy is such
As you too shall adore,
I could not love thee, Dear, so much,
Loved I not Honour more."

—Lovelace

Mrs. Cartwright's intuition had been perfectly right.
Jack Awdas was up during the raid over London. He was up to some purpose, as his comrades and three other airmen (prisoners of war) could tell.

But here is his own version of the affair, as told by him, on the following day, to his young wife.

"When that warning came through, you see, I felt that it was for me too. I don't know what my own idea was when I went off with old Ross. He said, 'What the something do *you* want to come along for?' I said, 'All right; shut up.' I didn't know, you know. Queer, wasn't it? All I knew was that I had got to go too, instead of bringing you back here as I'd thought. . . I'd *got* to leave you, girl."

She listened, leaning back now in his happy arms. She listened, all eyes. His own blue eyes had been deep in hers, locked to them with the lover's look that is another embrace. But now he took them from hers. He glanced aside and away, and into Jack Awdas's eyes there crept back one of those two other looks which were characteristic of him. It was the "yonderly" look that sees what is not for all to see.

"Somehow," he said, "I knew I just couldn't stay with you. I'd got to go up, and Lord only knew how it was going to be managed, or how I was going to get out of the 'drome in time, even. There wasn't a taxi in sight. Ross and I walked on to the Honeycomb, or half ran, half walked. Going up Whitehall he said, 'Jack, you darned fool, go back; what's wrong?' I said, 'Nothing; shut up, old thing, if you don't mind.'

"In the courtyard of the Honeycomb we nearly ran into a tiny little dispatch-rider girl with a side-car. I didn't know until just now that it was young Brown's widow that he was going to marry, that we'd heard about at dinner! She'd brought some man in, and was just starting up; I said to her, 'Where are you for?' She said, 'Home! and time, too.' 'Where's home?' said I, and I believe she told me it was Baker Street. . . But just as I was asking her I began to see what I'd got to do. It began to come to me then, d'you see?

"I said to the girl, 'Look here, I'm sorry, you can't go home yet. You've got to drive me out to my 'drome, and I told her where that was. Half an hour's ride into the country. We did it in less. I told her I'd got to get to my 'bus, and that she'd got to go hell-for-leather; and we did it in less. . .

"You see, I'd got to take that machine across at ten o'clock next morning. Had to: duty. (You knew about that, of course.) But if I could only get her up a few hours before that! I thought. . . There she was, waiting. There were dozens of our chaps up already, I knew. Here was I—and I couldn't stand it, somehow. Not last night. Just because it *was* that night. It would have spoilt it. You see, don't you? Yes; I thought you would. I wouldn't think of you then; except to think 'It's *her* I'm going to give Them.' I don't even know what 'them' meant—(This sounds such rot, girl, that I couldn't possibly tell anybody else, but there you are. . . I won't kiss you again until I've told you the end of this.)

"Well, we chased along the roads in the moonlight at the deuce of a lick, coming round the corners on the edge of one wheel. Just imagine it! Me and that side-car, and that girl of Brown's—No more idea it was his girl—! She's only about so-size; I thought she was a kid of fifteen like one of those little brown messengers with pigtails that go trotting about the corridors, and by Jove, I tried to *tip* her! I did! I didn't know. I hadn't any silver on me after all those tips and things in the afternoon, after we were married. I just lugged out my note-case and got out a couple of John Bradburys—the last. I stuffed 'em into her hand. 'Here, thanks awfully!' I said; 'do buy yourself a hat-pin or some sweets or something—' She did laugh! 'You won't?' I said—she stuffing them back for all she was worth. 'Oh well, sorry if I've made a break,' I said, 'can't stop to explain now—thanks awfully—Good night!' and up I legged it to the gates, holding those notes in my hand all the time. . .

"You know, I hadn't my papers or orders or anything! Neck, wasn't it? *I* didn't know what on earth I was going to ask the Adjutant! Sometimes when you want a thing it's a good deal better not to ask. . . just go and grab it, and explain afterwards.

"Well, then I had a bit of luck.

"Scurrying through the gates, I ran straight into Dashmold himself; that is the Adjutant. (A stinker on duty.)

"'Ha, Awdas!' he said, 'can't stop now, the Colonel's just rung me up from his house. See you in half an hour.'

"'Rightoh,' I said, and dashed ahead, thanking my lucky stars—for this only left me with our assistant adjutant, always a bit of an ass. I chased off to the orderly-room and found him.

"'Hello, Awdas,' he squeaked. (Voice rather like George Clarke at the Empire; pink and white face.)

"'I suppose you know there's a raid on?' I said. 'I've come for that 'bus.' He said, 'What about your papers?' I said, 'Yes, hand 'em over, that's all right. I've just this moment spoken to Dashmold.' (So I had; just said 'Rightoh' to him.) 'Those are my orders,' I said, 'in that pile there. Chuck 'em over. Thanks.' So that was *that*. . .

"Then off I streaked to the Officers' Quarters to get into my things. Not a soul there. You know. It's a long corridor with a row of little cubicles not much bigger than the dressing-rooms at the swimming bath. Just hold a camp-bed and a chest of drawers and a row of pegs. . . By Jove, if some thief hadn't pinched my kit. Some one got into the first that was handy, I suppose, when they got the warning. I'll have his blood for that, later. So in I nipped to one cubicle after another. All empty. I thought I wasn't going to find a stitch. However! At last I came to one; there it was, a lovely outfit all hanging ready on the pegs. Man called Jackson. He'd got leave. Well! I plunged into his coat and overalls and flying-cap and goggles, all the lot! quicker than anything I've ever done in my life. I remember I'd got those blessed pound notes still in my hand. I shoved them into my teeth while I dressed. Then down I doubled to the hangars.

"About a dozen of the ac emmas—those are mechanics, dear—were waiting about there. I switched the lights on.

"There was my 'bus all ready for tomorrow morning—ah, a beauty! Yes, the one you saw on Thursday, that I'd been making the trial flight in; the single-seater Scout monoplane. I'd always fancied her. She ran a little light, but I liked that. I'd got her balanced; just right for me. I.T. All ready, tanks filled up and everything. The gun was on her, but— Dash it! No ammunition, of course. That did me.

"Then I saw Smithers. (He's the Quartermaster's nephew.) I said, 'Smithers! Jump to it. . . here you are, take this' (the last two quid I had on me, that Brown's widow refused), 'and get me two drums of ammunition. How? *I* don't know. Somehow. Off with you and give you five minutes to get back in.' Off he streaked. Then I said to the others, 'Now, you men, get a move on. Get her out.' They wheeled her out of the hangar and into the moonlight.

"Oh! I nearly forgot to tell you all about something, though. Even at the time I noticed it. (The sort of funny little thing you do notice when you aren't really thinking of anything except getting on with what's on.) It was tied round the joy-stick! You know, dear, your bit of ribbon that I've always kept as a mascot since that day on the beach. I'd tied it on just before the trial flight. It's always been on, you know, on whatever 'bus I've been flying. I meant it to, until you were mine, and then I was going to give it back to you, Girl, because it wouldn't matter which of us two had the Luck *then*; it would be the same thing.

"I looked at it once as I was waiting, and I remember thinking to myself quickly, in the sort of rum way, like you think of things in dreams, 'By Jove, I suppose that's the most precious prize I've owned, up to now.'

"But after that I just looked at my watch and stamped as I stood waiting for those blighted drums. I'd given Smithers five minutes. Lord, if he couldn't do it. I—It seemed a thundering important thing to me, you see: the most important I'd ever had to do. You do know why, don't you? You do understand?"

Golden's great eyes upon his face were as full of understanding as the tone of her simple "yes." Her young husband gave a short, contented nod, then he went on:

"Well! So then I saw Smithers, coming running back. 'Got 'em?' I shouted. 'Right, sir!' he shouted back. Up he came with those two drums he'd got (God knows *how*). I fixed one on the gun myself, and put the other handy.

"'Start her up,' I said. I climbed in, and the boys swung the propeller. I gave 'em 'Contact,' and then I was up and off. . . Hadn't been off the earth for a week. And, by the way, I hadn't gone up to fight since the time I crashed.

"Yes, of course, it was a perfectly idiotic thing to do. I hadn't got the night's Orders any more than I'd orders to go and stand by with Ross, where you thought I was. I didn't know if we were fighting with guns or planes or both, nor where nor when nor anything about it. However!—.

"What did London look like from up there? Oh, just all dark, you know: like a great turned-up field below you, with the river winding through it. What you do see very plainly is that silver ribbon of the Thames, reflecting the light of the sky.

"You think the sky's big, don't you? Well, it isn't so big when you can bumble into your own barrage at any moment, or when a Hun you can neither see nor hear lets fly suddenly. But I could see shrapnel breaking away to the south-west, so I just beetled off after that. . .

"Then I'm dashed if those three blighters in their big plane didn't nearly run me down. Yes, I s'pose she'd be the plane you and Mrs. Cartwright heard over the house. Was she missing it all?"

"Missing?" repeated the fascinated Golden. "Why, how could I know?"

"Well, anyway, she was somewhere over that part of town. They'd jumped the barrage and got in. I circled round, climbing all I knew, and then I guess they dropped those two bombs to lighten themselves.

"The searchlight fellows down below were dazzling away to beat the band. You could see nothing but jumping flashes all over the show, putting 'em off their aim. Me too. Perfectly poisonous. I cursed, but I knew I'd no business there. . .

"Well, that Scout of mine could climb as quick as any Gotha built yet, so I gave them twenty rounds or so right into 'em. They didn't like that, so I gave 'em some more. They fired back, but nothing to hurt. The next go, they decided to give it up, I think. They headed for the south-west again. Evidently they were going to chance the barrage. Bon! Anyway, if they were, so was I.

"And oh, Girl, if you knew how I wanted to get them! I wanted to get those raiding Huns, if I had to chase them to the coast and across and right to Berlin. As Ross says, 'I wanted to let 'em have it where Dora wore the beads.' I felt 'I must. I'll die if I don't, and I—'

"D'you know what I did? This is one of the most idiotic bits yet, but I'm going to tell you the lot. . . Generally, I don't think I'm superstitious. Some fellows are; well, I'd known one perfectly sane and sensible fellow, who, when he was mad keen after something he wanted, winning some event, or something—he'd turn money out of his pocket—a sovereign, say, in the days when we had sovereigns, or a handful of silver—and throw it away. Pitch it right away, you know, to buy him luck. Well, I thought of it then. If I could buy that German plane! So—

"I pulled off my glove as I buzzed along after 'em and made a dive inside my jacket for money. Then I remembered I hadn't a bean on me. I'd given my last two quid to Smithers, and here I was, and I wanted to buy that Gotha, I tell you! I'd have bought her with anything I'd got, money, ring, every last thing—

"Then I remembered.

"It was on the joy-stick, the thing I valued. Your little mascot! I ripped it off. I gave one look round to where those beggars were heading for the barrage, and then chucked that bit of ribbon out over where I guessed you might be. (Perfectly absurd, of course. The wind whisked it away.) . . . And as I chucked it I shouted something out. Somebody's name.

"No! You can't guess whose name it was. Nobody'd have thought it. The funny thing about it was, it wasn't even the name I meant to shout. I meant to shout out 'Cheer O, Girl!' I heard myself yelling out instead, 'Cheer O, *Ferris*!'

"He was the observer I used to have. Killed, last year. . . Somehow, just then, I forgot that; I felt as if he were with me. Then! I thought 'Good Lord, fancy if old Ferris—'

"Then I didn't think any more; I settled down to business. Well, as you know, I did have to chase 'em to the coast, those dashed Archies popping all the way. *At* the coast the Archies were—say really hot. Then those sea-planes took a hand, but it wasn't the seaplane that got her. *I* got her! Got her right over Beachy Head.

"I knew I'd done it the moment he turned about. I'd put half a drum right into her engines, and she wouldn't want to land in the sea (rather Irish).

"Suddenly a searchlight blazed right on the pair of us, and the Archies stopped, just like the band stops and the limelight concentrates for the really tricky bit of the show with those acrobats at a music-hall. . .

"But this was dead easy, the rest of it. I just circled above her like a buzzard, driving her down, down, all the time. I didn't fire at her any more, because you could tell within twenty yards where she was going to land, and I knew the lads of the village were all ready and waiting for her. One bad wobble she gave and pitched straight down. I sheered off a bit for fear of getting any bombs, but she'd drop her last one on the way. She simply came down end on like shying a lump of clay at a board. Then I landed, tumbled out, and legged it up the slope as fast as I could; just in time to see 'em getting out all the three Huns alive.

"'My bird, I think,' says I, running up all out of breath.

"Then a chap beside me spoke out of the dark, 'Hi! Who are you?'

"I couldn't see him, so I said, 'D'you mind telling me who *you* are?'

"He pulled a torch out of his pocket and showed it on himself. A Staff-major. So we shook hands, and he congratulated me. . . Then I felt rather a fool," laughed Jack Awdas, "for he asked me my name.

"'Well, as a matter of fact, Sir,' I said, and stopped.

"'Well what?' he asked.

"'Well, as a matter of fact, I'm not supposed to be here at all.'

"'Oh?' he barked. 'Got any orders on you?'

"I had; from the Assistant Adjutant. I pulled 'em out and he read them by the light of his torch.

"'H'm,' he said, 'taking a machine to France, but I see by this you're not due to start until tomorrow morning. It's now two, ac emma. How's this?'

"Well, when you're cornered like that I always think there's only one thing for it; pure cheek. So, as bold as brass, I gave a look at the orders myself, and then said, 'I rather fancy this must be a clerical error, sir. My verbal orders were to start today, and I can't have been two hours on the way yet?'

"I fancied I heard him give a chuckle in the dark, but all he said was, 'Well, this will be a serious matter for you.'

"'Oh, I hope not, Sir,' I said.

"'A serious matter,' says he. 'If you'd been sent up to chase Hun planes you might have got the D.S.O. for this. But you see what it means now?'

"'What?' I asked.

"'Well! This being an act outside the course of your duty,' he said, 'it *may* mean the Victoria Cross!'"

Golden Awdas gasped. "Then, think of it, Bird-boy! You'll only have traded *my* ribbon," she exclaimed, "for that wonderful other! Now wasn't that a prize—"

But the wide and distant stare had gone now from her airman's eyes. These had returned to her; his sweet American who had journeyed across a world before he had found her, his love whom he had loved enough to leave, knowing that it might be for ever... His blue eyes were locked into hers again for a moment with his lover's look that now sent a wave of pink fire flaming into her face and down her throat. Against that perfect throat he buried eyes and lips.

"'Think?' I needn't think of anything else now, Girl," he whispered. "*You're* my prize!"

THAT WAS JACK AWDAS'S STORY of his share in the raid.

The evening papers announced:

"Bombs were dropped in several districts, but no material damage was caused. A woman and two children were slightly injured.

"One German aeroplane was brought down on the coast by a pilot of the Royal Flying Corps."

The German account read:

"A successful raid was carried out by our airmen over London last night. Good results were obtained, and large fires were seen to break out in various districts.

"All our aeroplanes returned safely."

XII

SHRAPNEL AND THE CHARM

"Never the time and the place and the loved one all together!"

—Browning

And what of the other people who had been at Mrs. Cartwright's party when that raid alarm came through?

Olwen Howel-Jones and young Ellerton had imagined that by taking "the Metropolitan" from Baker Street Station they might arrive at Wembley Park before the raid started in earnest.

This hope proved to be vain before their train reached Willesden Junction. Out went the lights as the train came to a dead stand between two stations. Up went the windows; above the iron bars that guarded them there craned the heads of passengers asking in every key what the matter was.

They were answered by the distant growling of those first guns.

"Bai Jove! Held up for the blessed raid," exclaimed the cheerful voice of young Ellerton, who was alone with Olwen in a first-class carriage in the front of the train. "How priceless! Here we are and here we stay until the blighters choose to finish their little call, I s'pose. That's all right. . . Hope you don't feel nervous, Miss Howel-Jones?"

The soft voice of little Olwen came to him out of the dark. (She was sitting in the corner seat, opposite to him.) "Oh, no! I'm not nervous at all, thanks. I think it's quite exciting! I only hope Lizzie (that's my Aunt) won't be worrying about me; but then she knew where I was; she'll probably think Mrs. Cartwright kept me."

"Ah, yes. She'll probably think Mrs. Cartwright kept you," agreed Olwen's companion. "I thought it looked a likely night for our friends."

He had made this remark, by the way, twice on their way to Baker Street.

"Yes," said Olwen.

Silence, punctuated by a nearer muttering of the guardian guns fell between the two young people in the carriage to themselves. The voices of other passengers could be heard further along the train; and the guard appeared to be exchanging repartee with the engine-driver, whose name (as that of all drivers of 'bus or engine seems to be), was Bill. Olwen gave a little laugh as "Bill's" comments were shouted forth on the night air, and her companion chuckled also. But he started no conversation about it. Or about any other subject.

The whole truth of the matter was that this quite good-looking and pleasant young man Harold Ellerton hadn't got very much conversation. Others besides Captain Ross (who was never inclined to be fair to him) had noticed this. Olwen herself had noticed it before now. It had been noticed by various girls whom he had taken out; for he was fond of taking out girls. But, unlike the majority of his sex, he preferred *them* to talk to *him*. He was perfectly happy to punctuate their treble twitter with his appreciative bass, "Ha!" "Bai Jove!" and "Priceless!" But (except for one other detail to be presently specified), he hardly knew what else to say to a young woman who was out with him. That was why he felt most at ease sitting beside her at a theatre (where, during two enjoyable hours, all the talking necessary was done for him by Mr. Owen Nares, or Mr. Leslie Henson, or somebody like that). Or at a restaurant, preferably at a table near the band; listening to that could always fill up any awkward pause. At dances, again, one could dance. At a little dinner party like tonight's, for instance, there was a crowd where everybody talked; made everything so much more cheery at once. But it was when these things came to an end, when one had the girl all to oneself to bring home—*That*, he found, was the crab!

Why was it, he wondered, that he found it so difficult to talk to her, except upon one subject?

He remembered delightful evenings, ending in these painful and tedious journeys *à deux*. Tonight, for instance, it was going to be the very dickens with this little Miss Howel-Jones. A jolly nice little kid, thought the sailor, a pretty kid! But here they might be held up together in this confounded train for another hour, perhaps, and he couldn't even see her face, and he was blessed if he knew what more to say to her—Why, he'd said everything as he sat next to her at dinner, he and that funny little Brown chap. He did envy the flow of chaps like that! Chaps who could yarn away upon this, that, and the other subject for three years or the duration of the War. Talk to girls for ever, they could, without repeating themselves!

"I thought it looked a likely sort of evening for a raid," he heard himself say at this point.

"Yes," said the girl opposite to him in the dark.

Of course he'd said everything there was to be said on the subject of air-raids in general and this air-raid in particular on the way to Baker Street. Yet he couldn't sit here in the dark opposite to her for the whole length of the raid, saying nothing?

Still the guns made distant thunder. . .

"I do hope you aren't frightened," he said. "It's quite all right, you know."

"Oh, I know. I'm not a bit frightened," came from Olwen; truthfully enough.

She was not frightened as she settled herself back against the padding of the carriage. She was only a little sleepy, a little anxious for the kind-hearted Lizzie, who would be waiting up for her in that pretty villa at Wembley Park; she was also excited and elated still after her lovely party.

She was thinking far more of that party than she was of her companion of the raid!

She was also wondering about Captain Ross.

What a *disgusting* temper the man had been in all that evening!

Positively scowling at her! Was he jealous, really? *Was* he?

Then she wondered what Captain Ross was doing at that moment.

If there had been no raid—! If it had been he who was seeing her home she might have asked him what she had done that he should scowl at her like that.

Or if only it were Captain Ross who was sitting with her here in this darkened carriage all smelling of engine-dust and cigarette smoke, waiting for the raid to finish. . .

Hurriedly Olwen put the thought away. It was no use allowing oneself to dwell on thoughts of things that were too good to be true. No, no, not too good. She told herself firmly that she did not wish Captain Ross were in this railway-carriage instead of Mr. Ellerton. Captain Ross would only be disagreeable.

Only—Well! She could imagine some girls feeling glad of a raid in these circumstances. Some girls to whom it would be as one long, long lovely dance "sat out" in a dark corner with their favourite partner of all. Perhaps there were girls "hung up" in this very train, feeling that it was the evening of their lives.

Whereas all she could feel was apologetic to Mr. Ellerton. He liked her, but she was sure he had never bargained for sitting out with her a dance of this length. Still, what was to be done? Here the train stuck. They couldn't get out and walk to Wembley!

"Shall we smoke?" suggested Mr. Ellerton. "You'll have a cigarette, won't you?"

He fumbled in his pockets and brought out his torch. Its tiny beams made rounds of light in the carriage and upon his face and upon the gold braid and gold rings of his uniform. He found case and matches. He lighted a cigarette for Olwen, who puffed at it with secret distaste (for the moderate smoker is not found among her sex; a woman being either a cigarette fiend or a passive objector).

The two red glow-worms winked and wavered in the dark carriage, their reflections shining in the glass of photographs over the rack. Outside the searchlights pointed, and now and again the sky showed the alien star of a shrapnel-burst.

Then, without warning, crash after crash seemed to rock the train on the rails. Some guns, very near, that had not yet spoken, were barking savagely, and between the barks a shrill "whee-you! whee-you!" hissed past the telegraph wires. . .

The start that Olwen gave made her drop her cigarette on to the floor of the carriage. She dug her little French heel into the spark. Young Ellerton threw his cigarette down beside it and rose quickly. Snapping up the arm of the seat by Olwen, he sat down close to her.

"You needn't be frightened," he said, encouragingly.

"I'm not frightened," she assured him. "Only it makes me jump."

"Brutes, frightening you!" exclaimed young Ellerton. "I say, I do wish I'd thought of bringing some chocolates or something for you."

"I'm not hungry either, thank you," laughed Olwen into the barking of those guns, but young Ellerton's voice repeated, "I wish I'd got any sweets for you. I've only this—"

She felt him move against her arm as he leant nearer to her to get something else out of his pocket: it was a phial of saccharine tablets, carried about since the sugar restrictions.

"Have some of these," he said. "Put out your hand. . . here, where are you?" He shook half a dozen tablets out into her palm.

As it happened, Olwen disliked saccharine worse than she disliked Virginian cigarettes, yet she munched the substitute-sweets to please this young man who, according to his lights, was being nice and kind and protective towards her.

For the severalth time he informed her that she was not to be frightened. . . Then, in a new tone, he added, "Dear little girl." Then, more softly still, "For you *are* a dear little girl, you know. Do you know, you're just about the sweetest I've ever met."

"Oh, pooh!" laughed Olwen, taken by surprise, nevertheless. She rather wished she could see the face of the young man sitting so close beside her. Had she done so, she would have seen it was what is known as "a study." For during the last half-hour or so the young man had become the prey to conflicting emotions indeed. Chief of these, perhaps, was a helpless fascination; the fascination of some one with a weak head who watches himself draw nearer and nearer to the brink of some giddy height.

Harold Ellerton knew he was drifting, as he'd done times and again, towards a fatal habit of his. Times and again, since before he had left Dartmouth, this thing had happened to him. It was as characteristic of him as was his lack of general conversation where women were concerned. In fact, it's not impossible that one of these characteristics may have led to the other.

HE DIDN'T KNOW WHAT TO say to girls unless he were making love to them, and his sole conception of love-making was to ask them to marry him!

He saw it coming now in the dark accomplice solitude of this railway carriage. He knew that he was going to say a few more tender things to this little Howel-Jones girl, about her eyelashes and how sweet she'd looked at that party and how she ought to have a bridal party of her own, directly—dear little sweetheart she'd make to any fellow!

He said these things.

He knew the other was coming.

It came.

"Look here, d'you think you could care enough to be *mine*?" he heard himself say. "Bai Jove, if you would—! If you'd marry *me*! Would you? Would you?"

There! He'd done it again.

Now came the agonizing moment.

Now again he'd have to wait for the girl's answer. That always seemed to him to be at least two hours in coming: except once, an anguished once when the girl had said, "Yes" directly. What would this one say; what? He waited in the dark; and sweat broke out on the young brow under the peaked cap.

In a long, uncertain breath the girl said, "Oh—"

Then, "D'you mean it, Mr. Ellerton?"

"Of *course!*" returned Mr. Ellerton, ardently, but digging his nails into the palms of his hands.

The soft voice beside him said, rather waveringly, "Wait a minute—"

The young man who had just proposed again set his teeth and waited. This was Hades. Serve him right for being such a double-blanked fool again! But this was the worst yet. Never before had he not been able to see the girl's face when he asked her to marry him. Never again, he vowed incoherently to himself, never again would he be such an ass as to propose to a girl during a raid with all the lights out! But then, never again would he let himself in for this with any girl alive! Not if he got safely out of this! Oh, Lord, the fool he'd been! . . . Could he possibly light a cigarette? . . . No, only wait. . . "A minute" this little thing had said. . .

Before she spoke again, æons seemed to elapse.

Actually they were a few moments only, during which the mind of Olwen Howel-Jones dashed swiftly through four distinct phases of thought. The first was pure surprise.

The second was a "No" that came from the bed-rock of woman's nature, that fundamental thing which Convention must blast and quarry into acceptable shapes.

The third was a "Yes" compounded of a thousand artificialities inherited, acquired, fostered, observed, and taught. Fear was among them; fear handed down from generations of dowerless girls who accepted the first proposal lest they might die as old maids. Why not! thought little Olwen. Engaged! Fancy if she were! What would her Aunts think, and Uncle, and her sisters! She would be the first of her sisters to become engaged! And she had got her leave, too, and would be going down to Wales; fancy going home to tell them! Fancy telling them at the Honeycomb; Mrs. Newton and everybody! What fun! Engaged to Mr. Ellerton. She did like him so much; she did, she did! He was awfully nice, and jolly with people, and so good-looking and so—it appeared, so fond of her! . . . More than could be said for Captain Ross. Wouldn't it be absolutely ridiculous to miss a real thing like this, for just a fancy like that? Girls had to get engaged while they could. It was the happiest thing; getting engaged and having a ripping time for a bit, then getting married and having everybody congratulating you. Getting engaged in the middle of a raid, too! Nobody could say that wasn't romantic. Love? . . . Well, Captain Ross had said that men couldn't bear "that Love-with-a-capital-L" business. It wasn't for everybody. And why do without all the fun of getting engaged, simply for the sake of some man who evidently didn't care two-pence. . . It would be awfully silly to say "No."

Swiftly as the flash of the guns this phase passed; swiftly as the following report there followed the fourth phase in the girl's mind. It flung her back to phase the second. But that had been composed of dumb Instinct. This was articulate.

No, no! She must not say "Yes" to this young man. However nice, however good-looking, however fond, he was not the man. She knew it. She did not love him. Golden said Love must be Lovely. What more unlovely than a loveless pact? The "fun" of this engagement? What would that be? A wretched substitute; no more real, sweet fun than the saccharine tablets which she had been munching were real sugar. Sugar in tea; Love in Life. . . Some people put up with makeshifts cheerfully; but not she. Some other people (she pursued the childish analogy) never did take sugar in their tea. The luckier they! They missed nothing; Olwen would crave it forever. But better a thousand times to go without everything than to accept the wrong thing!

She came out of her swift inner reverie, back to the dark railway carriage and the young man.

"Oh, Mr. Ellerton," she said hurriedly and remorsefully. "I am dreadfully sorry but I can't possibly. I don't care for you. Not that way. I do like you ever so much. But if—if you don't mind, I *couldn't* marry you."

She heard the young man near her give, in the darkness, the profoundest sigh that she had ever heard torn from any human breast. . .

Remorsefully she repeated, "I am so sorry—" Then stopped abruptly. She seemed, in the darkness and the vibrating atmosphere, to have caught a floating idea that startled her somewhat.

She began again gravely. "Will you lend me your torch for a minute?"

She felt it put into her hand.

Quickly Olwen said, "It's very rude of me, but I *must* look at you, please: I must see your face!"

Then she turned the little beam right upon him.

Then she exclaimed, "Mr. Ellerton!"

"Yes—" he said, unmistakably sheepish.

Olwen burst out laughing. "You are a fraud," she exclaimed gaily. "You aren't one bit sorry that I refused you. You're trying not to, but you're looking—yes, *relieved*. You're glad! Don't pretend!"

"Oh, I say—"

"No! Don't pretend! You were laughing. You're feeling gladder than you've ever felt over anything in your life because I don't want to marry you! I *know*!"

Young Ellerton dragged his handkerchief from his cuff, pushed back his cap and wiped his forehead. "Bai Jove," he said with the sincerest admiration in his tone, "you *are* a clever little thing. I—I don't think any of the others have ever tumbled to that."

A moment later he found himself talking to her with more real ease and enjoyment than he had ever talked to a girl in his life; with real fluency. To her (during the second hour for which they were hung up) he confessed that no, he didn't want to get married. There were people—anyhow, men, who *didn't*. Not to the sweetest and prettiest girl in the world. Not to *anybody*. To tie himself up like that for life, declared the young sailor, was what he wouldn't want to do for anything under the sun; certainly not for anything under a hat. Never!

Olwen, finding she had ceased to be bored by him for the first time since she had left Mrs. Cartwright's turned her face towards him in the dark and plied him with question after laughing question.

"But you ask people to marry you!"

"Can't stop myself! It's the devil!"

"And none of them have accepted you?"

"Yes; one! A girl who was at college with my sister. A nice girl. I did get to loathe her!" with feeling. "We were engaged for one whole awful week!"

"How did you break it off, then?"

"She did. I loved her for that. She said I was too much like the young man in Stevenson who said being engaged was all right as long as her sisters were there. So she chucked me. And after that I've been lucky—I mean, you know what I mean!"

Olwen shook with laughter. "But, then, why d'you *do* it?" she persisted.

"I tell you I can't help it. It happens!"

"Why? For instance, why did you let it happen tonight? Quite frankly, *why* did you ask me?"

"Oh, you—!" he began, and he paused for a minute. "Oh, come," he said, "you are an awful nice little girl, you know. Anybody might be excused for losing his head. You were looking extra pretty at the party tonight, too. Some *peach*, you looked, if I may say so; and it wasn't just looks either. There was *something* about you. Sort of disturbing. . . I swear there was. You attracted me till I—"

"Don't propose to me again," Olwen warned him. "I might think better of it."

"Oh, no," laughed Harold Ellerton. "You're an absolute little sportswoman, I know."

The little sportswoman, while she continued to laugh and chat with him in the friendliest way until the signal sounded for the train to start again, the little sportswoman had been really arrested by one of his remarks.

"*Something about her*" tonight, he thought. She'd heard something like that before. She thought she might know what it meant.

She went back to early on the afternoon of that eventful day.

VERY LATE SHE HAD FOUND herself as she was dressing for her tea with Mr. Brown at the Regent Palace; even as she was putting on her nicest silk stockings she had known that it would mean a scamper down the drive if she meant to catch that train. . .

Then in her hurry a suspender had snapped.

"Dash!" she had cried.

No time to stitch it.

She had cast round for the nearest bit of ribbon wherewith to garter herself securely, and had snatched it up from where it dangled on her dressing-table, hardly seeing which bit of pink ribbon it was with what satin sachet attached. She'd wound it hastily about her slim and silk-sheathed leg and forgotten all about it. That's how she had come to be wearing it that evening, not in the orthodox way round her neck, but wearing it nevertheless; the Disturbing Charm!

Hidden thus, it almost seemed as if it had done its work again?

AS THEY SAID GOOD-BYE AT the wicket gate of her Aunt's house, she found herself quite affectionately promising to write, while on leave, to this young sailor who never would be anything but a friend to her. She found herself submitting quite naturally to one of those flavourless and definite kisses on the cheek, of which the entirely brotherly quality can never be mistaken by the recipient.

A looker-on may be more easily mistaken.

Olwen's Aunt Lizzie was coming up the Drive behind her, having been delayed in another carriage of that very same train, since she had also been dining in town. From some distance she had observed the farewell at the gate. But she exchanged greetings, quite unprejudiced, with the young sailor who passed her. She was a modern Aunt. . .

At the house she found her niece already in the bedroom, so busy with her little straw work-basket and two lengths of pink ribbon, that before any talk even of the raid, she asked, "What have you got there, Olwen?"

"I'm just mending something," returned the intent Olwen, "that I've got to wear."

XIII

Vigil

"The raid is still in progress."

—Morning Paper

To other members of the party that raid had been less (obviously) eventful.

Little Mr. Brown, after he had seen Mrs. Cartwright's niece, the nurse, back to her rooms, trotted back to the Regent Palace Hotel all in a dither of undeniable funk.

Not funk for himself! Gallipoli and the Somme had found him "sticking it" with a music-hall joke between his teeth. But here he had something to be frightened about. The danger-zone was no place for women. At once he rang up his *fiancée*, Mrs. Robinson, in Baker Street. There was no reply! . . . On duty still? And Lord knew where. . .

[The little dispatch rider was at that moment, as we know, scorching along the road out of London and past the Kilburn Empire.]

Mr. Brown, M.C., took his cold feet and his pipe to another man's room, and sat there talking feverishly to drown the guns; from here he rang up at intervals, getting through to her at last.

"Worrying? . . . What about?" her cheeky little voice called back to him. "Been? Why I've been carting some young lunatic who's lost his 'bus or something, back to his 'drome. . . I say! He tried to give me two pounds. Got off again, didn't I? . . . Yes, and I'm just going to turn in. . . Silly ass. . . Worrying about me? Well, drop it. I'm not marrying any worries, they're too old-fash. Go to bed!"

"Right you are," called back her future lord on the note of cheery docility which was to resound throughout his married life. "See you demang. Good night, Pet!"

"Good night, Pug."

She rang off; he sought his room, and slept through the rest of the raid.

Miss Agatha Walsh sat up for it. She sat up in the private sitting-room of her hotel, where there was also staying, on business, the old family lawyer who transacted her business. There she sat with him and her *fiancé* at midnight, feeling delightfully emancipated if not "fast," drinking stone ginger-beer and translating the lawyer's remarks to her half-dozing sergeant. Agatha was entirely happy, for the talk was all about arrangements for her approaching marriage, settlements for her husband, and so on. What, compared to these things, was the noise of gun-fire? The only attention that she paid to it was to exclaim once, "Oh, I do wish I could have a bit of the shrapnel set in gold as a paper-weight or something for Gustave, just as a souvenir of the first raid we've been through together!"

And now we come to Captain Ross.

Captain Ross would have allowed no questions as to where he was and what doing whilst that raid was in progress. Suffice it to say that he was on duty.

Not active duty; not strenuous duty, but duty which, unfortunately for him, gave him plenty of leisure to think, and to feel, as he himself put it curtly, "sick."

Very sick he felt.

First there was the standing grouse of his not being able to take a man's job, ever, in that sort of show. They would never allow a one-armed chap to go up in a plane, of course. Not even by altering the mechanism of the whole thing so that he could work the controls left-handed—that was off for good; and he was sick of it.

He also felt sick with young Jack. What on earth had he been trying to play at? He had no duty. He was married that morning; hadn't he, Ross, seen him married? What the something did he mean by leaving his wife and chasing off like that? Saying "All right; shut up—" What did the young fool mean by it?

Further, there was that little hussy that Captain Ross was sick with. Sitting—wherever he was sitting while the raid-guns scolded outside, he went over and over in his mind the many grouses that he had against that little hussy Olwen Howel-Jones. She didn't know how to treat him right.

She was a darned little flirt.

Look at her at Les Pins with that ass young Brown!

Look at her here in London, with that even worse ass, young Ellerton!

Scandalous. . . Scandalous. . .

To Ellerton he meant to give such a telling-off as the young man had never heard in his life before.

And to the girl he was going to speak about it this very evening. Then the raid had come. . .

Of course Ellerton would see that child all the way home.

He'd done it before. . .

She admitted that herself.

She practically admitted that the fellow made love to her on the way home.

No doubt he was doing it again at that moment! Captain Ross could picture it. He did picture it. . .

Nothing could have been less like his picture than the reality of that proposal scene in the railway carriage of the train held up outside Willesden Junction at that moment, but how should this jealous brooder be expected to guess that?

He continued to brood so intently that it is unlikely he heard any of the firing. . .

That little hussy! How was it she always contrived to irritate him so? Always! Every time she spoke! The more meek and mild she was in the office the more downright impairrrtinence she managed to infuse, somehow, into the very meekness and mildness of the tone in which she spoke to her chief. Yep! Even if she were only putting somebody through to him on the telephone, she managed to convey an impression of—of—of *something*.

And why any busy man should waste a moment thinking of her the finest judge of women in Europe did not know. . . How had she done it?

Yes; she was pretty; confound her! Awfully neat. . . but weren't other girls? Why think of her, more than of all the others, dozens, scores, yes, hundreds of 'em that he'd known? What he demanded of a girl's society was that it should be kept in its right proporrrrtion as a relaxation for when a man wasn't occupied with a job.

Woman, it could not too often be reiterated, was the Plaything of Man—but not of young Ellerton, by the way. Why should any sensible man be obsessed by one more than another of these toys?

Let them keep in their places.

Dashed pretty she was! Taking little face, dandy little figure, hands and feet it. . . Still, if she thought that he, with all his experience, was going to say that Miss Olwen Howel-Jones was the best-looking girl he'd ever struck, she had another guess coming to her. Casual little ways she had! Those spoilt her. Pursing up her mouth—which was as red as if she shoved on carmine by the stick every five minutes, though he could see she didn't. It would sairrrrrrrrve her jolly well right if a man (not young Ellerton) were to catch ahold of her and kiss her good and hard a couple of dozen times running and then leave her, having had all he wanted of her. That other maddening habit of hers, too; looking 'way over a man's shoulder when he was speaking to her! Refusing to meet his eyes. . . though she could look straight enough into young Ellerton's. . . What colour *were* her eyes when all was said: brown, green, or hazel?

He had arrived at this point by the time that the rushing by of cars began to be heard up the Strand, down the Embankment and along every street within earshot; cars containing joyously important children in Scout's kit who "*woke to find that Noise was Duty,*" and who now roused London's echoes with their bugle calls of two long notes:

"*All clear—! All—clear!*"

Yes; the raid was over. Captain Ross of the Honeycomb found himself drawing a long breath and realizing that he did most bitterly resent these raids on account of the women that he knew who were in the danger zone. That child Olwen, now; had she been frightened? Very likely indeed. Scared to death, no doubt.

Poor wee girl! . . .

With the return to the thought of her, there suddenly stirred within him a feeling that lay so deep down and under so many other mere immediate things that he seldom allowed himself the chance of leisure to delve towards it. . .

It was—how express it? A gentle, reverent unspoilt tenderness. It was That which makes the difference in the ingrainedly sentimental mind of Man, between Woman—and his own women-folk. The key to the hearts of these finest judges of women in Europe is to be found held in the hands of a mother, a wife, or (most surely) of a baby-daughter. . . This particular Scot had denied *in toto* that that chit of a Welsh girl could ever have part or lot in any of his jealously-secret dreams.

But denied it he had; yes! Already he was so far gone as all that.

Therefore it will be seen that he had reached the moment when a man pulls himself resolutely together and determines that having gone so far, he will go no further.

The moment had arrived when he told himself that, having taken all things into consideration, he had done with the girl.

Yes; he had done with this Olwen.

What was meant by this could only be judged by subsequent events. One cannot but surmise that it meant the following:

To come to that office on Monday and, as usual, to treat her as part of the office furniture. To speak to her as usual with the charm of manner of a bear with a sore head. To glower at her as usual in the Strand if she passed him with young Ellerton. To have lunch on Friday as usual at that restaurant where she had lunch and, still as usual, to spar and wrangle with her until it was time to get back to work. To meet her as usual at Mrs. Cartwright's; to meet her perhaps with her friend Mrs. Awdas; to—well, to carry on in the usual way, as he had done up to now, and so, indefinitely, to continue. . .

"Yes! I've done with her," he meditated aloud in the solitude of whatever place it was in which he found himself. The sound of his own voice pronouncing these resolute words was balm to his irritated, exasperated mood. "I've done with her. *That's* sett—"

Into the word there broke the shrill whirring call of the telephone.

He snapped it up. The silence of the place where he sat seemed to ring to the now irritated bark of his voice, answering.

"Spikkin'! Who is that?"

"Ell—what? Oh, Ellerton? Yes; what is it?" He listened, scowling, to the clear boyish voice that came through, obviously in the joyous high feather. "Oh, yes; I know the raid's over, yes. . . Nothing of consequence; nothing at all. . . You saw *what*? Miss Howel-Jones home safely? That's all? . . . You were held up? Is that so? Where? For *how*—For two hours, was it? All the lights turned out, I suppose? . . . Indid. . . Ah. . . Well! I don't know that I was worrying specially about either of you; not so as you'd notice it. But thanks all the same for reassuring me, Ellerton—"

(This with the bitter sarcasm which, the Celt maintains, is ever lost upon the Saxon.)

"And I suppose Miss Howel-Jones will make it her excuse for turrrning up late on Monday morrrrning. . . *Whatt*? She won't be coming Monday? How's that? . . . *Leave*?"

His voice jumped up three notes.

"Going on leave? . . . Where's she going? Wales? . . . What part of Wales? . . . I said what part of Wales. . . Aber-*which*? . . . Ah. . . Night."

The finest judge of women snapped up the receiver and sat for a moment motionless: only the shapely feminine mouth under the hogged moustache moving to the form of inaudible words.

Then he sprung up and grabbed a paper-covered book from a shelf of reference books. He stood holding it.

Ellerton and she!

Held up for two mortal hours in the dark!

And the cub sounded in racing spirits. . .

Proposed to her! Not a doubt of it! And would he sound like that if he hadn't been acc—?

Here he slammed the book down on the table (it was an A B C), and, with his one hand, began violently fluttering the pages. Aber—Aber—

Gone, had she? Without a word. . . How dare she? Got leave without telling him. . .

Leave, indeed. . .

He'd got some leave coming to him.

Right now was where he'd take it, and at this Aber-where-was-it— ah, here. . .

Done with the girl? He realized that he had not yet begun with her.

XIV

Home and the Charm

"A charm from the skies seems to hallow us there,
Which, seek through the world, is ne'er met with elsewhere."

—Still-Popular Song

There was one thing that struck Olwen very forcibly as soon as she got down to that house of her Aunt Margaret's in Wales.

It was the first time for many months that she had entered a dwelling-place that was also a home.

Where had she been all this time? In places of which the keynote was "Here today and gone tomorrow"; places that she had never even seen a year ago; places without associations, without responsibilities for the pilgrim-guest.

There had been Les Pins; its hotel. . . Cap Ferret and its charming inn. Other hotels in Paris and London. There had been the Honeycomb; its busyness still informed by the hotel spirit of *"Dwell as if about to depart."*

Then there had been her Aunt's villa at Wembley Park; delightful little red-roofed, rose-wreathed doll's-house! There was an impermanency about that, too; it looked as if a gale of wind would carry it off, with the row of other red-and-white toy-dwellings in the midst of which it stood. It was a place to picnic and to sleep in, and of one which one turned the latch-key without giving it all day a further thought.

The same note was struck by Mrs. Cartwright's prettily-arranged flat. In three hours, perhaps, she could pack up and move. . . somewhere, anywhere that suited her! (People lived where they liked, after all, instead of making it a religion to like where they lived.)

The same could be said of Mrs. Newton's rooms at her hotel, and of the bachelor-diggings of half a dozen War-working girls whom Olwen knew in London. The new note was spreading. Domestic life as lived under Queen Victoria seemed at a discount. And to more and more of England's young womanhood one might apply the plaintive remark of the straphanger to the other occupants of the crowded 'bus: "Ain't *none* o' you got no 'omes?"

But here, on the outskirts of this provincial town where generations of the Howel-Joneses had been born, had lived and married and died— here one found oneself swept back to the domestic conditions of more than half a century ago.

Ah, the solidity of this square grey house, padded with ancient ivy and roofed with purple slate! Oh, the density of that laurel hedge, screening its lawn from the road that wound up towards the mountains! Heavens, the ponderous comfort of the furniture; every mahogany "piece," every *portière*, every vast Landseer steel engraving upon the walls seemed to remind Olwen "We were here in your grandmamma's time, and your great-grandmother's and you, little superficial upstart, what right have you to turn up your nose at what was good enough for them?"

Yes; it had taken three reigns to bring these things together; details that dragged the generations behind them as they settled down, heavily, into a permanent, complete and dominant whole, which it would now take an earthquake or a revolution to shift.

But Olwen, as it happened, felt no desire to "turn up her nose." She was enjoying this return to the days of old. It was a rest and a refreshment to her after all her war-time gipsying, after her eating in Soho restaurants, after her coming and going, after that whole life of the bird on the twig. For there is no place like home, the old, established, sturdy, stolid British home. . . when one knows that one is only there on ten days' leave.

Then there were the home-dwellers. Olwen had never before realized how pretty and amusing were her young sisters Peggy and Myfanwy; especially Peggy, in her V.A.D. kit! She had wrested three days' leave from her hospital in the town in order to be with her sister from London; and there were also gathered together on a visit in the old home a selection of cousins—Howel-Joneses, Pritchards, and little Llewella Price—to welcome the wanderer home. Never before had they "made such a fuss of her," or she of them.

Even Auntie Margaret (who was THE Miss Howel-Jones, the head of the household, and a despotic version of the Professor in petticoats), even Auntie Margaret did not seem nearly as "trying" to Olwen as in those pre-War days when the present Honeycomb war-worker was a girl at home.

Why, Olwen had been in the house for two whole days, and Auntie had only been really exasperating once! And even then she had almost immediately afterwards bestowed upon Olwen an exquisite old coral brooch and a bristly kiss. After all, there were no people like one's home-people. . . once one wasn't obliged always to live with them.

Yes; Olwen enjoyed them. She enjoyed the accent of the young creature who brought up hot water to her old bedroom (and who was described by Auntie as "no servant, but a colt off the mountains!"). And she enjoyed the forgotten ambrosia of the Welsh butter, and the family tea to which they all sat down about the family table, and the family jokes—all as old as her beloved hills.

There was no news, except of a bazaar in aid of comforts for the town's recruits; that had happened a month since, but it seemed still as important to the family as anything that Olwen could tell them of what had been happening in London. It was only on the Sunday when this function had been described to the last detail by each relation in turn that they left it at last to enquire about what raid; had Olwen seen anything of this?

The question was put to her at tea-time.

Olwen, munching Auntie's hot cakes, told them of the interrupted party and of her delayed journey home.

"In one of those wretchedly draughty trains! I wonder you didn't take your death," was her aunt's aghast comment.

A Pritchard cousin added, "In the dark! Weren't you terrified all alone?"

Olwen explained.

"Oh! *With* somebody," exclaimed another cousin.

"Sitting with a man from that place of yours. . . In khaki, then? No; a *sailor*? Oh, how *lovely*! . . . How old; twenty-four—five? It must have felt just like being at the Cinema. Olwen, what *did* he talk about?"

"Asked me to marry him," Olwen replied, tranquil in the assurance that this unembellished truth would never be believed.

A gale of girlish laughter broke out round the table; a clatter of feminine questions.

The Welsh speaking-voice, which normally resembles the coo of the ring-dove (*vide* a paper on "Timbre" read by a college-friend of Professor Howel-Jones), is capable of rising, in excitement, above the corncrake note of the average Saxon, to the parrot-screech of the Continental. It did so now, as the stay-at-homes cross-examined their wanderer.

"No; but really?"

"Do tell us what sort of a young man he was?"

"Yes; come on, Olwen *fach*. We never see a young man down here; might as well describe to us what one looks like—"

It was at this very moment that the young man who was passing the dining-room windows on his way to the front door caught a glimpse of clustered black heads all alike and heard a breaking wave of talk and giggling. This tide rose until it swamped the sound of his ring at the bell.

Presently, without warning, there burst into the dining-room that aproned colt from the mountains who had answered the door.

IN AN EXPLOSIVE WHISPER SHE announced, "Some *genttleman*! Some gentleman is in the drawing-room!"

"Who is it?" asked the mistress.

"Some gentleman wanting to see Miss S'olwen," the little maid hissed on every "S." (A sudden quiet fell upon the party.) "Some *Captain*, or something, he say."

"Of course!" shrilled Olwen's youngest cousin Llewella, in a voice that could (and did) carry easily across the hall into the drawing-room and beyond the lawn outside, "This *must* be her *sailor* young man!"

But Olwen (rising from the tea-table with the sudden sensation of having had no tea or any other meal for about a fortnight) knew better. She was the only one at that tea-table who had not been too absorbed in talk to notice the caller passing the window. Against the dark green laurel hedge and the lavender mountains beyond she had caught the flash of gayer colour, scarlet on khaki.

Captain Ross—!

"He's come," she thought in a whirl of happiest flurry. "What did Golden say!"

Her heart seemed to stand still as she crossed the hall. On the mat she waited for one second. She must look as if absolutely nothing had happened or could happen. Then she opened the heavily-draped door and went into the drawing-room.

Captain Ross had planted himself just where she had expected that he might; he was standing on the hearthrug with his back to the log fire.

That hearthrug was wide and white and fluffy; there was a brass-edged glass screen before the fender. The mantelpiece was of white alabaster and hung with looped drapery of peacock-blue brocade, lustrous and pompous and ball-fringed, dating from 1889. Upon the mantelshelf itself there stood under a tall glass shade an ormolu clock, with figures of nymphs and Cupid. On each side of this gleamed candlesticks with dangling prisms.

There were also china ornaments, a miniature of Margaret Howel-Jones at eighteen and another glass shade protecting a branch of white coral; the whole reflected in a gilt-framed mirror.

Everything in that drawing-room was in key with that mantelpiece. And into that complete and Victorian harmony there broke the Neo-Georgian note of a girl wearing the little modern serge frock, the pert effective shoes, and the hair-dressing of the instant.

But Captain Ross, turning abruptly did not see the dramatic contradiction of that girl to this room.

What he saw was the girl at last in the background that suited her. Yes; here she was, where she should be. None of your gimcrack hotels or grimy offices or fly-blown, cotton-glove restaurants! A girl like that ought never to leave a place like this. The place into which any decent man instinctively wants to put the sweetest woman he knows—A Nice, Comfortable Home of her Own.

(That the woman invariably longs to be "put" there has never yet been questioned by this type.)

To him every detail of the place seemed in league to "set" her; sweetly, worthily. For the first time he saw her as in a shrine—therefore to be worshipped, yes! worshipped.

But there was nothing of this to be read in Captain Ross's face as he returned her soft-voiced, surprised-sounding greeting. He was positively scowling.

And why was the finest judge of women in Europe scowling like this?

It was because of the unforseen way in which all his plans were going astray. On the way down in the train he'd had everything beautifully planned. He'd intended to tell this little Olwen casually but quite authoritatively that he'd something to say to her, and that "as he was in Wales" he guessed he'd look in and say it right then. (These women had to be handled—firmly.) He thought that a darned good opening. . . in the train.

But suddenly that "was in Wales" didn't seem the strong card he'd thought. It seemed, in fact, remarkably weak. He admitted that as he glanced round that immutably Victorian room. It might have done for the Honeycomb, but not here. Set-back Number One.

Next, he must look as if he'd come down here on purpose to see this aggravating chit. Which of course, he had not done. Or at least hadn't meant to. Or, anyway, wouldn't have done if there had been any other way. Captain Ross could explain this position to himself, perfectly. But appearances were all against him. . . Set-back Number Two.

For Set-back Number Three, had he not just heard half a sentence (before a door closed), in a shrill girlish voice, about a "*sailor* young man"?

Damn young Ellerton!

His anger against the sailor gave the send-off to the very first sentence that he addressed to the girl.

With a forward jerk of his head he brought out the startling abrupt remark, "Look, Miss Howel-Jones, don't you think this has gone on long enough?"

XV

The Charm Acknowledged

"'Even he that flies shall follow for thy sake—
Shall kiss that would not kiss thee' (yea, kiss me),
'When thou wouldst not' (when I would not kiss thee!)"

—Swinburne

Olwen's bright eyes opened in real astonishment. Here was a bewildering sex!

"Long enough," it said. *"Hasn't this been going on long enough."* . . . When—well, whose was the fault that anything had been *long*?

Or did Captain Ross mean that? Or what did he mean?

"I don't know what you mean," she confessed, standing there all at sea. Then she put out a hand to the draperies of that door. Bewilderment gave place for the moment to a stronger impulse; hospitality. The little Welshwoman must feed her guest. "Do come into the dining-room," she begged, "and have some tea first, anyhow—"

But Captain Ross stood rock-like. He had seen that rookery of black heads through the dining-room window.

"Thanks; I had tea in the train," he said curtly.

"I came to ask you something, and I'd like to know about it right now."

"But—oh—very well," murmured Olwen.

"It's this," said Captain Ross, peremptorily, "are you or are you not engaged to that—to Ellerton?"

Olwen had known her Chief sharp and abrupt before. For weeks she'd never known him anything else. This was his sharpest yet. She was intimidated. . . Then suddenly that went, and she had all the boldness of the kitten turning to face the big dog.

"Engaged?" she repeated. "What do you mean?"

"What do I mean? Engaged to be married." Captain Ross explained. "May I have a straight answer to that, please?"

There was a pause. Perhaps Olwen was sorting her thoughts. She smiled, at first uncertainly. Then, also uncertainly, she said, "But surely,

Captain Ross, you didn't come down from London specially to ask me that?"

With ominous patience Captain Ross nodded that sleek, black, Tom-cat head of his, almost as if to some old enemy he had expected to see cropping up at some time. "Why, of course, it's a lot to ask of a woman, a plain answer to a plain question. Right away, that is. But perhaps in haff a minute or so?" he suggested, adding, at once, "Are you engaged to him or are you not? Yes or no?"

Olwen, wondering at her own boldness, parried with, "If—if it *wasn't* worth coming down specially for, h-have you the right to ask me?"

"Say I came down specially, then," Captain Ross conceded reluctantly. "Now are you going to tell me?"

"Who said," asked Olwen, with a glance out of the window, "that there was anything to tell?"

"He's asked you to marry him, I know that," said Captain Ross with such conviction that Olwen coloured a little with surprise. How did Captain Ross know about that? It was true, of course. . . But he couldn't know quite *what* had happened. She almost laughed at the memory of Harold Ellerton's face in the light of the torch.

She hesitated. . .

It doesn't always follow that because a man is obstinate he may not be quick as well. It was very quickly that Captain Ross seized upon Olwen's hesitation, declaring, "He asked you on the night of the raid."

As quickly Olwen asked, "Did he *tell* you?"

A pause. Then "There was no nid, Miss Howel-Jones. I thought, somehow, that there'd be somebody else I'd have to be congrrrratulating very soon," said Captain Ross, with a sort of grim triumph in his tone.

He straightened his back, giving that little forward shrug of an armless shoulder that Olwen could never see unmoved. But her eyes were on the window and on the glimpse of variegated Welsh landscape beyond.

"Since that is so," concluded Captain Ross in his most final tone, "will you allow me to offer my very best wishes to yourself and to Mr. Ell—"

"No! Please don't!" protested Olwen quickly.

She felt that this misunderstanding had gone on long enough. Long enough. She turned from the window and looked straight—not at Captain Ross, that she couldn't do! but at a water-colour drawing of Carnarvon Castle on the wall. She said, "You see, I am not engaged or anything to Mr. Ellerton!"

And even as she said it, she knew what a change her words had made.

Without looking at him, she knew that Captain Ross's dark face had lighted up like a lantern into which a candle is put. She knew what he meant by that quick movement that he gave, as if rolling aside some weight that he'd been carrying. She knew, for sure and certain, why he'd come. Would he have cared about her being engaged to Mr. Ellerton if he hadn't wanted her himself? Of course he did want her. . .

Hadn't Golden said so? Wasn't that serene and lovely American always right?

Hadn't Madame Leroux thought so, too?

And hadn't she, Olwen herself, always known it too, in the very depths of her heart? Yes! Hadn't she always, always suspected his curt speech and his off-hand manner and his judgment of women?

Always!

A great and glowing delight filled the girl. For if he wanted her—oh, wasn't she his! Hadn't she been his all that time ago? All her denials of him since had been fibbing to herself, they had been making the best of things, they had been the hybernating sleep from which Love awakes as a giant refreshed! It had all been camouflage, and now there was no more need of it. . .

But even with this sweet and thrilling knowledge warm at her heart, the woman's Will-to-Prolong was strong within her, too.

She was a human little person enough and she had her dignity, she thought. Also she had to have her laugh—oh, quite a little one! over this man.

He said, "Then—" in a voice that there was no misunderstanding. His surliness had vanished like a mist. His eyes shone. He said, happily, "Then if you aren't engaged to him—!"

He seemed to think that she could take for granted what must follow.

But Olwen was mutinous. Had he come down here to propose? Let him do it! she thought. She resolved that she would not be cheated out of a single word of it. "Then—" in itself was not going to count as a proposal. "Then—," indeed!

"*Then—!*" Oh, dear no.

Immediately Olwen put on that look which is scarcely a look, but is for all that a defence past which no man's love-making may come. Immediately Captain Ross's own look changed to one of dashed and angry surprise. He had put out his arm. It dropped to his side while he watched this girl.

She sat down, her little figure almost lost in the embrace of a chair like a cretonne-covered bed. "Won't you sit down?" she said in the voice of a hostess, pointing to an opposite chair.

He did not move.

She, feeling that never before had she been mistress of the situation, and that perhaps never again would she have the opportunity, spoke first with a composure which startled herself.

"Why," she asked, "should it be supposed to have anything to do with you whether or not I was going to marry Mr. Ellerton?"

And now Captain Ross moved so abruptly against the mantelpiece that he shifted one of the handleless china teacups out of its place and set the prisms tinkling on the candlesticks.

He opened his mouth, then shut it as if he'd thought better of the answer which he meant to make to this chit. And then, in the tone of stinging reproof which he reserved for some careless error in the reading of some letter at the Honeycomb, he said, looking down upon her, "I should have thought that a girl of your intelligence would have had the sense to guess by this time what my object was in wanting to know what your ideas were on the subject of getting married."

Olwen, with a tiny turn of her head, remained silent, watching the sunset, which could just be seen over the Rival mountains out of the other window. This last remark of Captain Ross's she was not going to take as a proposal either.

From the lack of expression on her small face no man would have guessed at the happy tumult in the heart under that ribbon-and-satin of a hidden mascot that it rocked.

"Well?" demanded Captain Ross with outward patience. "How much longer do you intend to keep me dangling around and guessing?"

"About what?"

"About whether you're going to marry *me* or not," said Captain Ross, dourly.

Olwen stuffed a cushion behind her back and laughed quite naturally. "But, Captain Ross! You said Marriage was a thing the sensible man looked at from every angle and then decided to cut out. I never imagined—"

"Ah, cut *that* out," Captain Ross begged her, with the unsmiling mien of one who sees himself about to be routed from his last defences. "You knew all the time; you knew."

"I didn't!"

"What?" Captain Ross thrust out his jaw. "You ought to know me well enough by this time. You've seen me plenty."

"Yes," said Olwen, with feeling, "and always being—"

"Well?"

"Perfectly horrid to me."

"'Horrid,' you think?" barked Captain Ross. "In the office? You don't understand that I'm as much on active service there behind a pen as I was when I was able to be behind a gun? 'Horrid.' Because I didn't make love to you there, and both of us on duty? If you imagine that I'm the kind of man who'd do that ever, I am afraid you are under a serious misapprehen—"

"But you weren't always in the office," protested Olwen, quickly, "and you were *always* horrid to me!"

"When, please?"

"Well, at lunch!"

"Because I only had lunch with you once a week?"

"You didn't 'have lunch *with* me,'" Olwen demurely reminded him. "You happened to be lunching at the same place on Fridays."

"That's hair-splitting," snapped Captain Ross.

Exactly as if he never split hairs! As if he had not been splitting hairs for the last six months. That is, the same hair. And with a hatchet.

He felt that he was burying that hatchet now—if she would only let him.

He declared, "You know I only went to that darned little eating-place to see you," and it was with the manner of one who hands over his revolver that he had said it. "I loathe fish."

(But this was not a proposal!)

Olwen, gazing not at him, but through the window at a cluster of yellow crocuses on the lawn, exclaimed softly, "As if you didn't know that this is the first hint you've ever given me of your wanting to see me at all!"

Captain Ross took a step back on the hearthrug. He gave a short and angry laugh. "The fairrrrrst hint?" he cried, as if aghast.

"Of course it is," declared Olwen.

"It's nothing of the kind," doggedly from the man. "Plenty of other. . . things of that sort."

They were both wrong, and they knew it.

It is unlikely that Olwen had forgotten that Elysian evening on the lagoon when Mr. Brown had pulled and she had sat in the stern-sheets with Captain Ross. To have your hand held in the moonlight tenderly, and for an hour on end, might fairly be called "a hint."

So Captain Ross was right on that point.

But he was wrong on every other.

In the whole of their acquaintance that had been the one isolated instance in which he had failed to be as forbidding as an Army order. But at that moment (and indeed for several months afterwards) that incident in the boat was not to be referred to by either of them. For some obscure reason both of them felt more shy of that memory than any of fresh experiences.

Quickly Olwen got on with this war in the enemy's country. "Hints? I'm sure I don't know what they could have been. That box of chocolates at Les Pins. But I've had other boxes of chocolates given to me—"

"I've no doubt of that" (with grimness).

"So you can hardly call that a 'hint,' Captain Ross!"

"Ah!" he said, impatiently. "It's not what one gives or says to a woman, as you know. It's the *manner*—"

There was real merriment in Olwen's laugh at this. "The manner! The *manner*! Well, really! After the scolding and strafing and disapproving! After the way you never came near me if we were out—"

"I did. I did. I sat next you at that concert when Jack Awdas's girl was singing."

"For five minutes; yes, I remember," said Olwen, tilting her chin. "It was the one and only time."

"It was not, pardon me. I was coming to sit by you at Mrs. Cartwright's party, and I wasn't allowed a look in—"

"So you had a look *at*, most severely," Olwen countered. "At Mrs. Cartwright's was when you were the horridest of all. You just sat opposite to me and glared—"

IN THE DINING-ROOM THE PARTY of Olwen's relations sat over their last half-cups of tea in a simmer of delighted curiosity.

This was shared, openly, by the hireling colt from the mountains as she clattered in at intervals with hot water or more butter. Breathlessly she asked at last, "Will I take a tray and some fresh tea into the drawing-room for Miss S'olwen and that t'officer?"

"You will not," ordered her mistress. Even she had been young once.

"—Yes! glared at me as if you hated the sight of me!" insisted Olwen.

He said, "And weren't you flirrrting with those two fellows, and simply out to make me wild?"

"No," said the girl, quietly and sincerely.

He could have clasped her for it. "Darling!" said his glance, but aloud he only retorted, "Maybe you were not out to do it, but you certainly pulled it off."

"As for *you*," continued Olwen, "weren't you talking at me to Mrs. Cartwright all the time at dinner?"

"No!" he retorted, flagrantly.

"You know you were! *All* about Woman being the Plaything of Man!"

"Don't rub it in," he entreated, with another glance down at this plaything so maddeningly near, yet not, perhaps, for him. Yes! If she had had the boldness of the kitten who strikes with soft paws at the Force which could annihilate her, he had the boding patience of that big dog who waits, sitting up, with the lump of sugar on his nose.

It was she who kept him so. . . She was—oh, she was getting her own back now!

She broke off as if by the way, to ask him, "Let me see, what was the first thing—almost the first I ever heard you say. . . *What* sort of a judge of women are you?"

It is not true that the Scot is inevitably without a sense of humour. At that moment Fergus Ross saw even the joke against himself, since he thought it would appeal to her. He responded, "What was that about women? Something I've hairred in a drim?"

Relentless, Olwen repeated her demand. "What sort of a judge of women are you?"

He looked at her, threw up and shook his head with the action of a boxer who drops his hands as well.

"I guess I'm about as fine a judge of women as a baby is a judge of mothers," he told her, frankly and ruefully. "One he knows; his own. And herrrr he's got to have!"

But she put it aside. *This* wasn't enough of a proposal! She harked back to that party at Mrs. Cartwright's which had witnessed the last losing fight of this prisoner of hers, taken now with horse, foot and guns.

"'What's Love? An amusement,'" she quoted, mischievously, his words upon that occasion. "That's what you said, four—no! only three days ago," she insisted, now feeling that she had got well into her stride and could keep this well-merited strafing of the young man for an hour yet. "Yes! Just to be horrid to *me*! How you talked! All about how bored a man got 'when some woman started in to Love' him—"

Here Olwen stopped, abruptly but too late. She coloured to the deep pink of the little coral brooch at her throat. She saw what she'd said.

So did he.

Very quickly the soldier took advantage of this break in the line of her defence.

"Ah!" His voice lifted. "Well, what of that? What has *that* got to do with my being 'horrid' to you? What—connection is there between you, and any woman starting in to love *me*?"

"Oh, *none*! I didn't mean *that*," Olwen assured him, laughing flippantly, but dropping her eyes to gaze so hard at the carpet that only the top of the head was to be seen. Glossily black and shapely enough was the little head upon which Captain Ross had heaped, in his mind, every anathema as well as every endearment that he knew, but he was dashed if he was expected to read what she meant out of the mere top of it. So—

If, a month ago, some one had informed Captain Ross of the Honeycomb that he would ever be reduced for any possible reason, to go down on his knees on the floor at a woman's feet, he would not have considered the idiotic prophecy was worth a laugh.

But his number was up.

Here he found himself kneeling on the carpet at Olwen's feet just because there seemed no other way at that moment of getting a really satisfactory glimpse of Olwen's face.

"Now! my lady," he began, firmly.

But just as he'd thought he meet her eyes squarely she turned her head sidewards and directed that bright gaze of hers, as she'd often done before, over his shoulder and away. She was ready to glance at the blaze of the log fire, at the wall-paper, at the oval china frame all garlands and Loves of the standing mirror, at the large portrait of Professor Howel-Jones in his robes, at anything, yes! anything rather than at the (late) finest judge of women in Europe, at her feet. It was too much.

The pent-up, exasperated longing of months broke out in six words.

"Look at me, you little demon! *look* at me—"

But even now she did not look; how could she, when she had shut her eyes before the change that had come into his own?

He caught her to him. With his one arm slung about her, he put a scorching kiss upon her throat, under her ear. Then he took her chin in his hand and turned her face round; he kissed the childishly red mouth until little Olwen, all shy and aflame, felt that the shape of his own would be moulded upon her lips.

For all his theorizings, his protestations, his boastings about Love, he was yet a lover. . . or perhaps it would be truer to say a lover at last.

As for her. . . The whole of her girl's nature seemed to stretch out gleeful hands to the gift that he made to her—of herself. Till now she had resembled—what? The sea-anemone that for weary hours of low-tide has waited self-contained and folded into itself upon its rock, an inert lump. . . At last the warm waves rise, and lo! the rosy fingers spread to welcome its own element have turned it to a lovely thing, a star-shaped flower of flesh.

Into her sigh of delight he heard her murmur, "No! I *mustn't*—"

"Mustn't what?" muttered the strange voice of him who was no longer the Captain Ross of this story, but the Fergus of their love-tale that was beginning.

And in Love, after all, all's well that begins well. (Even though there was no real "proposal" after all.)

He coaxed, "Mustn't what, Honey?"

"Mustn't like you any *more*, or you won't like me as *much*!"

It was Woman's dearly-bought wisdom—but he laughed at it until his teeth gleamed across his vivid face.

She? Do anything he would not like? Even if she loved him and showed it, even that could not cool this man off, now he knew. The chit had got him going sure enough. Whatever she did or said only added to her attraction, to her long-contested, her triumphant, her Disturbing Charm!

Postscript

The Charm Confessed

With regard to the three words with which the last chapter closed:

The Disturbing Charm. . .

What was its story, after all, apart from the tangled stories of those people into whose lives it twined its thread of rose colour?

Perhaps it was all summed up in a letter that came, one February morning of Nineteen-Eighteen, to Professor Howel-Jones.

The old botanist was sitting in his study. It was a wide, cleared room with a table as chaotic as that had been at Les Pins, set, as at Les Pins, before a window; but the view here was not of a lagoon with a belt of dunes and a lighthouse. It showed the roofs of Liverpool.

Professor Howel-Jones had just returned, after various wanderings, to find a big mail awaiting him. He sighed, as he opened the letters, for his little niece and secretary. (Olwen had not been replaced.)

Then he knit his brows over the letter in his hand.

It said:

Dear Sir,

"The writer of this letter has reproached himself more than once over the rather stupid practical joke that he elected to play upon a man of your attainments by sending to you what was alleged to be the discovery of a love-germ, or Disturbing Charm—"

"Dear me! What and when was that?" pondered the Professor. "Ah, yes. I have it. Some lunatic that wrote to me in France. Something about '*half the trouble in the world arising from people falling in Love—with the wrong people*.' Yes, yes. And what was this 'Charm' supposed to do? . . . Ah, it says now that the Charm was spoof. . ." He went on reading the letter; the belated apology of some pupil at some University where he had once lectured. . .

He took it in, half thinking of the next letter as he read. . .

Fern seed, it appeared, was all that the "magic" packet had contained. . .

The Professor scarcely remembered that there had been a packet! What had he done with it now, and with the letter? Burnt them, he thought, before that little Olwen got hold of that nonsense. . .

It would have been just like a very young, imaginative girl like that to have believed in it!

Well, this last letter would have to shatter that belief! thought her Uncle, as he crumpled the practical joker's apology into a ball and tossed it on to the fire.

At the moment when her Uncle's thoughts were turning to her, his niece, young Mrs. Ross, was watching rather a pretty scene.

She stood at the window of her husband's rooms in Victoria Street, his old bachelor rooms into which she had brought the new element of her girlish belongings, her love, herself. . .

Behind her on the table, above a pile of his books on "Reconstruction," there trailed a dainty litter of her sewing: the lacy whiteness of a garment that was being reconstructed, feminine-fashion, into some other garment.

Beside her stood another war-bride of but a few more weeks' standing, young Mrs. Awdas.

Both of them were looking down into the street, where a crowd lined the pavement to right and left, waiting, watching to see a company of American soldiers march past on their way to Victoria Station.

Ah! Here it was, the stream of clean khaki cleaving the motley of the crowd. Here they came, the boys, tall, fit, and splendid, drilled to the minute; the pick and cream of the new belligerent country. . . Here they came, spare and useful looking and ah, how faultless in kit and accoutrements, from straight-brimmed hats to spotlessly-polished boots. And as they swung past with the unison of a machine in which every part is perfect, there hove into sight, straggling, slouching towards them out of the station, a knot of British just back from the firing line. An officer walked along beside the men.

Over these there brooded the spectre of three years and more of War. Their eyes were heavy with lack of sleep as they lurched heavily along, blinking around them at London once again; they were dirty and loaded down with gear, they were strung about with mess-tins and water-bottles and boots and brown-paper parcels and battered shrapnel helmets. One or two of them had Hun helmets tied to their knapsacks. They wore greasy remnants of caps, disreputable goatskin coats. All over them was thickly caked the foul mud of the trenches.

What a contrast. . .

The mob of straggling scarecrows turned to give a friendly stare, a "Cheerio" to their smart American comrades as they swung past in their immaculate fours.

"See you in ten days!" shouted a Tommy.

Olwen Ross, up at the window, thrust out her little black head to watch the Americans.

"Oh, they are magnificent," she breathed excitedly. "Aren't you proud of them, Golden?"

"Am I *proud* of them!" laughed her friend.

But while the Welsh girl was all eyes for these new troops, the American girl's wide gaze turned upon the others with whom they must soon be standing shoulder to shoulder; the war-worn soldiers, muddy, tattered, scarred, exhausted, cheery still. . .

"*They* are magnificent, Olwen, I guess," said she.

And her opinion seemed to be shared by a countryman. A quick and graceful thought struck the officer in charge of those Americans.

Suddenly and clearly, above the buzz of the street, the rhythmic tramp of feet, there snapped out his order:

"Company—eyes—RIGHT!"

Every head under the straight-brimmed hat turned sharply towards those heroic scallywags their allies.

Perhaps that young American company officer would have explained, diplomatically, that the word of command had been for his men to give the Eyes Right to that British subaltern who was passing with the leave-men; a white-faced, hollow-eyed stripling with two gold stripes on his cuff and the black "flash" of the Royal Welsh Fusiliers fluttering at his nape. But if it were ostensibly for him, it was also for his men. The new Allies, equipped for Victory, saluted the old, all but broken, but carrying on. . .

And the bright eyes of the two girls at the windows above shone suddenly, mistily brighter at the sight.

As they watched the two bodies of men disappear—those marching towards Victoria and the boat-train, these straggling towards a soldiers' hostel in Buckingham Palace Road, Golden said softly, "My people, Olwen, honouring yours."

Olwen said, "Yes; but mine are yours now, and yours are mine."

She turned from the window and into the little sitting-room with her guest's arm in hers.

"What's the time?" asked young Mrs. Awdas. "I'm due to sing at the hospital at four. We'll have to hurry—"

She lifted, on Olwen's blouse, the tiny pin-on watch which was one of her friend's wedding presents. Then she exclaimed, "What have you got tied around here?"

Golden did not recognize any similarity between this sachet of pink-and-mauve and the sun-faded ribbon trifle she had picked up on Biscay beach. But Olwen smiled as she tucked into the place the mascot that she wore and always would wear, even had she read that letter which her Uncle held would shatter any belief in that "magic." The old scientist summed her up as faultily as if he, too, had set out to be the finest judge, etc. . .

"Golden," she said, "if I tell you about this, will you promise not to laugh?"

And as they walked along to the hospital, she gave to her friend the outlines of the story which you have just read. . . so far as she knew them herself.

Golden, listening, smiled above her leopard-skins. "Do you think all these things would not have happened just as they did happen without the wearing of a Charm?"

Olwen, with happy dreams in her eyes, did not reply.

After a pause her friend went on, softly, "When I look at you," she said, "and when I look at your Fergus, and at my Jack, and at any one else who is lovely and loving. . . why, of course I believe there's a Charm really, though it just can't be anything you could make up out of a pinch of powder and a bit of ribbon. A Charm? Why, the world's full of it! Didn't it send me over the sea to my Bird-boy? Didn't it bring your men from Canada and France to you? Didn't it let us all meet in a country that was sweet and friendly, though none of ours? Didn't it work—why, all the time?"

"Sometimes—Often—Half the time," suggested Olwen, "it is supposed to make such mistakes. It takes the wrong people. . ."

"We hear of those, just because they're the exceptions, I guess," smiled her buoyant friend. "We aren't so talked about, we with the happy love stories, that the Charm has worked! . . . Olwen, it's making stories now for each of those splendid boys we saw go marching by, and for each of the pretty girls who wishes them Luck. It never stops! . . . But you can't see it. You can't hold it. You can only feel it is—"

"But then what is it?" Olwen asked. "What is it in itself?"

"Who knows?" Golden replied. "Does it matter if we *never* know?"

THE END

A Note About the Author

Berta Ruck (1878–1978) was a British romance novelist. Born in Punjab, British India, she was raised in a family of eight children. After moving with her parents to Bangor, Wales, Ruck completed her education and embarked on a career as a professional writer. She began submitting stories to magazines in 1905, publishing her first novel, *His Official Fiancée*, in 1914. Adapted twice for the cinema, her debut began her run as a bestselling romance writer, spanning nearly 60 years and dozens of novels. In 1909, she married fellow writer Oliver Onions, with whom she had two sons. Ruck published her final work in 1972 and lived to the age of 100.

A Note from the Publisher

SIA information can be obtained
.ICGtesting.com
.n the USA
√081744250521
110BV00010B/151

9 781513 282862